To Kathy Brooks,

# WHERE WE ARE

Keep looking for dimes!

Annie Mac

# WHERE WE ARE

*by*

## Annie McDonald

2019

# WHERE WE ARE

ISBN 13: 978-1-63555-581-3

THIS TRADE PAPERBACK ORIGINAL IS PUBLISHED BY
BOLD STROKES BOOKS, INC.
P.O. BOX 249
VALLEY FALLS, NY 12185

FIRST EDITION: DECEMBER 2019

CREDITS
EDITOR: BARBARA ANN WRIGHT
PRODUCTION DESIGN: STACIA SEAMAN
COVER DESIGN BY TAMMY SEIDICK

# Acknowledgments

This story is wholly inspired and devoted to Sharon Rochelle Little. The seven dollars and twenty cents might as well be a million.

Thanks to Laurie Danowski, who stood in my corner through each chapter, over and over again. Soul sister. Eagle eye. Big heart.

Thanks to Heather and John, who pushed me into the deep end—NaNoWriMo—and convinced me that I could swim.

I'm grateful to my beta readers, Fiona, Maria, and Marlene, whose encouragement buoyed me.

I'm indebted to the expert folks at Bold Strokes Books, most especially to Barbara Ann Wright, whose guidance was instrumental and whose patience was unfathomable.

Special thanks to Sandy B. for holding my hand and steadying me through the grind. Words matter. So does love.

For Sharon.
Thanks for the dimes.
Ebby.

## PROLOGUE

Mia Jarvis caught a glimpse of herself in the shiny silver metal of the trailer and considered wiping the black streak of grease from her cheek. Instead, she pulled her hair back into a ponytail and tried again to set the sway bars on the hitch to the recommended tension. Better to be safe than sorry, she thought. Her determination and caution might have merit, but she accepted that hypervigilance was both overkill and part of her process. After one more minor adjustment, she smiled and stepped from behind the trailer, satisfied that she was ready for the open road.

"Are you sure? Absolutely sure?" Leah asked.

"I'm not sure of much right now," Mia said. "The past year has been a blur, but I need to lay a new foundation."

"Can't you lay it here?"

"Riley's gone. I know that. But our life was here, and it's still too hard."

"I get that, but in a trailer? Mia, are you sure? Alone?"

"I won't be alone. I have Flynn."

"You know what I mean."

"Yes. And I know you're throwing up fences to keep me from harm. And I love you for that. But I'm forty-six, Leah, and I need to find out what the rest of my life will be."

Mia circled the small airstream trailer, stopping here and there to check compartment latches and signal lights as her best friend and Flynn, her smooth-coated collie, followed.

"I'm pretty self-sufficient, and you and I both know how to use cell phones, so we'll never be out of touch. Well, except for those long stretches through the prairies and some spots in the mountains."

Noticing her friend still hovering anxiously, Mia changed tack. "Hey, what do a divorce in Alberta, a tornado in Saskatchewan, and a flood in Manitoba have in common?"

Leah was already rolling her eyes.

"Somebody's fixin' to lose a trailer!" As she always did at her own jokes, Mia laughed. Leah joined in with a groan, as she had so many times through their long friendship.

"You're not running away?" she asked when her groan ran thin.

"I know you think I'm taking on too much too soon, but no, I'm running *to*. I just don't know to what, or where, exactly."

"Love you, Mia Jarvis."

"Love you back." They hugged, and she climbed into the cab of her Ford F-150.

"Find some dimes," Leah said through the open window.

The inexplicable appearance of the coins brought Riley to mind, and she smiled. "You know I will."

## CHAPTER ONE

Mia couldn't believe how quickly the next twelve months passed by. She had travelled west from Ontario across Manitoba and Saskatchewan, a distance equivalent to driving across the breadth of Texas at least twice. Her trailer was not only her home but also served as the mobile headquarters of her dog training service. Specializing in herding techniques for canines and their owners, she worked with ten young dogs, migrating more or less westward after each client through the livestock-rich farms of central Canada. More important than the respectable income was the time it afforded her. Time for grieving. Time for healing.

And now, a whole year of smooth sailing churned into a maelstrom as ATVs roared over the banks of the creek where she was walking, the machines side-sliding to a stop in tandem not twenty feet from where she stood.

"It's impossible that you *didn't* see the fence!" the lead driver bellowed over the deafening engines, gesturing toward a gap in the nearby trees.

"I saw it, but to a dog," Mia said, "cedar rails are just a bunch of fallen trees. Milo's curious. And fast."

Milo, a sweet but undisciplined black and white border collie and her most recent client, had cowered from the noise and size of the trail-runners, abandoning his dreams of chasing the distant cattle he'd spotted from the other side of said fence. Now his natural curiosity turned to the driver on the lead vehicle. He moved forward and pressed his nose against a leather boot, then nestled it into the cuff of the overlaid jeans. It was only when Mia let her eyes follow the blue denim upward from where Milo sniffed, along muscled but undeniably curvaceous thighs, that she realized the rider was a woman.

"Is the dog yours?" The tone was not so much angry now as it was cold and sardonic.

*What kind of a question is that? She can't use his name?* The interrogator pulled off her black leather riding gloves, draped them over the handlebars of her still-rumbling all-terrain vehicle, and pushed the peak of her trucker's cap back on her forehead. Mia recognized the move as a power gesture but not before it had its intended effect. She found herself staring quite helplessly into hypnotic hazel eyes or maybe green or dark grey...it was hard to tell. Regardless, they unnerved her. She silently chastised herself for allowing this stranger's eyes to distract her, and refocused on resolving what was now an unnecessarily escalating dispute. Before she could formulate a plan, repeated vitriol was hurled her way.

"I said, is he yours?" The words *he* and *yours* were emphasized, with a pause in between that infuriated Mia enough to break the spell. Rather than react as usual, in terms that would not exclude several of the four-letter variety, Mia instead took a breath to compose herself.

*Be nice, Mia. These are Beth and Owen's neighbors.*

She looked calmly to the other driver, a handsome young man wearing a ball cap that looked similar to the one his partner wore but backward, and directed her response at him.

"He's in my care, yes."

Before backward hat could respond, his partner did.

"Then care for him. I can't be responsible if he gets hurt. My cattle aren't used to herders."

The way the woman stressed the word *care* rankled Mia. There was really no need for the attitude.

"He's hardly a herder yet. And he didn't get hurt. He's just young and impulsive." Mia stressed the last word but bit her tongue, knowing better than to draw an obvious comparison between Milo and this rancher anywhere but in her thoughts. "We're working on it."

As if to undermine Mia's fading authority, Milo sat up and placed his paws on the rider's leg, tail wagging rapidly as if she had bacon in her boots.

She stroked Milo's head, wrapping long fingers around his ears and rubbing the sweet spot under his neck. His gratitude was obvious, but the kind gesture did nothing to soften the woman's next words.

"Well, work elsewhere." Mia could see that the eyes were unquestioningly grey. Without waiting for a response, the woman fired up her ATV and—pulling on the long penny-brown mane of hair held in place by the hat band—pulled her cap tightly back into place.

Mia couldn't hold her tongue any longer. She had given nice a chance. But neighbors didn't always have to be neighborly. "Look, I don't know who you are, but there's no need to be rude." She raised her voice above the engine noise. At the sound, Milo moved from beside the machine and took a stance in front of it. He lowered his shoulders and stayed square to the vehicle as its wheels began to slowly turn, and the machine edged forward.

"I'm Sid Harris," was the terse response. "I don't know or care who you are either, but you're standing on my family's land. And in five minutes, I'd prefer you weren't." She pulled on the leather gloves. "I trust you can find your way back to wherever you and your dog came from."

*Again with the* dog.

As the vehicle began to power forward, Milo stood his ground, staring at the headlights, swaying side to side. This was instinct for a border collie, the breed naturally standing and facing the lead cow, a herding strategy called heading. Borders weren't predominantly nippers—dogs who used small leg bites to enforce movement— though a cow would be ill-advised to test them. Instead, they mostly opted to command cattle with a head-to-head, strong-eye stare, using intimidation to move the herd.

Mia was pleased to see Milo's breed intuition in action.

*Now we just need to teach you the difference between an ATV and a cow.*

She was also consoled that the rider—as abrasive as she was—at least had taken care to move around him before gaining speed and spraying gravel away. Maybe there was a human being somewhere under that cap. *Too bad her behavior doesn't match her looks.*

As the ATVs disappeared, Mia found herself transfixed and oddly breathless, trying to make sense of what had just happened. Yes, she was trespassing. But she wasn't doing any harm, and Milo had obeyed her command to retreat in spite of how excited he was when he spotted the cattle on the Harris side of the fence. Yes, the landowner had a right to ask her to leave. But Mia hadn't done anything to provoke the level of rudeness shown by this Sid person. Replaying the event in her mind left her wondering what else might be going on with the Harris woman to have elevated the intensity of what could have, and should have been, a polite request but was instead a diatribe. She also wondered why she was giving such consideration to someone so inarguably undeserving.

Walking back through the band of trees along the Miller-Harris property line, Milo easily vaulting the rails ahead of her, Mia chose to focus on the matter at hand. She was now two weeks into training eleven-month-old Milo. His agility and tirelessness were excellent markers, and she felt confident when she told his owner, Jack McCann, that he would be ready within the month to start working with herds. Her next lesson was to create a healthy appreciation in the pup for all things big, including—now—ATVs. Milo had already shown an appreciation for a certain driver.

*What a bitch. But those eyes. And her hands. Damn.*

The cultivated fields of the lower foothills opened up and rolled for acres in the morning sun as they came out the other side of the narrow forest. Mia gazed at the hills which built into a spectacular range, the eastern edge of the majestic Rockies. The snow was no longer visible on the peaks, the latest Alberta heat wave finally melting the last remaining glaciers. To her right, the wheat fields were well short of being the paler shade of yellow that signalled readiness. Now, midsummer, they shone and gently swayed like a vast green-gold ocean.

Mia retraced her steps along the east side of the south-flowing creek, its bed rocky with gravel and its water clear. She recalled from her childhood, having grown up less than ten miles from here, that there had been some mining along these cuts way back in the day, but when the mines dried up, all that was left were unusable extracts from the deep pits and a few legendary caves, home now to a protected population of bats.

Beth and Owen Miller's acreage was impressively large, and it extended from the far ridge of the foothills on the other side of the creek, cascading down before flattening out, crossing the road in the south, and reaching farther than the eyes could see. The only livestock they managed were the fifty or so head of beef cattle that were currently held in a stockade on the lower tier of the property. This was the reason Mia had set up her trailer here instead of at Milo's owner's ranch. This spot was far enough away from cattle which would distract an untrained dog, but when the time came, and Milo was ready, he would have access to a small, manageable number of cattle to complete his training. Provided he achieved his training goals, he would then be handed back to the McCanns, whose herd numbered in the thousands.

Beth Miller's daughter Leah was Mia's best friend. The two bonded as eleven-year-olds when Leah's dad and Mia's mom died in the same tragic winter pileup on an icy mountain highway. Now remarried, Beth had invited Mia to set up on their property when she heard that the nearby neighbors, the McCanns, had hired her. Neither Miller would have had any qualm with having Mia—or her dogs—staying with them in their home, but Beth respected Mia's independent streak and was satisfied just knowing Leah's "bestie" was within the realm.

As the trailer came within sight, Mia saw her own beloved boy in the shade. Flynn was at attention, his ears raised and his body crouched in the stalking pose, watching for movement in her direction. Milo saw him, too, and Mia anticipated quickly.

"Milo. Stand." He stopped.

*Pretty good. Now praise.*

"Good boy."

As fond as she was of Milo, Flynn would always be her baby

boy, and seeing him in guard mode, she realized how much she loved the way he remained determined to retain his alpha status in the company of the much younger dog.

"Flynn. Come."

Flynn abandoned his predatory stance and came forward, slowing as he neared, his tail wagging with unmitigated joy. Normally he would have joined her on walks, but Flynn's presence would have been one more distraction for Milo. Now that there was distance between her and the Harris land, Mia regretted that she hadn't seen the tumbled rail fence or the cattle in the field on the other side of the trees, and she had no issues taking full responsibility for her charge's behavior.

*No matter. That woman was over the top.*

Mia smiled and imagined there were many women who would enjoy being under Sid Harris. And quite possibly men. She laughed, recalling that her gaydar had always been horribly inaccurate. Even Riley had to wave a rainbow flag in front of her face before Mia let her feelings be known. A risk taker she was not. At least not then. Now, well, it had been so long since anyone of interest flirted with her that it wasn't something she had cause to think about. Her stomach fluttered for some incomprehensible reason. Hunger maybe.

Giving rein to more rational thought, Mia allowed the two dogs to run back to the trailer. Milo bounded with the unfathomable energy of youth, tripping over Flynn, who was a good ten pounds heavier than the border yearling and used his advantage to push the youngster away with his snout while maintaining shoulder checks every few steps to ensure his owner was following safely behind.

"Be nice to your little brother, Flynn; he's had a rotten morning." But she knew that Milo's impression of Sid Harris was far from her own; he seemed happy indeed with the ear scratch. She considered it no less than an act of treason and felt that the whole encounter could simply be chalked up to the misdirected behavior of someone with other issues nipping at her heels, a person she hoped she wouldn't run into again any time soon.

## CHAPTER TWO

Sid knew her cousin. And she knew what was coming. When they returned from their foray to the creek, she watched Aaron pace contemplatively while the ATVs were powering down and the dust settled in the barnyard. She knew there was no point trying to avoid him when something was gnawing at him. Especially when the gnawing had something to do with her. It might have been a year since they'd seen each other, but Sid was sure he wouldn't sugarcoat his words. Most often, in the Harris clan, there was no simple way to make things sweet.

"Sid, what the hell?"

"What do you mean?" she replied, removing her leather riding gloves and brushing the dust off her shirt and jeans. She knew exactly what he meant but was stalling for time to consider her defense. She took off her hat, folded the peak, and tucked it into her back pocket, letting her hair fall around her shoulders before flipping it to the side and securing it into a ponytail. She wiped her brow with her forearm and took a breath followed by a short, stuttered exhale.

"Are you okay?" His words were softer, as if sensing that her mind was on other more important matters. Even so, it seemed he wasn't going to let her off the hook.

She leaned on the quad. "Yes, why?" She tried not to sound as annoyed as she was.

"That wasn't like you. I mean, well, you went a bit hard on her...don't you think?"

*The woman and the dog. Trespassers.*

"How many head, Aaron? Dad wouldn't say, exactly. So tell me. In the past month, how many head of cattle have we lost?"

"Ten." He seemed to resign himself to the fact that Sid would rather change the subject than address her behavior. "I'm going to circle back, Sid, I know what you're up to."

Sid loved and hated how well he knew her. He recognized her knack for redirection and distraction, and even she couldn't help but laugh when he pointed it out by yelling "squirrel," referencing the animated dog in the movie *Up*. Given the present circumstances, though, Sid knew that neither of them felt like laughing.

"Ten head, all gone, God knows where. Stolen. No sign of predators." She didn't wait for a response. "Since I've been here, three more. Right? And then a stranger shows up with a lame excuse for being on the step, and you think I'm overreacting?" She stood, putting her gloves over the handlebars of the ATV and walking toward the barn.

The "step" was the local vernacular for the plateau of a low escarpment that extended along the back of the Harrises' grazing land, pushed into place thousands of years ago by either a landslide or a plate shift. The mountain stream cut the granite before the ridge rose again, creating another step on the Rockies side of its bank. Trees had rooted in the sediment, making it unsuitable for crops but just right for the hundred head that grazed there. The stream then opened into a four-acre lake at the south side of the step before taking its leave on the south side and carving its way through the foothills toward Pincher Creek.

"Still, Sid, that wasn't like you. I know you have a few things on your mind, but she seemed apologetic. Kinda cute, too. I mean, if you're into that kinda thing." He paused. He scanned the barn behind her as if looking for an escape route. "Girls, I mean."

"Women, cousin! I prefer *women*."

She refused to continue reacting. She took out her hat and hung it on the hook inside the barn door. She continued past the stalls toward the feed room, hoping that by creating physical distance, she could put a quick end to his teasing. Instead, he followed.

"Just sayin', maybe you should think about being more neighborly."

Thinking more about anything was the very last of Sid's objectives. Her mind was already spinning, her list of things to do a mile long. The stolen cattle were top of that list, but with the exception of who was committing the crimes, it was no real mystery why and how. Each head was worth a good chunk of change, and if a rancher was not vigilant, they were readily targeted. Maintaining fences around a thousand acres—some at elevations—was a job demanding more than two men, let alone one. If only she had been called home earlier, before her dad had his surgery, maybe they could've been proactive and wouldn't be scrambling to try to plug the leaks. But her dad was stubborn and independent, an inherited trait that she realized had not skipped her generation, and asking for help was not easy for him. In fact, if it weren't for Aaron sending her a text two weeks ago, he would still be trying to secure the fences alone. And settling the new bull.

In addition to things at the Harris ranch, Sid was also juggling her job at the gallery. And her relationship or what remained. Nothing left, perhaps, to salvage there.

And now, a trespasser. Not really in the suspect pool, Sid reckoned, trying to avoid being sexist but thinking that a woman and her dog in broad daylight did not constitute a likely criminal pairing. Kinda Cute, as Aaron called her, and she did show some bravado, standing up the way she did. Slightly more petite than Sid and well-rounded in the spots that mattered, Kinda Cute hadn't so much as budged as Sid laid into her. Instead, she held her ground, setting her jaw and riveting her ice blue—*no, flame blue*—eyes on Sid, fiercely determined to defend herself and her furry sidekick. *Milo, was it?* Curious that she'd noticed more about the kinda cute trespasser than she ordinarily might have under the circumstances. As if she didn't have enough on her plate. Best to keep her attention here. And definitely not on women. Any women. *Especially the kinda cute ones with flame blue eyes.* Maybe, though, she could manage neighborly.

She nodded. "Message received. Did you hear back from the breeder?"

"Yes. Well, your dad has. He told me we could pick him up tomorrow morning. He negotiated a great price." Aaron grabbed a bale of hay off the stack and walked it toward the stalls. "We'll have a great spring if things go well. Replace our losses plus a lot more."

"Makes better sense for us to have a new bull than to have to pay the insemination fees. Prices have sure gone up since I was here last." She hauled a large sack of grain off a pallet, dumped it into a wheelbarrow, and rolled it over to the stalls, discarding the burlap into a barrel almost spilling over. "And what about you? Still sowing your wild oats?"

Aaron laughed. At thirty, he was ten years Sid's junior and, unlike his cousin, had been living out loud since he was a teen. He openly shared his outrageous exploits—from his almost legendary status as a bronco rider in the Gay Rodeo, to his winter white parties in Miami—with whoever would listen. And people loved to listen. Aaron was quiet at first, but once he stuck to people, they became equally hard to peel off.

Sid wished she had a bit of his easygoing nature, but she found it difficult to separate her mind from her work long enough to downshift. The few close relationships she had outside of Aaron came as a result of her work. The people she knew there, more acquaintances than friends, filled in whatever personal time she managed to carve out. And those pieces were thin. In fairness to Aurora, her most recent girlfriend, Sid knew she only had herself to blame for her newly single status.

"Yes," Aaron said, "but I'm slowing down. I might stay here this winter."

"What? Really? What's his name?"

She envied the younger generation so much more freely expressing their lifestyle than her, a transition for the better in almost all respects. She had been on the cusp of that social change, living her truth selectively. In Toronto, in the art circles she traveled in, people hardly blinked at same-sex couples. But here, her childhood home, things felt blurry. *Probably my own lens.* She'd never truly been herself in Green River, Alberta.

"I'll tell if you'll tell," he challenged, breaking up the bale and serving it to the hungry heifers. "You haven't said much about Aurora...can I assume things with your painter friend have derailed a bit?"

"I'd say entirely. No surprise, given my track record. Our relationship is...was...more open for her than for me." With that, Sid turned her muddled mind to the grain she was shoveling into the troughs, forgetting to insist Aaron share back as her own thoughts of Toronto, the gallery, Aurora, and that kinda cute blonde with the dog were all successfully excised by the welcomed distraction of physical labor.

## CHAPTER THREE

The sun crept over the wheat fields through a veil of thin fog, the heat of the earth barely a few degrees warmer than the air for the moment. But along the base of the Rockies, especially in August in Alberta, the peaks warmed much sooner than the flatlands, creating a valley breeze that would soon dry up the mist and push the warmed winds uphill. The sky was a blue that reminded Mia of the wild flax she had seen yesterday on one of the south-facing slopes near the stream behind her trailer.

The flash of a hubcap caught her eye, and she turned to watch a pickup truck drive up the north road, turn onto her makeshift dirt driveway, and bounce its way slowly into the field where they were standing, the dust clouding in its wake. *We could really use a good rain.* As the brakes squeaked to a stop, Flynn left Mia's side and trotted toward the opening door. Milo rose to follow.

"Milo, stand." This was a test for the young dog, who was still in the basic command stage of his training. Mia was pleased to see that even with Flynn taking the lead, Milo was holding his spot in front of her. She could sense his eagerness, but he needed to adhere to commands to keep not only his future charges protected but himself as well. Only when the enormous cowboy boots of the driver swung out of the cab and hit the dirt did Mia release him.

"Milo, steady."

As commanded, Milo slowly approached the figure stooped behind the door, and Flynn's tail wagged jauntily in response to the massive hands giving him a thorough petting. Mia observed Milo's intense caution; he hadn't yet recognized the driver. As soon as Jack McCann stood up and stepped from behind the door, Milo's focus snapped like a pretzel stick, and he bounded toward his owner.

"Hey there, little fella! How's my boy?" Jack bent to tousle Milo's ears, his hands as big as the dog's head. Mia thought that everything must be "little" to the massive man, a friendly giant whose stature was as huge as his gentle soul.

Milo danced around Jack's boots, tail fanning like a black and white palm frond, hindquarters carried along with it and almost lifting the small dog out of his own furry white boots. After a few long strokes of his body, Milo began to calm as best a pup could. Flynn had long since abandoned the reunion, his temperament for the intense energy of his buddy having worn thin over the weeks. He found the shade of a nearby fencepost and sat to watch from a distance.

"Hi, Jack! Milo has been great."

"I can see that, Miss Mia. And how are you today? You're looking ready for action." He smiled, and Mia took inventory of her fashion choices: skinny jeans tucked into olive green Hunter boots and a white tank top barely visible beneath the lightweight M65 field jacket with shoulder Air Force patch and name tape still intact.

"Did you serve?"

Mia could tell he was trying to reconcile the name tape, Frigon, with her surname, Jarvis. "No, sir; a very dear friend did." *Riley.* "I'm sure I won't be wearing it long. It's going to be another hot one. Oh, and before I forget, Beth and Owen said to say hello to you."

"I'm grateful for your friend's service. You make sure you say hi back to the Millers. And thank them for not only putting the two of us in touch but for giving you some space for this training. I would've happily had you camp at my place, but I gather Milo's still not quite ready for cattle yet."

"Well, you may be surprised. We had a breakthrough yesterday."

*Break*through, *more like it.*

Mia told Jack about Milo's first few minutes on the Harris property before the ATVs roared up, and how he had approached the distant cows with tail down, showing amazing maturity for such a young dog.

"He clearly has excellent instincts, and naturally, as a young dog, he's still very prone to being impulsive. But most importantly, just from his address of the cows, I can tell he's equated cattle with work. Some dogs don't figure that out until they've been thumped by a hoof or worse."

*Speaking of being thumped by a hoof...*

"Do you happen to know who lives on the neighboring land?" Mia briefly described the unpleasant encounter from the day before.

"Oh yeah, that sounds like Sid. Can't mistake that girl's hair; red like chocolate, as my wife says. Rubbed you the wrong way, did she?"

"She wasn't exactly...neighborly."

"Well, she's here to help her dad. All the way from Toronto. I heard he had some shoulder surgery...story is that a bull almost tore his arm clean out of his socket. Happens around cattle sometimes. And bulls are unpredictable as the weather."

Mia flinched at the thought and mentally acknowledged that perhaps Sid possessed a more generous nature than she'd been willing to share under yesterday's contentious circumstances.

"And her boyfriend?"

Jack looked puzzled.

"A blond guy? Maybe a speck younger."

Jack laughed. "Oh, that would be Aaron. Definitely not her boyfriend. In fact, he used to be my son Greg's boyfriend." Mia could feel her eyebrows rise, not because she was shocked by the story but rather impressed by Jack's obvious comfort level sharing it.

Jack seemed to pick up on her surprise. "Times are different now. More important *that* you choose to love, not *who* you choose to love."

"Glad to hear it, Jack. We'd have a problem if you felt otherwise." Now it was Jack's turn to raise an eyebrow. Mia was a girly-girl. She certainly didn't match the stereotype many people still—in spite of all the Ellens and Portias in the world—held regarding lesbians. She loved and indulged in her tattered jeans and her Doc Martens and her flannels, yes. She enjoyed playing on the paradox in her personal style, gender-mashing old school like kd lang in her Reclines days. But even in leather, Mia Jarvis exuded lace.

"About Sid, not to excuse her rudeness, but I'd be pissed, too, if someone was walking away with my family's property." He went on to explain that the whole community was on alert because of cattle losses, likely from rustlers targeting the western part of the region. Mia not only grew up but also worked in the farm community, so she was aware of the problem. It wasn't limited to Green River. Good-natured and trusting, farm folks' steadfast values often put them at the mercy of organized criminal enterprises. Short of fencing off entire acreages with ten-foot-high electrified barriers or sensors, a cost-prohibitive measure out of reach of virtually every family farm, there was little to prevent middle-of-the-night poachers from trucking away a few head here and there before moving on, always ahead of law enforcement.

"Day and night." He shook his head disapprovingly. "It's like the Old West, but these guys are very clever. They don't sleep. And depending how many head you own, keeping yourself in business is hard when your bread and butter is disappearing right out from under you. Farm margins aren't as wide as city folks think. We've all been victims around here, but the Harrises? My gosh! I know Duncan wouldn't leave his land unless he was hog-tied to a trailer hitch and dragged off it, but at the rate he's losing head, well… suffice to say we're all keeping our eyes peeled for taillights in the night."

Milo put a paw on Jack's boot, indicating that the attention should be back on him. Jack got down on a knee and gave him a thorough petting.

"So now that he's had a taste of cattle, when will I start my work with him?"

"It won't be long, but just to be clear, the relationship of working dog to handler is not of primary importance. Yes, you will need to learn basic commands, which aren't too complicated or time consuming. But unlike the kind of obedience training you might see on TV, we're trying to teach the dog to react to the herd, not to the handler. Too much obedience can divide a working dog's attention, so once Milo's around cattle regularly, you almost have to ignore his demand for attention so that he stays on the herd."

Jack seemed genuinely engaged, but Mia sensed her passion for talking about training might have overwhelmed him. More than sensed; Mia had developed a skill for observation that was applicable to people as well as dogs, one that had been fine-tuned by years of sign and signal interpretation. *Enough for today.* "I'll keep you posted. I have your number."

"I'm sure you will. And I haven't forgotten...I'll bring a package of meat and a few bags of grain by in a couple of days if that works for you? Oats, right?"

"Absolutely. We can start on the commands then. Even though you're not the dog's central focus, the two of you are still a team. And someone has to make sure his impulsiveness doesn't end up getting him or the cattle hurt."

As Jack's pickup bounced back down the road, Mia found herself thinking about what she'd just said. Milo's behavior reminded her of the Harris woman's, excessive and erratic, led more by instinct than by self-awareness.

*Did she really think that Milo and I were intent on stealing cattle?*

Sid looked to be in her mid-to-late thirties, so her rudeness couldn't be excused by youth. No, they were all likely characteristics of a lack of discipline.

*Or arrogance.*

Sid didn't strike her as someone who would ever admit she was chasing the wrong rabbit. Too much ego. She was distractingly beautiful with her wavy auburn hair, fair skin, and grey-green eyes. *Worth staring into over a glass of merlot. Maybe distraction is how she's managed to get away with such acrimonious first impressions.*

"Take heart, Milo," she said, "You're not the only one who could use a little training."

# CHAPTER FOUR

E vening in the foothills was a stark contrast to its August mornings. Now the winds descended from the high ridges down across the farmlands, and regardless of the official sunset time, the shadows of the mountains started their brushstroke across the wheat fields well before then. It felt both dark and cool enough by 7:30 to justify a bonfire. Not that bonfires required justification; they were one of Mia's favourite things. And besides, tonight she had non-canine company.

For over thirty-five years, Leah Fleming had been a constant breath of fresh air in Mia's life. Regardless of how much time passed between visits—months, sometimes even years—they were deeply bonded and fell into a comfortable groove without having to work at it. Even so, Leah's visit was unexpected, and Mia found herself wondering what had brought her back to their hometown without an obvious occasion or agenda. Something was up, and before the night was over, Mia intended to know what it was.

"So, this whole dog thing is still working out, eh, Mia?"

"Totally. Ever since I associated with the Kennel Club's training collective, I've moved from dog to dog and town to town everywhere between Ontario and Alberta. I really have to thank Mom and Owen again for putting me in touch with Jack and Milo. Both are sweethearts. Please tell me you didn't come all the way from Vancouver to check up on me?"

"Speaking of sweethearts, how is your dad?"

Leah had sidestepped her question, but Mia gave her latitude for the moment. She stepped into the trailer and talked out the open door. "You know Dad; the grass doesn't grow under his feet. We Skyped last night, and he's living it up with his pals on a river cruise in Prague. He's thinking of coming back in time for Thanksgiving, but we'll see!"

"I'm so happy for him. I was worried he might never push through his grief."

The devastating accident that claimed Mia's mom and Leah's dad resulted in the two surviving parents sharing responsibilities for each girl. And so while Mia and Leah weren't sisters by blood, Beth was as much Mom to Mia as Mikka Jarvis was Dad to Leah.

"Speaking of changes, Owen seems really nice," Mia said.

"He's a great guy. Adores Mom. I think he's farming over a thousand acres so during summer, he's busy. It took a bit of time, but she's adjusted to farm life." Leah poked the coals beneath the firepit grill. "She and the neighbor, Isabel, have become close friends. Mom's becoming quite a cook thanks to her."

"Beth cooking? Well, that's new! Speaking of which, the salmon will be a few more minutes. I hope you're okay with Buddha bowls. Maybe over dinner you can tell me why you're here." Mia descended from the trailer and put two large bowls on the pop-up, fold-out picnic table, then grabbed a set of fish tongs and began probing the fish that had plumped beautifully over the crimson coals of the hardwood fire.

"You know, it's not just our parents I've been concerned with over the years. I've been worried about you, too." Leah paused as Milo poked his nose under her hand until she gave him a face rub. "But I'm worrying less now."

*Another sidestep, albeit sweet, noted.*

"I may have been wrong about you striking out alone on the open road," Leah continued. "It seems to be giving you what you need for now."

"For now." Losing Riley had cut her legs out from under her. For the first year, she'd felt devastated, shocked by the suddenness of it all, and utterly impaired by heartache. But as she'd hoped when she set out, the passage of time had helped her stand up and create a new set of bearings. It didn't mean she missed Riley any less, but she was feeling the ground again and on occasion even dreamed that there was a path ahead of her. Tears began to well at the thought of both the loss and the hope. She swallowed and allowed herself to move through the feelings.

"Is Isabel a Harris?" she asked once composed.

"Not exactly. She started off as the Harrises' farm manager. I'm not sure this is public knowledge, but she and Duncan Harris are romantically involved. Why are you asking?" Leah cocked her head.

"I met someone named Sid Harris yesterday." Her tone was as matter-of-fact as she could make it.

"Oh? That's nice. Duncan's boy?"

"Girl, actually. Woman. And not exactly nice. Bit of a bitch, it seems. Certainly doesn't like this neighbor." She jerked a thumb at herself.

"Do tell."

Mia recounted her brief run-in as casually as possible, knowing that even so, Leah—a lawyer with well-honed discourse skills—likely noted her pretense and filed it away for future inquiry. She had only herself to blame. After all, Leah had learned a great deal about the intricacies of nonverbal communication from her during their time at graduate school. She'd even proofread her thesis on digital microgestures. So unsurprisingly, Leah not only listened to what was said but read body language with a critical edge that served her well in her practice.

Happy to end the discussion about Sid Harris, Mia lifted the fish and set it on top of the rice and veggie bowls. "Salmon's ready."

"How old is Flynn now?" Leah asked, stroking the head he'd parked on her lap, impeding her route to the table.

"He's seven. Still quick enough to stay clear from hooves, but he's been slowing down a bit lately. Might just be the heat."

Once she poured the tahini lemon dressing over salmon, they set about enjoying their dinner, the dogs shifting from near the warm fire to more lucrative spots under the table.

"Ever hopeful, eh, boys?" Leah teased.

Mia was as responsible with her dogs as she was with her own diet: clean, organic much of the time, with room for the occasional indulgence. Table scraps for the dogs were a no-no unless they were veggies.

In between bites, Leah talked about work and the weather and moaned in occasional ecstasy at the odd kale chip or almond or dried apricot in her bowl. Mia listened quietly until the dishes were cleared and they were back in front of a newly stoked fire.

"So, what brings you here?" Mia looked directly at her, cutting off her escape routes with a visual version of the same trick she'd witnessed Milo employ with the ATV.

"What do you mean?" Leah cautiously replied.

"I think we've known each other long enough to know when chitchat is being used as a smoke screen. And this trip is a drive-by; you flew in this morning and are leaving tomorrow. Something's up. I know you love me, and I know you agree that time should be spent wisely. So spill."

Leah slumped in her camp chair, and her eyes moved again to the dancing flames. "It's Jim. His last physical showed elevated PSA, the antigens associated with prostate cancer."

Jim was Leah's husband. *There's that damned C-word again!* Mia felt a wave of dread coursing toward her.

"And they found a small lump." Leah's voice tightened, and her eyes dropped toward the ground.

Mia let the wave crash. Cancer. Lump. The words settled uncomfortably, and she was silenced by the fear that echoed in her heart. *Stay with it, Mia. And breathe. Be here for Leah.* "Jim has always been religiously adherent to annual physicals, right?" she began calmly. "So whatever it is, it's early, *if* it's anything."

She put her hand on Leah's knee, tilted her head to gain eye contact, and then gently raised Leah's head with a finger under her chin. She could feel her fear as tears built and fell. Platitudes were just that, and Leah was a planner, so the best thing Mia could do was give her an opportunity to lay things out so that the overwhelming whole was made smaller by the piece. She took a deep controlled breath. "Okay, what's the next step?"

"He had a biopsy. And now we're waiting. I feel odd about crying like this; early indicators are that most of the PSA's are free, so the prognosis is likely very good. Not like...well..." She stumbled over her words.

Mia jumped in, clear on where her friend was going. *Riley.* "I know. But you need to let yourself feel it all. Be angry. Be afraid. But also keep in mind that we have no evidence to suggest Jim's prognosis won't continue to be good and every reason to believe that it will."

Leah sat back and took a deep breath, finishing off her white wine. Mia was immediate with the refill, topped her own glass up, moved her chair closer to her friend, and took her hand before sitting back and staring into the flames. The two had grieved together over the deaths of their parents, shared their fears, lived their lives, and loved each other through it all. Even when they lived thousands of miles apart, there was never any real distance between them.

"Jim is one tough nugget, Leah. He'd have to be to put up with you."

"You're one to talk! Do you remember what you were like before Riley? Less like Flynn and more like Milo. Hyper. Always distracted. Bit of a mess, if I'm being honest."

Mia looked at Milo, who conducted a thorough sweep under the table with one ear tipped toward the crackling fire and the other on the treetops swaying with the cascading winds. "Can't argue."

"But she tempered you. Miracle worker, that woman. Tequila?"

At the mention of their traditional nightcap, Mia dashed in and out of the trailer, returning with a bottle of Jose Cuervo and two shot glasses. She poured, and the two held hands, raising their glasses to the fire.

"Limes are for cowards!" they said in unison, shouting at the stars, throwing back the golden liquor, grimacing, and then laughing along with Riley's favourite toast. Riley had forever espoused the virtues of drinking tequila without the cumbersome accoutrement and taught Mia early in their fifteen-year relationship that "drinking it clean" took bravery but always warmed the heart.

"You know, she is still leaving dimes. Even two years later."

"That's crazy." Leah squeezed her hand more tightly.

"She doesn't need to…I'll never forget her."

"I know. And she knows that, too."

Two enthusiastic toasts later, Mia felt wonderfully mellow and guessed by Leah's contented sighs that Jose had done his job. They sat, still holding hands, dogs at their feet, all parties temporarily mesmerized by the coals and flames. Then Milo and Flynn's ears shot up, and the two leapt up, noses pointed toward the farm buildings whose lights were barely visible the valley.

"Is that thunder?" Leah asked.

"Too patterned. Horse or wandering cow maybe?" Mia got out of her chair and calmly took Milo's collar. "Flynn, trailer." His obedience was a testament to his breed's willingness to please, a quality that made her work much easier than people typically thought. Flynn moved toward the trailer and stood, rigid with vigilance, at the base of the steps. Milo, too young to have reached a comparable level of understanding, began tugging and pawing at the dirt in his struggle to investigate.

"Milo, that'll do." Mia's tone was calm yet authoritative—surprising given the tequila consumption—and Milo refocused on her command. He looked toward Flynn and followed him into the trailer without a further glance at the source of the noise, which was getting clearer.

"Good boy." She shut the door behind them and turned back to the sound. "Horse?"

She strained at the darkness, seeing the blacking out of the farm's lights and listening as hooves clicked up toward the camp, then made out the unmistakable shape of an approaching horse and rider in the arch of the firelight.

❖

Aaron had been right. Sid had been rude. She was rude lately. And exhausted. Lots of excuses but not any one of them worth making. Just get it over with, she thought as she saddled up Annika, her fifteen-year-old Tennessee Walker. It was a beautiful evening for a ride, but she hesitated, wondering how Annika—not ridden since last summer—would respond.

*Is there anything or anyone I'm not failing?*

At dinner, Isabel let it slip that the McCanns' dog trainer was camped near the step. Sid suspected Aaron had mentioned the incident with Kinda Cute and her dog, and this was Isabel's way of suggesting without suggesting that a truce was in order. Sid had always appreciated Isabel's subtlety, but it wasn't until she was an adult that she recognized it.

When Isabel first arrived at the Harris ranch, Sid was twelve and had just lost her mother. Grief had charged into her adolescence like an angry bull, thrashing and bucking and kicking until she could do nothing to protect herself other than curl into a ball. She knew the loss changed her. She'd been a happy, intensely curious, courageous girl who'd become sullen, sad, and remote. And she would have rebelled if anyone had tried to take her mom's place. In retrospect, Sid could see that over the years, Isabel had carefully led a delicate dance managing all aspects of the ranch's finances, personnel, and household. Without trying to take anyone's place, Isabel had managed through loving care to buoy both her and her devastated father.

Sparked by Isabel's mention of the trainer, once Sid saw the small fire burning toward the back end of the Miller's west acreage, she felt her own conscience ignite and went to the barn to tack up. Mounted and taking a slow, steady pace up the south side of the Miller's fields near the Harrises' fence line, Sid saw the fire clearly through her field glasses along with two figures seated beside it and their flickering shadows on the shiny silver trailer.

Ten minutes into the ride, Sid stopped and assessed Annika's stamina, making sure the gradual ascent wasn't too taxing. Another look through the binoculars revealed Mia, easily recognizable by her shoulder-length blond hair, and another person, a guy perhaps, with short hair. Another ten minutes and an echo of women's voices reached her. So, not a man. Another look. The two were holding hands.

*Oh. Okay. Kinda Cute is kinda taken.*

She felt a quiver in her gut. Disappointment? No. Jealousy? Ridiculous. She certainly didn't have time to distract herself with another miscalculated dalliance, but her attention—against her own better judgment—was riveted to the intertwined hands, so by the time she arrived, she was no longer as resolute in her reason for being there as she had been fifteen minutes before.

"Limes are for cowards?" she said aloud, taking inventory of the camp.

*Well, that was stupid. Admitting to eavesdropping. Not particularly neighborly. A bit stalky.*

"Oh, it's you." The response from Kinda Cute was almost as frigid as the tops of the mountains behind her.

She and her friend had come to the edge of where the light reached. While the greeting sounded commanding, perfectly fitting for a dog trainer, Kinda Cute's body language betrayed her. She was shifting somewhat, almost but not quite unbalanced. Her eyes were locked on Sid's, but her hands were brushing off the front of her jeans and then shaping her peasant top into a respectable shape.

"Yes, it is. My name, if you've forgotten, is…"

"Sid Harris. My territorial neighbor. Yes, I recall."

The air between them grew several degrees colder, and Sid settled deeper in her saddle and lowered the reins so that her hands rested on the horn.

"Chilly. I deserve that." she said.

"And more," Kinda Cute replied, crossing her arms and nodding as if her point had been made. This was followed by an awkward silence. A long awkward silence.

When her arms uncrossed, Sid took the opportunity to end the stalemate. "Sorry if I've interrupted something. I saw the fire. Wanted to make sure things were okay." *Kind and polite.* She was doing her best to put out of her mind the tiny bit of whatever had disturbed her when she saw them holding hands.

"Well, they are. You realize that you're the one trespassing now, right?"

*Even cooler.*

Sid spent the second awkward silence biting her tongue. She

lowered her head and looked away from the fire, hoping that the brim of her hat hid her expression, which she hadn't quite settled on. She was, after all, trying to be nice, and Kinda Cute was making that difficult. She was amused at the spunky retort and didn't want her smile to fuel the fire. *Screw it.*

Sid locked eyes with Mia. She couldn't help letting loose a smile as she watched Mia's reaction. Spunky looked ready to combust. Sid tightened a grip on the reins, expecting that at any moment, she might be tackled clean off her mount.

"Yes, you are quite right. My apologies," Sid said.

"Anything else you'd like to apologize for?"

Sid lifted a hand to her ear and tucked back the hair that had fallen forward as she rode. She knew exactly the apology expected, but this was too fun. "Only that I haven't asked your names. And I'm still wondering about the limes."

"Are you...do you know what...how..."

Sid was pleased to have unnerved her and was disappointed when Kinda Cute's friend stepped in, presumably intent on rescuing Kinda Cute from herself.

"Hello, I'm Leah Fleming. Beth Miller, your dad's neighbor, is my mom. And this is my friend, Mia Jarvis."

*Kinda cute Mia.* "Leah. Mia. Cute." Sid looked again at Mia, whose mouth was now shut, but whose eyes narrowed.

"Yes, we get that a lot." Leah raised her hand to Sid, who removed her glove to shake it.

"Nice to meet you. I've heard..." Leah faltered. "Well, I've heard some about you." Leah's emphasis was on the word *some*, and her tone was apologetic.

"Mostly good?" Sid looked at Mia, expecting a reaction.

"You should feel free to imagine," Leah said with an odd tinge of optimism.

"Thanks, I will." Sid held her smile and kept her eyes on Mia. *I'm imagining a lot about her right now.*

Sid looked around the camp, taking a slow inventory of the setup as she turned her horse down-range. "And I think I'll also take my leave. Three's a crowd. You two have a good night."

❖

"Why on earth did you say that?" Mia flared as soon as Sid was out of earshot.

"What?" Leah smiled, "Oh, you mean that I'd heard some about her? Well, why not? It's true."

"It's true all right. Didn't I tell you? She's even more arrogant than I first thought. And nosy. What's with her checking out my stuff like she owns the place? And not apologizing. So rude!" Mia turned on her heel and marched back to the chairs by the fire. She poured another two shots and held one toward Leah.

"I think I know her," Leah said.

"You probably just know her type. Did you hear how she said 'three's a crowd'? What do you think she meant? Honestly!" She downed her shot and poured another.

"Okay, slow down there, darlin'." Leah grabbed the bottle and set it down a long arm's length beyond Mia's reach. "What's got your panties in a knot? Or who?"

Instead of answering, she stared at the fire and then her glass, looking for a way to redirect the conversation and hoping Leah was drunk enough to forget. Was it that obvious? Hopefully it wasn't so obvious to Sid. Hopefully she hadn't noticed how Mia's stomach had strangled the words in her throat or how her palms had become white hot in her clenched hands. At one point during the exchange, Mia's heart was pounding so loudly in her ears that she almost couldn't hear Sid's voice. But what a voice it was. The velvety alto carried through the night air like tumbleweeds across sand before hanging like a perfectly struck, barely-below-C chord on an acoustic guitar. More than once, she had to steel herself against the captivating resonance of its timbre. She cursed Jose Cuervo. When all she wanted to do was knock the annoyingly beautiful woman right off her horse, and the cocky smirk off her gorgeous face, Jose had undermined her resolve.

"So, what's up with your sex life?" Leah asked.

"Where did that come from? What do you mean?" Mia feigned

innocence, but her own tequila consumption made pretending increasingly difficult.

"You know, that thing that you and other women do? With each other? I'm guessing, in your case, rarely. Weren't you talking about dating that breeder you met in Calgary?"

Mia drank her shot. "Not the right fit." She looked at Leah's expression of doubt and calmed herself. "Seriously. She wasn't. I feel like I'm almost ready to date again. Really. Maybe."

*Maybe with the right woman. Maybe with one who's not so right.*

"Okay, okay. But, Mia, I swear I know Sid. I can't help but think *we* know her. Do you still have your yearbooks? We should look. No, on second thought, she's too young for our high school years. Maybe we saw her at the Stampede? Do you think she's a barrel racer? She has the body for it. Long legs and broad shoulders. Nice biceps, too, did you notice? And she looks great on a horse. A regular Alberta Amazon."

As Leah espoused the inarguable physiological virtues of Sid Harris, Mia retrieved the bottle, filled their glasses, and looked out over the valley. She found herself rubbing the finger where her wedding band used to be and turned toward the faint sound of retreating hooves.

"Well, it certainly seems like you're ready to me," Leah said softly, raising her glass.

*Limes really are for cowards.*

## CHAPTER FIVE

It was no mystery where the sweat came from. In the heat of the morning sun, tequila oozing from her pores, Mia had only herself to blame. After all, she had done as much of the pouring as Leah had the night before, and the early morning run might have been a decision made while still under the influence of the evil *gusano*, the mythic tequila worm. No T-shirt, no matter its promise to wick, stood a chance. She was dripping.

As Mia started up the dirt road, the breeze against her back tempered only a fraction of the sun's heat, which was rising eerily, surrounded by the deep red of a blood orange. Rain was sure to come, which would be a relief to the crops and help settle the dust collecting in her shirt, but the forecast meant that if Milo was going to get two hours of command training, she would need to get it done this morning.

She smiled regretfully, remembering a sign she saw over the door of one of her favourite dive bars in Key West. "This tequila tastes like I'm not going to work tomorrow." She wished she had that option. Like humans in the heat and humidity, work dogs fatigued more readily. Since Milo was at the end of his second week, he wasn't conditioned for the endurance required for long sessions, so fewer hours for consecutive days were in his best interest, and Mia didn't feel it fair to deny Milo simply because she hadn't been her own liquor control board.

*Maybe I made a few bad choices over the past twenty-four hours, but at least I fueled up.* She credited herself for drinking two large glasses of water before her head hit the pillow last night and for downing a double dose of an electrolyte hydrator and a protein bar before heading out into the morning.

Approaching the base of the T-junction, Mia first considered taking a left and heading north past the Millers' homestead, her usual route. But today she was on a schedule and couldn't take the chance that Beth might stop her for a chat, so she turned south and continued on the shoulder, focusing as best she could on her breathing and stride in order to distract herself from the river of sweat tickling between her butt cheeks.

❖

Sid liked to drive, especially in her dad's pickup and most especially in the country, even pulling a livestock trailer. There were no taxis or cyclists or streetcars to contend with, and she felt pure exhilaration to roll down the cab's windows and settle in for a trip to anywhere. The nearest such "anywhere" was thirty or so minutes from the Harris farm, and this morning's "anywhere" was another fifteen minutes beyond that. The stockyard she and Aaron were headed to was near the main highway heading south into Calgary.

As they cruised toward the interchange that would put them on course, Sid could make out a figure running on the opposite side of the road in the same direction. It was a rare sight given that the typical farm day provided a workout far and away more rigorous than a gym could and left the hardworking with little extra energy to spend. Starting the day with a run, well, that seemed a bit much.

Sid slowed as she closed the distance to the runner. If the sweat-blotched fabric sticking on the glistening toned and tanned curves didn't make it easy to see it was a woman, then the ponytail bobbing up and down with each stride did.

*Of course. Mia.*

Sid's suspicion was confirmed when she felt her own breath catch at Mia's quick shoulder check.

*Damn. She saw me. Oh well, of course she did.*

Sid felt oddly cornered, which she knew was ridiculous given that she was driving in a big truck, and Mia was, well, just running. Size and speed were on Sid's side. But she nonetheless hoped against hope that the pickup hadn't slowed so much that Mia would know it was her.

*So what if she did? Why does it matter? I was just being courteous by slowing. It's how we do things. Why did I have to have the window open?*

"See something you like?" Aaron's words popped Sid's ballooning contemplations like a thumbtack.

"Not interested in women at the moment," she replied quickly, her heart racing, and her foot already pressing heavier on the gas as if to catch up. She was lying, of course, and she suspected Aaron knew that. He was the only one who had ever beaten her during family poker games, though only rarely. In the business Sid was in, keeping emotion in check was a necessity and a skill she had mastered in order to survive her teens. But as steely as she could be, it was impossible not to notice the tight physique, the sexy arch of the woman's back as it flowed down into muscled but nicely rounded glutes and sculpted thighs and calves she had only seen on serious cyclists.

"Oddly enough, neither am I." Aaron's laugh was enough to check Sid's distraction, but she knew he'd rally if she didn't steer him in a different direction.

"When are *you* going to settle, cuz?"

"Maybe sooner than later," was Aaron's cryptic, almost musical reply. It was the kind of baiting intended to create drama, a conversational equivalent of glitter, and Sid refused to sparkle along.

"Speaking of sooner, do you think we'll be back with Bullwinkle before the rain hits? Not that I'll melt if we're not, but it's been a while since I've hauled a trailer and on slippery roads…"

"No worries, Sid, I'll drive back. So, you're going with Bullwinkle now?"

"Yes. Why? You don't think it's a good name for our new bull?"

"I think it's great. I also think it's great that you're all hot and bothered by that girl you didn't notice back there. Sorry, *woman*. Makes me feel like I've got someone to keep me company on the lust train." More glitter. This time, Sid was happy to give over the drama.

"Okay, cuz, what's his name?" She smiled broadly as they turned onto the highway access road.

"Greg. Yes, again."

## CHAPTER SIX

By the time Mia returned from her run, changed into dry clothes, and wrapped up her session with Milo, it was late morning, and the clouds, though still in the distance, were on a direct path for the area. She could hear Leah bumping around in the trailer, a signal that she was up even though the blinds were still down. Some things never changed; Leah knew how to sleep.

Mia swung open the door, and daylight filled the Airstream.

"Oh God, Mia, please! The light!" Leah shielded her eyes with her arm, Garbo-esque, leaving it there until the door fell shut. She stood in the kitchen, chewing on a protein bar, her head wrapped in a towel turban. "What were you thinking? And why did you let me sleep so late? I have a flight this afternoon."

"No worries; at least you're already showered and dressed. You have plenty of time. To be honest, my only thought this morning was how to keep the Alberta dustbowl out of my mouth. Tequila! Why?" While she ranted, Mia dropped a handful of ice cubes into a large glass and filled it with iced tea.

"I know." Leah laughed, sliding last night's jeans and hoodie, both immaculately folded, into a vacuum pouch. "Why do we do it?"

"Tradition. Want one? It's bergamot. No sugar."

"Please." She peered out the window and shook her head. "No, wait, on second thought, no time. I'd like to stay ahead of the rain. It's been so dry. I don't want to chance washouts on the road." Leah sat down on the space-saving travel bag, and the air whooshed out; she zipped it closed and tucked the rigid envelope under her arm.

Mia was filling a travel mug with tea and ice while Leah unwrapped her head and towelled her hair, worked in a bit of product, and pieced it into place with her fingers. With her pixie haircut, she reminded Mia of sportscaster celebrity Robin Roberts whose hair, even when messy, still looked perfect.

"I had the craziest dreams," Leah said over her shoulder, sliding small bottles of shampoo and various makeup off the bathroom counter into a toiletries bag. "I knew something was percolating when I met Sid last night. Remember? Well guess what? When I woke up, it came to me."

Mia was pouring a second glass for herself—having already downed the first in one gulp—as Leah headed for the door, bags in hand, still talking at a pace as quick as she moved.

"I was at the opening of the Vezina Gallery in Montreal in the spring, and Sid was there. She was one of the guest speakers. I think it took me a while to figure this whole thing out because in art circles, she goes by Cassidy."

Cassidy Harris. Not possible. The incongruity was beyond Mia's belief, and her brain worked to banish the notion.

*Sid. Cassidy. Fancy. With her big truck. So subtle.* Mia could still feel the woman's eyes on her sweaty ass.

Milo bounced at Leah's feet as she stepped out of the trailer. Mia scanned for Flynn, who normally would have joined in but who had opted for a shady spot under the table. Mia took the opportunity to change the subject.

"Come say good-bye to Leah, Flynn." At this, he slowly got to his feet and sauntered over, his tail wagging barely.

"Cassidy Harris. Sid is *Cassidy* Harris." Leah was unstoppable, continuing her story as she popped open the back of the rental Range Rover. "The art curator from the Northern Lights Gallery."

Mia knew the gallery. It was one of the most respected in the country. Surely its curator and the maniac on the ATV were not the same Sid Harris. Mia tried to imagine Sid traveling in art circles, clinking glasses with the sophisticates and breaking bread with the bon vivants of the Toronto art scene. Maybe with a change of clothes. She mentally dressed her in evening wear, then considered undressing her. Sid's hair, that lovely auburn hair, flowing down her shoulders. Jewelry. Dark green emeralds. Like her eyes. Mia found herself parched again, and she took a swig of her own tea to quench the thirst. The curator of Northern Lights Gallery? Maybe when spit-shined. But her temperament? No way. It had to be a different Sid Harris.

"And she was at the gala *with* Aurora St. Germaine." Leah didn't wait for Mia's reaction, as she carried on. "Yes, *that* St. Germaine. The one with the fresco in the new ferry terminal on the island. Can you believe it?"

Mia was glad Leah hadn't looked because as aware as Mia was of her facial cues and gestures—a skill required for her work—she knew she wasn't hiding her response to what felt like a kick in the solar plexus. No need to think a moment more about Sid, who had already occupied too much of her headspace over the last twenty-four hours. Besides, Mia had a hard and fast rule about dating people in relationships: She didn't.

Leah unzipped and flipped opened the enormous hard-sided travel bag in the truck and tucked her plastic-sealed clothes and toiletries bag in, then squeezed it shut as if she'd done it a million times. Mia suspected she probably had; as a senior partner in an international legal firm, Leah was always here or there. In fact, she'd met Jim in Amsterdam while on a business trip. She continued to talk as she walked toward the driver's side and opened the door, almost knocking the travel mug out of Mia's hands.

"The colleague I was there with is Aurora's counsel. She mentioned that the two are dating. Curator by night. Rancher by day. It's like she has a secret identity. And her super power is her sexy gorgeousness. Aurora St. Germaine and Cassidy…Sid. Dating. Crazy, right?"

*All three?* Mia, always her own best audience, nearly laughed out loud.

Leah wrapped her arms around Mia, petted the dogs, and settled into the Rover. She put on her seat belt and lowered the window before closing the door. Mia handed her the traveler mug of iced tea through the window. She tried not to look as disappointed as she felt.

"Damn, Mia, I'm sorry. That wasn't very sensitive of me. I saw the way you looked at her. And we all saw the way she looked at you, didn't we, boys? In fact, I might be a superhero too, because last night while she was here, I was invisible. You two only had eyes for each other. If I hadn't been tipsy, I would've been embarrassed for the both of you."

"Are you still tipsy? Maybe you shouldn't drive. Can I call you a cab?"

"Hilarious. I'm perfectly fine. Thanks for the tea. Just remember, Sid may be taken, but there are plenty of fish in the sea."

Mia shook her head and couldn't do much else but smile. Her friend's motives were well intended, just seriously misdirected. There wasn't time to reset. "I don't even know where you're off to. Toronto?"

"Not this time. I have discoveries in Calgary starting Monday, and if my case prep goes well, I'm hoping to catch the Emily Carr exhibit tomorrow night to break up the weekend. Should wrap up by next Friday, and then I'm home to Jim…to celebrate."

Mia smiled, noting her friend's revived optimism.

"But if any of that's going to happen, I have to make my flight. I'll give you a call when hubby's results are in; they tell us next week. Thanks for being here for me. Love you, Mia."

Mia gently touched Leah's cheek, knowing that while she was all business on the outside, she was turmoil inside. "Love you back."

Leah nodded and put the Rover into gear.

Mia watched, sipping her tea as her friend pulled to a stop at the T-junction at the bottom of the slope. Flynn was still under the table, ears perking up now and again, signaling there was likely thunder in the distance. She was pleased to see that Milo, happily chasing a rolling ball of twigs and grass, still had some energy. Provided the weather held, she hoped to do another hour with him this afternoon. As she watched the Range Rover across the landscape, she noticed another vehicle heading toward it.

*Sid's truck. Cassidy's. Whatever. Aurora St. Germaine's girlfriend.*

The Harris pickup and trailer moved slowly past, an arm waved from the passenger side, and Leah's arm raised in greeting. Mia turned and headed back to the trailer, again parched.

"Come on, Flynn, Milo, the air conditioner is on, and I think we could all use a cooldown."

## CHAPTER SEVEN

It was only after her third glass of iced tea that Mia began to feel less jittery and more like herself. Learning about Sid's world had startled her and left her feeling unsettled. It had been a long time since her hormones had been stirred by a beautiful woman, and Mia realized with some sadness that she yearned for touch, for the tenderness of a woman's hand on her shoulder, the sweetness of soft lips on hers, and the smoldering passion she hadn't felt since her years with Riley.

She stepped out of the cool trailer into the heat, leaving the dogs behind so they wouldn't be underfoot as she gathered things in preparation for the weather change. The arched storage tent had proven over the years that it could withstand some pretty tough winds, so she confidently moved the table, the fold-up Muskoka chairs, and the grill into it, zipping up and pulling down the side awnings and securing them to the spiral ground pegs. She was about to head into the trailer when a dusty Ford Ranger pulled up. Mia smiled, remembering from her childhood that it was impossible to keep anything white during a dry prairie summer.

"Hey there!" Beth Miller called from the cab. "You're in my bad books, little girl. How dare you steal my daughter's attention? I think I saw her for all of ten minutes this trip."

"Well, you have Jose Cuervo to thank for that. He always has his way with us."

"Don't I know it."

Beth gestured to her companion, who walked beside her carrying a small square straw basket, its contents hidden by a white linen cloth. "This is my friend Isabel. Isabel, this is Mia Jarvis."

"Hello, Mia, I've heard so much about you!" Isabel's words seemed genuine, and her smile shone from a face warmly weathered and tanned in a way that said she laughed a lot. Mia was instantly drawn to her and, knowing that she was a friend of Beth's, ignored both the Harris connection and her proffered hand to give her a hug.

"So nice to meet you, Isabel. What on earth smells so delightful?" Mia's stomach was growling, a sign that her hangover was subsiding.

"I made some tortillas this morning. These are for you."

"Wow, homemade tortillas? Corn?" Mia accepted the basket and pulled back the linen cloth, breathing in the delicious, earthy aroma.

Isabel looked at her as if she'd asked if there really was a man in the moon. "Of course. Where I'm from, there's no other kind. Only two ingredients needed, *masa harina* and water."

"Where are you from?" A pause, then Mia continued, "Originally?"

"Asunción Ocotlán. It's a very small place in the south of Mexico. I've been here with the Harrises a long time now."

Mia stiffened at the mention of the Harrises and noted a glance between Isabel and Beth that suggested there was more to the story. Before she could inquire, Isabel looked her in the eyes.

"Please accept my apologies for Sid's behavior. I heard that she behaved badly. She's as headstrong as her father at times, but like him, she has a good heart." Isabel looked again at Beth, who smiled slyly, then back at Mia.

*Somebody has a secret. Wait a second…how do they know?*

As if reading Mia's mind, Beth stepped forward to explain that Leah had called from her cell on her way to the airport and told her about Sid's confrontation with Mia the day before last.

"Don't worry. When it comes to secrets, Isabel is a vault." Beth winked at Isabel, confirming what Mia suspected. There was clearly something going on that they weren't about to share.

"Next trip, I get time with her first," Beth continued. "You and your damn tequila have a way of monopolizing Leah's home time." "Deal. I don't like her much anyways," Mia lied, and Beth and Isabel both laughed.

Once they gathered around the kitchen table, iced teas in hand, Mia set some shredded chicken, salsa, and guacamole on the table. She hoped Isabel wouldn't be offended that the latter two were store-bought. Unable to politely wait and still starving from the morning's activities, Mia peeled one of Isabel's tortillas off the top of the stack, noting that it was soft as a pillow; the almost nutty fragrance reminded her of mushrooms. The thin pancake melted on her tongue, and she was astonished that something so simple could taste so amazing. They ate, but it wasn't long before the conversation turned back to Sid Harris.

"She wasn't always like that, our Sid. When her mama died, she was devastated. Teenagers already have such a tough time. I'm sure you know." Isabel rested her hand on Mia's. "She pulled away from her friends and especially from her papa. Duncan. Years later, she went away to university and didn't come back other than Christmas except to help in the spring with plowing and planting. I think it was hard for her to be here when her mother wasn't."

"What a terrible coincidence," Beth said. "Sid lost her mom around the same age you lost yours and Leah lost her dad, my Bruce."

Mia wasn't sure how to respond. She wanted to stand her ground, rationalizing that grief or sadness or whatever Sid might be feeling didn't excuse rudeness years later. But she also felt a twinge of empathy and compassion for another girl who lost her mom too soon.

"You haven't met the real Sid, the one on the inside," Isabel continued as Mia dug into another tortilla. "Just now, so much stress. The stolen cattle. A new bull. Many fences that need fixing. And she has a big job in the city that she's still trying to manage from here." Isabel shook her head. "I'm not sure how she does it all. Well, I guess I do. Not very nicely right now."

Big job was a bit of an understatement. The Northern Lights

Gallery was top-shelf, their exhibits unparalleled in terms of heritage and contemporary Canadian art. Leah and Mia would always include an afternoon in their itineraries whenever Leah came to visit her—and then her and Riley—in Toronto. A curator would have responsibilities beyond what Mia could have imagined Cassidy Harris capable of, given her encounters with the woman thus far. *Tact, for one example. Diplomacy another.*

"That's okay, Isabel." Mia could tell she felt genuinely bad, and that was not hers to bear. "We all have bad days. I'm sure that if she was influenced at all by having you in her life after her mom passed, she has a more endearing side. We all do."

Isabel smiled, relieved, it seemed, to have made some sort of amends.

They continued to share stories over lunch. Beth asked about Mia's dad. They'd maintained their friendship after he'd moved to Calgary to support Mia through university, but she caught her up on his most recent travels and promised she'd pass along her best when they spoke next.

A deep grumble of thunder rolled outside. Flynn, never a fan of storms, whimpered and put his paw over his eyes. Milo took it as an invitation to annoy his buddy and licked Flynn's face. Mia could easily imagine what Flynn was thinking.

"Isabel, we should think about going soon. Mia, please tell me how you're really doing." When Beth used her name with that tone and an emphasis on the *really*, Mia knew what she was asking.

"I'm okay. *Really*, Beth." Mia smiled at her imitation. "Of course, I'll always miss Riley, but I don't want to miss out on life; she'd kick my ass if I chose that path. You know she would."

Beth smiled and hugged her. Isabel smiled empathetically, so Mia gathered she had been made aware of who Riley was.

As Isabel collected the empty tortilla basket, she continued—unnecessarily but kindly—to make amends. "Duncan and I would like you to feel free to use the show arena whenever you like. It's covered and will come in handy for you and the dogs if the rain lasts. Aaron and Sid just moved the new bull into the far pen, but there's plenty of room for your training. We have no events requiring it for the next few weeks. Oh, and mark your calendar for two weeks from now. I'm throwing a big fiesta for Duncan's seventieth birthday. You must come!"

"If I'm here, I may just do that. Milo is a quick learner, so I may have moved on by then, though I'm not sure where to next."

"Please promise me. I'm making tortillas. So much food. And I will put Sid on notice that she must treat all the guests like royalty."

Mia smiled, but on the inside, doubts stirred that Sid would take kindly to seeing her. Maybe that was as good a reason as any to go.

## CHAPTER EIGHT

Mia chose, wisely she thought, to take a short nap after lunch. She had not been a napper in her younger years, but now that she stood close to the fifty-year threshold, with the rain pounding on the trailer and the thunder rolling across the fields, it would be easy and wise to reenergize before taking the extra hour with Milo. Both dogs usually curled at the foot of the bed, but today it was just her and Milo, Flynn preferring the added protection of the kitchen table above his head.

Awake by midafternoon, she had successfully put the post-tequila jitters and thirst behind her, and the rain let up enough to get from trailer to truck without rain gear. She set out with Milo to take Isabel and Duncan up on their offer of the arena.

She passed the first driveway into the compound, noticing that the second entry ran up directly beside the arena. The ruts were deep, and because they were made by a truck with a double-wide wheel base, her pickup slid in the mud from one trough to the other, jostling her and Milo in spite of her seat belt and his harness vest, and eventually coming to a slick stop beside the main south opening under the building's overhang. As it did, she recognized Aaron as he stepped up to the passenger window and knocked. She pushed the button on her armrest, holding Milo's harness in case he felt the need to lunge, bark, or lick the handsome, friendly face.

"Hey, there! Isabel told me you might be coming. I'm Aaron, and as I understand it, you're Mia." He pushed his tanned, muscled arm into the cab, letting Milo give him a thorough sniff, thus gaining permission to shake Mia's hand.

"We did meet a few days ago." Mia was unsure of whether the two cousins were of a feather, so kept her tone formal. "But I'm certain you had no idea then that I was a guest of the Millers."

"No, ma'am, I certainly did not. And I do apologize for the behavior of myself and, of course, my cousin. Sid had a very, very bad morning that day. Not to excuse her, but well, we've been having a few challenges lately."

"Cattle disappearing in the night? Yes, I heard. That's terrible. Any idea who?"

"No, ma'am." He walked around the front of the truck and opened Mia's door, offering a hand which she ignored, but as her foot sank inches into the mud, she accepted with thanks.

"Mia, please, Aaron. I'm nobody's ma'am."

The two walked around the pickup and into the mostly open-air arena. Mia brushed off jacket sleeves that had become speckled with rain before giving up and setting it down on a bale near the door. The building was beautifully equipped for work and show: eighty yards or so long and at least forty wide. Whitewashed walls ran along three sides of the building, not quite halfway up the height of the beautifully hand hewn, two-foot by two-foot fir posts that supported the main beams and roof. Above these half walls were vertical metal rails that effectively deterred an animal that might have notions of escape.

The show building had two large entryways on each of the sides, their locations mirrored to facilitate off-loading, enabling a vehicle to go in one side and straight out the other. These each had a standard cattle swing gate, and also electric pull-down iron fences that would contain animals, but most importantly—especially in August heat—would facilitate air flow throughout the stadium.

Around the inside perimeter, along the half walls of the two long sides and one short side, were three-level stadium benches. All along the remaining short side—the only full exterior wall—was a heavy gauge pen roughly ten yards deep with gates on the three open sides. Stacks of hay bales walled off almost the entire left half, and Mia assumed the enclosure, like others she had seen in arena barns when the facility wasn't in use, was to segregate sick or injured cattle.

"My gosh, it's so still. That rain has done nothing to drop the temperatures or the humidity." Mia was pleased that she'd decided on a sleeveless, collarless cotton shirt.

"It's always that way here. When the rains come, it's as if the winds forget to. Except during Chinooks!" Aaron possessed that good ol' boy charm, and as much as she'd tried to dislike him—unfairly—by association with Sid, she found herself enjoying his company. "If you're looking to cool off, there's a small lake up on the step just south of where you're camped. Maybe you saw it on your walk the other day?"

Mia shook her head, wishing she had. It would be a lovely respite during days like these, and the dogs would enjoy a plunge more than a walk in the creek to cool off.

"You can cut through woods beyond where we met you and stay on the game trail. There's a gate Duncan built so that the neighbors could access it...I think he's too afraid to tell Sid about it."

"Don't they get along?" Mia was undoing Milo's harness, setting him down on the arena side of the mud that surrounded her truck.

"Oh heck, they get along. But Sid reacts like a mama bear when folks take advantage, and she's trying her best right now to hold down the fort, so to speak. Uncle Dunc is just so friendly, and I think she's caught up in trying to protect him from his own kindness."

*That's understandable. Mama bear indeed.*

"Between you and me," he added, "Sid loves this place more than she probably knows. And she's worried that if things keep up the way they're going, well—"

"Cuz! Let's go. That grain isn't going to pour itself." Sid stood in the doorway on the far side of the barn, one hand on her hip and the other holding a pair of leather gloves, which she was slapping on her thigh. At the sound of her voice, Milo stopped sniffing the ground and beelined toward her.

"Milo, stand," Mia called.

Milo stopped, his sights still on Sid, but his desire thwarted by training that had started to seep into his young brain.

"Howdy, neighbor." She tipped her head, and Mia caught a slight smirk beneath her hat brim. "Impressive. Good dog."

Aaron passed Milo, who held his spot, and joined his cousin. "See you later, Mia. You too, Milo."

"Bye, Aaron. Nice meeting you...this time!" Mia turned, refusing to acknowledge Sid by pretending she had something urgent to get out of the truck. She felt the glare against her back.

*Get a good look. That's all you'll get.*

By the time she turned back, Sid and Aaron were headed toward the barn on the other side of the courtyard, seemingly oblivious to the light rain that still fell and the mud puddles they sloshed through.

❖

Mia and Milo worked together at the open end of the stadium near the gates, happy for a late afternoon breeze that at long, hot last had started to work its way down the cooler mountains. Milo had done well, and Mia's jeans pocket was empty of treats in spite of the fact that she used them sparingly. She kept a small reserve in her glove compartment and was walking to the truck to fetch them when a sharp staccato of barks caused her to spin back into the arena. Milo was at a full run to the pen at the far end of the building. He covered the last bit of distance with a dive, flattening to squish himself between the muddy floor and the lowest metal bar. He darted back and forth in the pen, barking at whatever stood behind the hay bales; her heart lurched as she ran toward the enclosure.

*Surely there's nothing in there. We would've seen it by now.*

A loud prolonged snort emanated from behind the stack of hay bales.

*Oh God.* The dread built as she remembered something Isabel had said at lunch.

"...new bull...far pen..."

"Milo, come." She fought her own panic, needing to keep her voice steady and commanding. The barking continued. By the time she reached the pen, the bull had shown himself. His massive dark body was hunched like a grizzly bear, his head bobbing and black eyes glistening as they followed Milo's ill-advised leaps with sickening intent. Mia had no time to think; she climbed over the bars, vaulting into the bull's domain. Milo continued to bark and dance, but the bull turned its attention to Mia.

She grabbed Milo by the scruff and tossed him behind her. If she had a plan, it wasn't a good one. She was in a very bad spot, the bull cutting off her escape, no doubt to crush her against the wall. *Keep away from his feet. Don't get trampled or kicked.* As her panic rose, he advanced like a tank.

Desperately, Mia leapt on the lowest rail of the gate, lunged, and grabbed his nose ring before he could pull away. She held tight to the snot-covered metal as the bull's head twisted grotesquely, and his body pressed her into the iron bars.

*Don't let go. Mia, don't let go.*

She wasn't sure it was her own voice, but it was followed by a sickening crunch as the bull pushed slowly into her. Mia felt as though a red-hot bowsaw pushed and pulled savagely through her torso. Her feet lifted off the rail, and she dangled like a broken rag doll. She was desperate to keep hold of the cold, wet brass, the spew of the bull soaking her hand and arm; she twisted the ring with all of her strength, and the bull jerked away. Her feet planted again, one on the rail, the other in the mud. Milo barked frantically, adding to the snorting, spewing, and grunting in the pen. With her arm extended to keep hold of the nose ring, each breath brought with it the searing cut of the saw.

The bull retrenched and pressed against her again. Her body lifted, and she lost her footing, putting her whole weight on his ring. Her arm twisted with his head as he shrieked with pain. A shower of warm mucus flew through the air. It twirled and twizzled and flipped above her like a slow-motion scene in a Tarantino film.

*Don't let go. Don't let go.*

She fell so he was unable to rack her again, bringing relief and dread; his hooves would kill just as easily. Her fingers slipped from the ring, and her head fell back, striking the lower bar with a strange clang that echoed like a bouncing ball through her head. Each echo brought with it a dizzying, nauseating thud that turned Mia's stomach. The darkness sweeping across her vision seemed to have also turned down the volume. Now everything slowed.

Bits and pieces.

Intermittent flashes. Slides in a carousel.

Barking. Voices.

"Hold on, Mia!"

More slides. Two hands wrapped under her arms, tugging, the bar now over her head, the mud cold and wet under her body but yielding like snow on a toboggan run. Jagged spears replaced the red-hot saw. Spears tortured her with each movement and each breath. A scream she thought sounded like her own. Then more spears.

Now warmth. Strong soft arms around her, down in the mud, cradling her. Milo licking the bull's spit off her hand.

Tumbleweeds. Whispers now.

"Hold on. I gotcha."

Copper-brown hair, like a worn penny. The smell of hay. Flannel.

"Dammit, Mia."

❖

"How goddam stupid, Aaron!" She was pacing frantically.

"Sid, calm down."

"I won't calm down. She could've been killed. She should've known better. At least she had the sense to hang on to that ring."

He nodded. "She'll be fine, cuz."

"She'd better be. I mean, what was she thinking? And what about Bullwinkle? How much longer until he'll settle now?"

Aaron didn't reply. He knew she wasn't at all concerned about the bull. Her focus was on nothing or no one but Mia. Sid had moved so quickly when Milo sounded the alarm that she was across the yard before he was even out of the barn. As he entered the stadium, he heard Mia's desperate cry and saw Sid scramble under the fence and single-handedly wedge and slide her under the rail and out from beneath the thrashing bull. He saw her face as she fell backward onto the sloppy, straw-strewn floor of the arena, holding the whimpering, mud-covered Mia in her arms. Aaron had seen more than fear in Sid's eyes. He saw a steadfastness he knew Sid possessed but hadn't seen since he was a young boy in the days at his sick aunt's bedside. The Sid of then had parked her emotions elsewhere when cancer visited the Harris house. She was always there, tending to her mom's every need, but she was absent, too. When Beverly Harris succumbed, maybe a bit of Sid went with her. Now, seeing such deep, undisguised tenderness in her tear-streaked eyes, he was reminded of Sid before those dark days.

Though it seemed like hours, it was only several minutes later when Mia was able to get to her feet, albeit unsteadily. He noted the smile Sid tried to disguise as Mia insisted she was fine, and that yes, she would go to the hospital provided Isabel drove her, and no ambulance was required.

*Girls*, he thought, then shook his head. *Check that. Women.*

## CHAPTER NINE

A cloud of red Alberta dust chased the pickup truck along the foothill. It grew bigger as the truck slowed near the Harris ranch turnoff. Mia had felt every stone beneath the tires and every hollow in the road from the moment she and Isabel left the hospital. She bit hard on her tongue, refusing to alarm her anxious driver, but as Isabel turned slowly into the Harris driveway, the front wheel of the truck dipped sharply into a mud rut, and Mia let out a yelp.

"I'm so sorry. I'm going as slowly as I can without risking getting stuck."

Mia could feel Isabel's eyes on her. When she caught a narrowed glimpse of her own face in the sideview mirror, she understood Isabel's concern: her eyes were creased in pain, and her eerily ashen face was scrunched up as she tried to thwart the feeling. Her breath came short through her nose at first, then as the pain subsided to what was just short of terrible, she was able to relax and take a few shallow breaths through her mouth.

"Please don't apologize; you're doing great." It was a miracle Mia could manage words. Her right arm was tucked in close against her side and abdomen, creating a natural splint that barely relieved her discomfort. Her right hand was bandaged, her fingertips sticking out of the end of the gauze so she was forced to use her left hand to grip the seat belt, doing her best to take a bit more of the pressure off her right ribs. Though corseted tightly, every movement of her torso sent shards of pain to her throbbing head. Nausea rose in her gut constantly, but the prospect of retching with her ribs so compromised was enough to arrest the notion.

"Are you sure that Milo is okay?" she asked, hoping the change of topic would make the next few hundred yards to the house bearable.

"Yes, please don't worry. Aaron texted while you were with the doctor; it took a bit to get him to calm down, but he seemed better once Flynn was brought down to the house."

"Flynn hasn't been around many men. I'm surprised he agreed. You know, I appreciate your offer to stay, but I'm pretty sure I can manage at the trailer."

"And I'm pretty sure you cannot." Isabel took her right hand off the wheel and put it gently on Mia's lap. "At least, not for a day or two. You're going to be even stiffer tomorrow, and we're happy to have you and the dogs. We have plenty of room."

Mia moaned as the car completed its stop in front of the main house.

"Are the drugs wearing off? I picked up the prescription at the hospital pharmacy while they were monitoring you. As soon as we get in the house, we'll top you off with a couple of Percocet; that should help you sleep."

"Thank you. Sorry to be a bother." Mia doubted there were enough drugs on the planet to keep the spears at bay. She felt helpless, and tears began to fall down her cheeks. She didn't have the energy to wipe them away.

"No bother at all. Just be aware that I will be poking my head into your room throughout the night as instructed by the doctor to make sure you don't have a concussion."

"I didn't lose consciousness. I just got a bit…blurry."

*Blurry? Or was I hallucinating?*

Images again flashed through her mind as if on an old-school carousel projector. The slick black hooves raised above her. Milo. Sid's hair. Green eyes, panicked. Tears. Shouts.

"Well, nonetheless, little girl, you'll be under observation." Isabel had adopted Beth's term of endearment, and for that brief moment—until the truck came to a stop in front of the house—Mia forgot how much she hurt.

*Could have been worse.*

The doctor told her how lucky she had been, and Mia couldn't disagree. She wasn't sure if her nausea was a response to the goose egg on the back of her head or the intrusive memory of fear as she struggled to protect Milo and escape. Either way, she thought with dread, it could have ended much differently.

Aaron and a man with a shoulder sling, no doubt Duncan, were there to greet them.

Aaron opened Mia's door. "Shall I lift you?" he asked.

"I don't think my ribs could bear that, Aaron. I can walk. But thanks."

He came around her left side, and she pivoted slowly, bringing her legs out of the cab and sliding out the door. She wrapped her free arm around his waist so that she could lean against him for support. His was a gentle strength, and Mia trusted him.

Duncan held open the screen door. The pain from every movement almost buckling her legs, Mia barely managed to acknowledge his kindness.

"We'll get properly introduced tomorrow, young lady. Let's get you to your room."

❖

The dime was shiny. Sid reached for it but couldn't quite touch it. It was stuck to a black velvet cloth outside her bedroom window. She stood on tiptoe, extending her arms as far as she could, but still, it was out of reach. Her mom's voice wafted across her shoulders from somewhere behind her, soft and encouraging. *You've almost got it, Cassidy Lynn. It's right there.* Goose bumps now. And warm tears.

*I can't, Mom. Mom. Mom?*

Sid woke with a start, her breath sudden and sharp. Her mom was gone, but she could still feel the goose bumps on her arms and see the dime through tears that fell softly on the pillow. This time, the dime was the moon suspended above the horizon. Sid grabbed her phone and looked at the time. It was after one a.m. She hadn't been asleep for more than an hour, and it had taken her at least that to will herself into the restlessness that defined her sleep patterns lately. The recurring dream no longer disturbed her as it once had, but she knew it would be hours before she'd be able to surrender to sleep again, so she kicked back what remained of the strewn bed sheets and shifted to work mode. Resignedly, she dressed and made her way to the stables.

Sid barely had the shovel in her hands when the flash of headlights shone briefly through the board walls. She moved to the doorway, obscured by darkness, watching as Mia was escorted into the Harrises' house. She knew her intense reactions toward Mia were rooted somewhere well beyond her current comfort zone. Maybe, sadly, her comfort zone period. True, Mia's second misadventure on the Harris property in as many days demonstrated a lack of concern for personal safety, but that was none of Sid's concern. And yet it was. For some indeterminable reason, the annoyance she'd felt had turned into something else. And as hard as Sid tried to focus on what was important—to balance the needs of her family's farm and her responsibilities at the gallery—images of Mia penned, in danger and wounded, swirled in her mind and made her stomach flip.

She was a lot tougher than Sid had first imagined: Even when confronted with unimaginable terror—a result of her own misstep—she'd had the presence of mind to grab the bull by its ring and preserve her life. Had she not done so, the outcome would have been worse. Much worse. Sid felt her throat constrict, and she fought the deep urge to follow the entourage into the house and make sure Mia was okay.

*She doesn't need you to worry about her. She has Leah.*

Sid managed a shallow breath of relief and tucked her hair behind her ears. Turning her back on the bright shiny dime of a moon, she walked back into the barn to finish mucking the stalls.

## CHAPTER TEN

It took everything Mia had to get out of bed. Every movement from the time she started lifting her head from the pillow—which she had little recollection hitting the night before—until her feet landed on the floor was a nauseating, excruciating negotiation. Her internal dialogue was not advocating in favor of the deal: *Can you do this without opening your eyes? Why does my earlobe hurt? Try again without using your core muscles. Try without your arms. Why don't you try again later? How many Percocet will this take? Who was the sadist who invented the childproof cap? Are you competing for a medal? You can hear people in the house, Mia. Stay put. Ask for help.*

The pain meds dulled the inner voice more effectively than they did the pain, and with what could be considered insanity as her driving force, she managed her way into the en suite bathroom.

*Well, that is quite the sight.*

Her reflection made her think of a drunk celebrity mug shot, her hair an almost comical combination of spiked and matted, with little resemblance to her usual neatly managed bob. Was that the remnant of a ponytail? No way to know, given it would take movement to get a better look, and movement was bad. Super bad. Better to direct what little energy she had to what she could readily see and reach. She stared at something that looked like a smear of mud on her neck and ear.

*Don't look too closely; just go with mud.*

The flash bomb of rib pain struck again as she reached for a facecloth from the short stack on the vanity. The spears were back. *Slowly. Yes. That's it. One thing at a time.*

Once she had given her face and neck a good once-over with soap and hot water, she felt better and stood back to see what else she could accomplish. She was wearing a loose-fitting, V-neck Tragically Hip concert T-shirt—not hers—that smelled like vanilla or maybe freshly mown hay. It was sleeveless, so she could see the top of the gauze that wrapped her torso under her non-splint arm. She was bottomless and completely indifferent to what had happened to the clothes she was wearing the night before or who had been involved in their removal. For a moment, she found herself thinking about Sid and what it might feel like to have those strong sexy hands remove her clothes.

*Okay, clearly the bull did no damage to your libido. Get a grip.*

The gauze and the bandage on her hand would make proper showering impossible for today, so she opted for a camp shower.

*Pits. Bits. And pieces. Well, one pit at least. And whatever is reachable without actually bending over.*

The roominess of the shirt made it possible for Mia to "shower" without stripping, a task that would take her to a level of pain she couldn't stomach. Wringing the facecloth was impossible with one hand, so she and the shirt were soaked by the end. Rather than withstand the omnipresent nausea to remove it, she improvised, using a hair dryer to pale the dark water splotches on the grey tee. She ran her good hand through her hair until the tangles surrendered into a reasonable shape.

She showed up in the kitchen wearing a thick terry robe over the tee and holding the bottle of meds imploringly out in front of her. Isabel and Duncan sat at the table, their hands intertwined beside their coffee cups. At the sight of Mia, they broke contact, and Isabel jumped up to greet her.

"Come sit down. I didn't hear you get up, or I would've come to help. It's so early…you mustn't have slept much."

"No worries, I managed okay. Except for this." She happily surrendered the bottle to Isabel and greeted Duncan.

"I'm guessing Isabel is the only one in this kitchen with the ability to open the meds," she said, nodding at his sling. "Good morning, Mr. Harris, thanks for your hospitality."

Duncan beamed toward Isabel, then back at Mia. "Duncan, please. And yes, if we want those dreaded pill bottles open, I guess we need to stay on Isabel's good side. No need to thank us. *Nuestra casa es su casa.*"

If the guest bedroom and the kitchen were any indication, the "casa" was nothing short of magnificent. The hallway from the bedroom opened into an impressive seating area with an obelisk pedestal table surrounded by four rail-back chairs. Two matching chairs stood against an interior wall near an arched doorway into what Mia guessed was a living room or possibly a dining room. On the kitchen side of the mission table was an L-shaped granite counter. The wall against the long side of the L was virtually all glass, with a sliding walk-out to the screened porch which faced the courtyard of buildings, including the livestock arena. She tensed involuntarily, then shuddered. The morning sun was half-risen on the horizon. The kitchen was not only comfortable, Mia had a strong sense that it was the hub of the home.

While Duncan and Mia commiserated over their injuries, Isabel set a plate of fruit and toast on the table, topped up the coffee mugs, and joined them.

"So, was it the same bull that got you?" Mia asked.

Duncan laughed. "Oh, heck no. It wasn't a bull at all, but once a rumour starts in this neck of the woods, well, it picks up speed like a spring wind. And it was hardly as dramatic as your adventure. I reached up to take down a bale of hay and came too far back over my head...ended up taking my arm down with it in not quite the right way. It's healing up pretty well now."

Mia looked at the bandaged hand on her lap and wiggled her fingers. Isabel cast a concerned glance her way.

"How are they feeling, little girl?"

"I don't feel any pain in my hand, truly. Maybe it's a relativity thing?" She leaned back in her chair and winced, sucking air through her clenched teeth. Spears in. Spears out.

"Let me see." Isabel took her hand and slowly lifted it, supporting the elbow and taking care not to overextend beyond what the ribs were able to endure. She felt the fingertips, pinching each gently. The blood flowed back. With good circulation confirmed, Isabel unravelled the gauze and turned the palm up, peeling back the dressing to reveal a long, thin red welt, something akin to a burn, with blue and purple along the margins.

Mia sighed with relief as the air hit the wound. "That feels much better, thank you."

"We can leave it off for a bit, but you'll have to keep it covered until it heals a bit more. I have some aloe vera that will speed things up. I'm starting to think I need to charge extra for medical care." She reached across the table to take Duncan's hand. He pulled back a bit, but Isabel was insistent.

"I take it not everyone knows about the two of you?" Mia ventured, recalling Leah's caution about public knowledge. *Does Sid know?*

"They will soon enough. Sid and I haven't spent much quality time together, but it's time." Duncan smiled at Isabel, and Mia felt their connection. She wondered when their relationship had turned romantic, thinking back to the grief support groups she had attended and how much discussion centred around what was a "socially appropriate" amount of time between the death of a partner and dating. The consensus amongst survivors was that reconnection was immeasurable by something as objective as time and that a solidly subjective sense of the grief process and where each individual stood within it was the best determinant.

"Well, your secret is safe with me. And I'm happy for you both. Is Sid around?" The memory carousel was spinning in her mind again, and she had a sense that she needed to thank her.

"I think I heard her earlier," Duncan replied. "Don't be shocked if she comes across as a bit grumpy today. I think she was pretty shaken up by the events yesterday, and I saw her working in the barn well after you arrived last night...rather, this morning."

*Great. More of grumpy Sid. Mea culpa this time.*

"I may need to apologize for that. I didn't realize the bull was there. Well, I didn't remember. He must've been behind the haystack until the very end of our session, and unfortunately, Milo saw him before I did. I'm sure it'll take some extra time to settle your new stud now. I can imagine the event caused some additional problems for your daughter. I'm very sorry."

Duncan shook his head and smiled. "That bull will be fine. And so will Sid. She has a way of getting things done in spite of herself. A million irons in the fire but my girl always knows which iron to pull and when. I'm sure this"—Duncan squeezed Isabel's hand—"won't really surprise her if she doesn't already know. She holds her cards pretty close to her vest." He laughed as if something just occurred to him. "I guess that's what makes her so good at poker."

"Poker? Really?"

"Absolutely. We all play. Well, I mostly donate. If Sid isn't walking away with the pot, then Isabel is. Aaron, too. Damn, everyone but me!"

"What's this I hear about poker?"

Mia felt a warm flush rise up her neck but pulled the robe tighter and higher. Sid was standing under the archway. Milo and Flynn wove around her feet. With her hair pulled back, she revealed classically high cheekbones and a strong but very feminine jawline. The mesmerizing eyes that had caught Mia's attention in the midst of their first encounter were made even more stunning by the morning sun that shone through the kitchen windows. She was wearing a faded, sleeveless denim shirt and an even more faded pair of casual-fit Levi's. These were tucked in to brown Blundstone boots that had clearly seen the inside of a barn with hay sticking out here and there around the soles. Mia felt conspicuous in her bare feet, T-shirt, and robe and wished she could fade away rather than be subjected to Sid's disarming presence.

The dogs were equally captivated, behaving as though the attractive woman was the only person in the room. It wasn't until Mia composed herself enough to make a direct appeal that they broke away and joined her in the kitchen.

"Good morning, Sid," Duncan said. "I was sharing with Mia how I so enjoy making donations, but before we play again, I must warn you that I've been practicing."

"Oh, is that so, old man?" Sid folded her arms, head nodding, feet shoulder-width apart as if in showdown mode. "Well, I guess you'd better bring a lot of practice money because I can win it just as easily as the real thing." At this, she smiled broadly—a big, genuine smile—and Mia found herself again entranced.

*I can see how she'd be good at her job. I'd buy a painting from her. Hell, I'd buy a used car from her.*

Sid turned to her. "And how are *you* this morning?" The smile was gone, the eyes now grey. The spell was broken.

"Terrific," Mia lied. "Thank you for looking after the boys. I hope they weren't any trouble."

"Not at all. I took them for a walk. I may have tired out Flynn; he's not nearly as energetic as the young one."

"Milo."

After a pregnant pause, "Yes. Milo."

She couldn't make sense of why, but knowing that Sid had taken the dogs for a walk disturbed her, as if a line had been crossed. Maybe not a hard line. *Fallen cedars, maybe.* Attributing it to her injuries, she accepted that nothing felt quite under her control at the moment. She noticed Isabel and Duncan exchange looks as if sensing the awkward tension, but her head felt as if it was stuffed with cotton, and she couldn't find words. She was relieved when Isabel filled in the silence.

"I let Beth know about your accident. She and Owen are in Edmonton buying equipment and won't be back until tomorrow, but Beth promises she will come over as soon as they're back." Isabel paused and moved an errant strand of hair behind Mia's ear. "She said to give you a hug, but I'll give you a rain check for that."

A hug would improve her spirits, but with the rails of the chair against her back putting more than enough pressure on her tender frame, Mia would take that check. She winced and leaned forward to give her ribs some relief, causing her to moan.

Sid looked away, poured herself a cup of coffee, and joined

them at the table. As she did, the vibration of a cell phone sounded from her pocket. She glanced at the screen briefly and returned it to her jeans. She had to have been aware of the curious looks from around the table, but she sat quietly. Mia imagined she was staring at the cream swirling in her mug.

At last, Duncan broke the uncomfortable silence. "Have you given any more thought to coming to my party, Mia?"

"Yes," added Isabel before she could respond. "You'll be able to come now, right, Mia? Clearly, Milo needs more training, and since you'll be recuperating for a bit, you'll still be here. I'm planning to make *pozole rojo* and *beef barbacoa.*"

"I have no idea what either of those things are, but if they're even nearly as good as your tortillas, count me in." Mia glanced toward Sid, whose eyes briefly held hers and darkened further.

*Grumpy is right.*

Mia ignored moody Sid. She turned her mind to happier things and directed her words to Isabel. "My mother was Métis, and I always found it interesting how cultures have so much in common, especially in terms of bread. She taught me to make bannock, but tortillas, crepes, West Indian roti, and even Asian steam buns... they're all so different yet tied to a similar tradition, don't you think?"

❖

Sid loved food and would have been quite content to listen in on Mia and Isabel's culinary discussion. She'd found it most curious when Mia mentioned having Métis heritage. With acute awareness of her own cultural ignorance, she wondered how Mia's blond hair and blue eyes could have come about. Adoption, perhaps?

When Sid's butt vibrated for the third time in as many minutes, she excused herself from the table and moved into the living room. A crisis at the gallery had been put on her radar, and she was hoping that the situation—which had the potential to ravage her business with the devastation of a windblown prairie fire—had been contained. Only time would tell, and while she knew this, she also realized it tested what little patience she possessed. Her phone buzzed again. Patience failed. She had to look. Food and blond hair would have to wait.

Ella texted, *It might be too late.*

*Not possible*, Sid replied.

*He should have known better.*

*I suspect he did. Text me when you know for sure. Check Europe?*

Sid didn't wait for her capable colleague's response. Instead, she sat down in an armchair and put her phone facedown on the ottoman. She adjusted it so that its edges lined up perfectly square with the cushioned surface. For the first time in her career, and only the second time in her life, she felt helpless. She pushed deeper into the chair, gripping the armrests, and closed her eyes. It was as though a line of dominos was falling. Her dad's injury, stolen cattle, a crazed bull, and now this…how should she put it? Fraud? Collusion? Deceit? Seen in perspective, was this dilemma any more destructive than any of these others? Not really. And with any luck, she thought with a glimmer of hope, perhaps the latest teetering tile would not fall.

"You okay, hon?" Duncan asked when she ambled back into the kitchen.

"Yep, fine," Sid lied, tucking a piece of hair that had separated from the ponytail behind her ear. "Okay to join you? Or are you wrapping up?" She looked at the bandage beneath Mia's tee and flashed a smile. "No pun intended."

Mia smiled, and Isabel pulled out the chair next to her. "Please sit. Your dad has to go to physio this morning, so we'll be leaving shortly. Excuse us, Mia. Let's see how that hand does for the morning as is. I think the air might do it a world of good, but take care not to get it wet or dirty, okay?"

"Yes, thanks."

As Duncan and Isabel exited, Sid took the seat across from Mia and put her phone on the table. She looked at Mia's hand and was aghast at the blisters that had formed across the palm where Bullwinkle's nose ring left its mark.

"So, your girlfriend has gone home?"

Sid watched a crease form between eyes that appeared much less vibrant than the day the two met. Given the medication and the residual shock of yesterday's battle, Sid was not terribly surprised. *Damn Bullwinkle.*

"Oh, Leah. Yes, well, yes and no. She's off to Calgary for the week, then headed back to Vancouver."

"Is it difficult to make a long-distance relationship work?" A vibration from her phone punctuated her query, but she resisted. *Ella could not know this fast. European markets haven't closed yet.*

"We manage. Against all odds, really, given how opposite we are in so many respects."

She was pleased to see what she thought was a glint in Mia's eyes and wondered if there was some coyness in the response. Before she could sort out how she felt about it, her phone vibrated again. She again resisted.

"Leah travels a lot. And her husband is patient," Mia explained, matter-of-factly.

*Husband?*

Vibration.

*What?*

"Husband?" she managed.

"Yes. Leah's husband. Do you need to take that?" Mia smiled, gesturing toward the phone that was vibrating toward the table's edge.

"No. Not yet." Sid knew that depending on what Ella had to report, her plans for the day could take a major detour. And there was no way her colleague would know how hot this fire was burning for another hour at least, when Pacific markets opened. Until then, Sid knew to keep from reacting. She moved the phone and put the sugar bowl on top of it. Better to deal with the fire that was smouldering in the kitchen.

"So, Leah is married?" She had to work at it, but she managed to keep from babbling.

"Yes, happily. Leah is Beth's daughter, you know. We grew up together, and she is my girlfriend, but not my *girlfriend* girlfriend."

Mia went on to tell the story of how, as teens, they were both *Charlie's Angels* fans.

"Embarrassingly, we were megafans. Leah loved them for their fashion choices. I had other ideas..."

Sid was quick to pick up the code. Declaring without declaring.

Mia went on to talk about their parents' tragic accident on the mountainous Coquihalla Highway and how that had sealed the friendship deal. Sid found it remarkable that Mia could open up so easily to someone who was still a complete stranger, but maybe that was a comment on her own wary nature more than it was an informed opinion on the state of Mia's grief. Sid still found it hard to open up the box that contained all of the emotions she felt around her own mother's death. As Mia continued, her words began to slur, and Sid recognized the cumulative result of fatigue and pain medications.

"Mia-Leah. That's what they called us growin' up. There was no end of teasing because of our rhymin' names, and I'm sure many people thought there was more going on than friendship. Mia-Leah. Gettin' back to your question, though, we do live far apart now, but I'm inchin' closer with every dog. Mia-Leah." She repeated the rhyme, eyes cast downward. Sid noticed her smile turn oddly sad. "We don't see each other often," Mia continued, staring at her injured hand, "'cep when Riley got sick. Then, Leah was like a Band-Aid. I couldn't peel her off."

"Riley?"

The phone shook the sugar bowl.

"She was my wife. We were married nearly ten years. Cancer took her almost two years ago."

Sid was rocked. Her mother. And her wife. And the girl was still on her feet. *No wonder she didn't let go of that ring. So much loss. She simply couldn't.*

"I'm so sorry." Sid reached across the table, past the vibrating sugar, and put her hand gently on top of Mia's uninjured one. "And I'm sorry for saying 'I'm sorry.' I hated it when people said that to me. Well, not hated, exactly. After all, people often don't know what to say, and something is better than silence. Most days."

Sid absently caressed the back of Mia's hand, lost in her own memories of when she was a child and her mom was sick. It wasn't until the sugar bowl tipped off the edge of the phone that Sid was back in the kitchen. She looked at her fingers on Mia's and pulled them away, chastising herself for invading someone else's personal space.

"I'm sorry…"

"No need to…" Mia's hand was warm where Sid had touched it.

Duncan and Isabel returned, and the moment was gone. Sid grabbed her phone and pushed back from the table.

❖

While Isabel pulled her chair next to Mia and opened a small green squeeze bottle, Duncan headed for the truck.

"Aloe vera. It will feel weird at first, but it will help." Taking Mia's hand, she spread the green gel along the line of the welt. The aloe began to tingle, and Mia could feel it cooling the heat of the wound. Isabel poured a tall glass of water before returning to the table, opening up Mia's medicine bottle, and pouring two capsules into her hand.

"I'm going to put these on the table beside the recliner in the sunporch. It will be a nice change from your bedroom. There's even an automatic control for it so you won't have to strain to get comfortable. Are you okay to make it there?"

"No prob'm," Mia slurred. She was tired, and the cotton in her head had turned to parade cymbals. As much as she'd love to continue talking with Sid, she knew she needed sleep if only to silence the clanging.

Isabel touched Mia's cheek. "We'll be back from town in a few hours. Sid, maybe you can get Mia's phone and put it on the side table as well? I think it's on the dresser in the guest room. Mia, text if you need anything."

"I'll get it now." Sid, who'd been hovering and texting nearby, disappeared down the hallway.

The sunporch wrapped around three sides of the house, but the recliner was conveniently located on the same side as the kitchen, so Mia didn't have far to go. Nonetheless, by the time she made it to the chair, her phone was already on the table beside the water and pills. Through the large windows, she could see Sid in the courtyard, standing in the dust left by Duncan's pickup. She was pacing, phone against her ear, gesturing in a way that suggested she was irritated? Angry? Passionate, at least.

Her girlfriend, perhaps?

Mia knew Aurora St. Germaine. At least, she knew of her. Her celebrity status as an artist was surpassed only by her legendary reputation as a woman's woman. She was infinitely creative, pushing the envelope in her mediums, mixing oils and welding works with chaotic but thought-provoking results. Mia had even seen her lead a performance art piece a couple of years back involving reimaginations of an AR-15 semiautomatic assault rifle in protest of school shootings. Her waist-length ebony hair was curly, and her eyes matched in intensity, like pools of black tar surrounded by eyelashes that went on forever. She was stunning. And to many, quite sexy. Mia imagined that Aurora and Sid would look amazing together. A lesbian power couple without question. And yet it was Mia's hand that Sid had just touched with surprising tenderness.

*She was just being kind. And you're on drugs.*

Maybe, but Mia still possessed the presence of mind to know that Sid's questions about Leah were of the fishing kind. And that perhaps, if the damn cell phone hadn't constantly sounded, she might have been quicker to set the record straight regarding her relationship with Leah. *Quite literally, straight.* But since she imagined it was Aurora on the phone, she'd impulsively decided to let Sid's fishing hook hang that little bit longer. With just one touch, though, Mia regretted playing games with her.

*You need to nip this whole thing in the bud.*

Mia drifted asleep—the dogs curled on the floor beneath her in a sunbeam—aware that now both of her hands were tingling.

## CHAPTER ELEVEN

Mia spent all day sleeping very comfortably in the recliner on the porch, the oversized leather arms providing just the right amount of support for her ribs and enabling her to stay inclined enough that her head stopped spinning or at least slowed. The nausea abated. Isabel woke her only to persuade her to eat some soup and grilled cheese before she and Duncan escorted her to the guest bed. Propped up on a collection of pillows and dosed with adequate pain medication, she slept remarkably well through the night and woke up feeling good enough to make her own way to the kitchen for breakfast.

Watching and listening to Isabel and Duncan reminded Mia of how the best of relationships appeared so easy, like gentle waves on a beach, never revealing the powerful currents that lay beneath. She could see that the two were not only in love but that they flowed with each other, moving and talking and laughing harmoniously. Mia wondered how it was possible that Sid could not see how her dad and Isabel, even as they resisted overt displays of affection, were connected. Mia wondered, too, if she would ever know that kind of love again, but seeing their example bolstered her courage to stay open to the possibilities.

Beth returned from Edmonton and stopped by later that morning, rousing Mia from a post-pancakes snooze.

"I'm going to run you into town tomorrow to see my doctor. No point arguing, little girl; she's already made room in her schedule for you. Tomorrow afternoon."

"I suppose I should have these ribs looked at. Everything else is coming along."

"Glad to hear it because, Mia, I love you...but you stink. I'm going to help you shower today."

"No point arguing?" She hadn't had the energy to think about personal hygiene, let alone do much about it aside from a sink shower. It was time. She was ripe.

An hour and a half later, Mia felt like a million bucks. A very tired million bucks but nonetheless... Beth had worked as if by magic to soap and rinse and blow-dry everything in need. In between the careful removal and rewrapping of the tensor bandaging around her ribs, Mia caught sight of the two angry purple red and blue bands— unsurprisingly the same dimension as the pen's iron rails—running diagonally across her torso from her lower back to the base of her right breast. The X-rays had shown a hairline crack in one rib, but seeing the damage with her own eyes, Mia couldn't help but wonder how she'd escaped with just that. Beth must've been reading her mind.

"Seems that Sid's actions did more to apologize for her terrible first impression than words could. I hope you accepted?"

"What do you mean?" Mia felt herself off balance even at the mention of Sid's name.

"You don't remember, do you, sweetie?" Beth shook her head. "The way Aaron tells it, Sid prevented you from suffering a worse fate. She pulled you straight out from under that bull just as he was lifting a leg to stomp you."

Mia was speechless. She had snapshots of the incident and a recollection that Sid was there and had helped her to the truck. She remembered arms under her, around her. Saws and spears and the smell of hay and manure. Her adrenaline had been pumping, and things were moving so quickly, but at the same time, so slowly. It was a jumble, and her current meds did nothing to fine-tune her thoughts about that day.

"I'll make sure we ask the doctor about that head injury. I'm not convinced you weren't concussed. You struck that bottom bar so hard that Aaron said he could hear it from the stadium door. Can't believe it didn't knock you out cold, little girl."

"Takes more than that, I suppose." Mia shrugged off the could-have-beens and considered instead what Beth had said about her rescue. Sid saved her?

*Hold on, Mia.*

She might not have passed out during the melee, but there were plenty of parts that weren't very clear. Like slides, the images popped up through a fuzzy fog: the crush and crack of her ribs, the grip on the ring slipping, the mud sliding beneath her, arms pulling, holding. Vanilla. A voice spoken through a fog.

*Hold on. I gotcha.*

If Sid had saved her, then why hadn't she said something about it? Was she so disinterested in Mia's well-being that her actions weren't worthy of mention? Was she more interested in rescuing Mia or calming her precious new bull? Or did she want Mia to be beholden to her for some reason? Mia knew she'd fallen down a rabbit hole and tried to quell her suspicions, but it was too late. She could already sense the whale-sized headache floating behind her eyes, attracted by thoughts of Sid that swam through her mind like a school of frenzied baitfish.

Beth didn't stay long. Even though Mia felt fresher than she had in days, the shower had taken a bundle of energy, the headache was breaching, and once lunch was finished, so was Mia. Before leaving, Beth tucked her into bed, and the dogs curled on the floor beside her. Flynn usually slept at her feet, but maybe he knew they were guests and needed to show more respect. Milo was happy for his company and pawed Flynn playfully until he found a comfortable position.

By the time hunger roused Mia, the headache had mercifully subsided. The kitchen was dark, and the microwave showed it was just shy of midnight. Near a small nightlight under the counter was a note: *Dinner in fridge. Wake me if you need anything. Isabel.*

As the bowl of pasta with chicken and mushrooms heated in the microwave, it occurred to Mia—not for the first time—that Sid hadn't been around since the morning before. Since she told her about Riley. Not so strange. Death had a way of making people feel uncomfortable, especially in North American culture where mourners were told, usually by people who'd never lost a loved one, to get over their grief instead of being allowed and encouraged to move through it. There were times when Mia felt that talking about Riley with the "get-over-it-gang," as she called them, put her own healing at risk, so she was careful with whom she shared her grief. Sid had seemed empathetic at the time, but maybe she hid her discomfort well. *Like she apparently hides so much.* Not that it really mattered, she reasoned, thinking back to the tense phone call she'd witnessed. After all, Sid seemed to have her hands full with a bunch of things, not the least of which was apparently her girlfriend Aurora.

The dogs followed lazily behind her as she took her pasta to the recliner. Her ribs were beginning to feel better. She still felt as though she'd been hit by a truck, but all in all, the acute pain had diffused. She was able to move a bit more easily, but most importantly was able to take a breath without being skewered with spears. Her head was clearer, the bump on her scalp the only source of pain unless she turned her head too quickly or forgot to keep her movements conservative. Speed was her enemy, but otherwise, the pain was manageable. Hopefully, tomorrow's trip to the doctor would confirm Mia's own positive prognosis.

She fell asleep for a few hours after her pasta and slept on and off. Halfway through the night, she stopped trying and opened her eyes, surprised to find Sid leaning against the nearby door frame looking down at her. She fought the instinct to stretch, knowing her ribs weren't quite ready to bear the movement.

"What are you doing up?" she spoke groggily, her mind thick with ragged sleep.

"Not stalking you, though I couldn't blame you for thinking so. I just got here. Thought I'd make sure you and the boys were okay. Did I wake you?" Sid's voice was so warm and soft that the sleeping dogs didn't budge.

"Not really. I can't sleep soundly at the moment. I feel like I've been sleeping for days, so I'm guessing my body doesn't need any more right now."

Sid sat at the end of the couch that ran perpendicular to the recliner, turning so she was facing Mia, and pulled her legs and feet up. She leaned forward and put her cell phone on the coffee table and relaxed into the big pillows. She put her hands on her thighs, rubbing her jeans beneath her palms. Her eyes were unfocused, and although she was looking toward her, Mia could tell she was not looking at her. In fact, she appeared to be staring at nothing in particular. She realized this was the first time she'd seen Sid sit still. Not reacting. Calm even. With the one small exception at the table yesterday morning, all their interactions had been filled with distractions or laden with tension or cell phones or anger or bravado. Right now, there was just Sid. Mia watched, matching the silence and keen to see how long it would last.

After ten minutes, Milo disrupted the moment by moving in between Sid and the coffee table and nudging her elbow.

Her eyes lifted. "Listen, I'm sorry about before. Not the hand. I'm sorry if I've been rude, is what I'm meaning to say."

"And I'm sorry for what happened with the bull," Mia countered.

"Please, don't apologize for that. It's the very least of my concerns." Sid looked at her phone.

Mia wasn't sure how to interpret Sid's words, but there was something in her tone that suggested she was struggling. Perhaps this was Mia's chance to return the favor. "You have a captive audience, you know. It's not like I can run off."

Sid smiled and looked back at her, apparently taking measure of the offer. "It's work."

Mia sat quietly, sensing that Sid needed to find her way.

"I work at an art gallery. Curating mainly. But it's hard not to get involved with the buying and selling end of the business."

Mia nodded. A curator's expertise would be extremely useful to art dealers, particularly when the market was hot. And the Canadian market was very hot.

"I've only been here a few weeks helping Dad, and already

someone at my gallery has apparently been involved in a questionable deal. To what degree, I'm not sure. But there may be some exposure at the gallery's end, and I'm trying to resolve things." Sid ran her fingers through her hair and looked again toward her phone.

"That must be hard from a distance," Mia said.

"It is, but there are two issues that make the situation more difficult. Do you know much about art deals?"

"A bit but help me understand as much as you'd like."

"I work at a gallery that exhibits post-impressionist and contemporary art. Canadian mainly. We act as a gatekeeper of sorts, an intermediary between the artists or their estates or benefactors... and the brokers or buyers. I chose to work at Northern Lights because it has a strong reputation for respecting a work's provenance and maintaining an artist's or movement's legacy. With Canadian art prices at an all-time high, some of these considerations seem to be falling by the wayside. Northern Lights has thus far managed to stay clean, for lack of a better word. But this week..." Sid trailed off, looking toward her silent phone.

"This week, things changed?" Mia offered.

"Maybe. Likely. We hired a new gallery associate, and it seems one of his first acts was to convince an elderly collector who has worked with our gallery in the past to part with a Group of Seven piece. We know that this particular work is of great interest to a European collector. We have evidence that the sale went through. What we don't have is a receipt by the gallery. It strongly suggests that he's been working with a broker to side deal. In spite of what he suggested to the seller, the gallery was never going to manage the piece."

"So, the first issue is one of trust and ethics? Maybe criminal?"

"Yes. Unconfirmed but it seems so."

"And the second issue? Is it that you'd have preferred the piece to stay in Canada?"

"No, actually. I think the nationalist notion, as romantic as it is, influenced many selling decisions in the past, especially where works of the Group of Seven and contemporaries like Tom Thomson were concerned. But now I think we collectively, no pun intended, feel a greater sense of pride when Canadian artists are appreciated abroad."

"I've heard quite a bit in the news lately about Martin Stephens, the American actor who's taken quite a shine to Lawren Harris?" Mia was also a fan of one of the Group's key members, especially of his many Iceberg depictions.

"Exactly! And you're probably also aware what a celebrity spotlight does to prices?"

Mia was fascinated at how the discussion had transformed Sid. Until this point, her passion seemed fueled by anger or tension, but as she spoke about her work, her eyes brightened and her focus sharpened.

*So, this is Cassidy?*

"Yes." Mia said. "Provenance is bolstered, and we end up with record prices for many of the Group's major works. Sadly, that's why I don't have an original hanging in my trailer. So, the second issue is..."

"Legacy. Legacy is vital. It helps preserve the story, and what is there to art but the story? Aesthetics?" Sid shook her head.

"Perhaps a bit. Yes. I would think so." Mia felt brave. "I like a work that is pleasing to look at."

Sid paused, and Mia could sense she was considering her next words. "Aesthetics are subjective, would you agree?" Sid asked. "What you find beautiful might differ from what my dad finds beautiful, yes?"

"Yes."

"And subjectivity depends on where the viewer stands relative to time and place."

Mia felt that Sid, Cassidy, had argued this case before. She also realized that having lived on her own for a couple of years, the opportunities for an engaging debate had been few and far between...Milo and Flynn angling for a treat notwithstanding.

"I would agree with that, too," Mia allowed.

"Story...well, the story of any true work of art is *objective*. It is bound by credibility, provability, and it is ostensibly sustainable. The story stands the test of time."

"Objective?" Mia was happy to present an opposing viewpoint. "But any work's story is subject to interpretation, too, no?"

"It is indeed." Sid reached for her phone and turned the screen toward her. "We could go on all night, at least what's left of it." She turned her phone. White numbers glowed 4:10. "But if you're not too tired, and you're still willing to be my captive, there is something I'd like to share, if only to explain and maybe excuse, my rather un-neighborly behavior. I had mentioned legacy earlier. The work that's in the process of being dealt by my *colleague...*" She seemed to have trouble with the egalitarian nature of the title.

"Of your coworker?" Mia asked.

"Yes." Sid flashed a satisfied smile before continuing. "The work is not a final painting as we think of it but rather a field sketch. On cedar shake."

Mia had seen several of these types of renderings at the McMichael Gallery and knew that the shake, nothing more than a wooden shingle, was used by the Group and other travelling artists because unlike paper and lighter than canvas, it stood up to the rigors of bush-whacking, train and canoe transport, and often harsh weather conditions, all of which the young artists endured as they forayed into the Canadian wilderness to record their visions. The shakes were perfect for fieldwork and made it back to the studios to enlighten the canvases.

"The partner piece, the finished canvas, is owned by one of my good clients. An American. He would never have approached the sketch owner or had any dealer approach them because he trusts that the tradition of first offer would be honored. He trusts us to ensure that happens, and we have never failed to do so."

"The right of first refusal for the corresponding field sketch goes to the final canvas owner. Sounds fair."

"Fair. And right. At least, as far as our gallery sees it. Absolutely, as *I* see it. Having the sketch and final canvas is the most powerful way to preserve the story. The differences, so evident when the two works are seen side by side, shows us more about the artist's intent than anything. The vision pops from the canvas, the story's words... well, they almost speak for themselves."

"And in this case, if the sketch goes farther afield..." Mia understood Sid's dilemma.

"Hopefully, it doesn't. I'll know as soon as the European markets close." Sid sighed and sat up, elbows on her knees and head in her hands for a moment until she pushed up from the couch, tucked her hair back over her shoulders, and headed for the kitchen. "I think I've kept you up long enough. I'm going to make you something that will help you sleep."

Mia wasn't about to argue. The aches in her head and body were again hard to ignore, and the meds could not replace rest. She must've dozed off because within what seemed like a second, Sid was kneeling beside her with a mug of something steaming.

"Warm almond milk with vanilla and a touch of maple syrup." Sid handed it over, remaining on the floor with Flynn and Milo, who were delighted to have someone at their level. Sid placed a hand on Mia's knee, a hand so wonderfully warmed by the mug that Mia could feel it through the blanket across her lap. The drink was equally soothing and delicious. Mia's eyes closed, and she exhaled deeply. She tried to turn in the chair, but as hard as she was capable of trying, she couldn't find a comfortable position.

"I'm guessing you'd be better off in bed." Sid's words didn't sound like a question, and in seconds, Mia was helped to her feet and escorted through the kitchen and down the hall to her bedroom.

She was able to slip the robe from her shoulders and let it fall on the edge of the bed. She didn't have the energy to manufacture modesty, and she noticed that Sid didn't flinch at the sight of her in the Melissa Etheridge V-neck tee. Instead, Sid placed the mug on the bedside table and gently swung Mia's legs up onto the bed, pulled the covers over her, and started toward the door.

"It's nice that you care about your artists," Mia managed, taking care not to slur as fatigue set in. She hoped Sid didn't see her scowl before pushing thoughts of Aurora out of mind.

"Somebody has to protect them. And their stories. I'm not alone in thinking so."

"It sounds funny to hear you say that. Not alone." Mia's eyes were closing.

"Funny? Why do you say that?"

Mia's eyes were now closed, and she felt her head sink slowly into the pillow.

"Not alone..." she mumbled again before falling into a fitful sleep. She dreamt of northern lights, white-topped waves lapping across canoe bows, warm hands, and a wild and dangerous woman with raven black hair wielding an artist's brush with flaming bristles.

❖

After turning off the light and closing the door, Sid stood in the hall outside Mia's room, leaning against the door frame. Mia's words ricocheted in her head. What did she mean by "not alone"? Why would she think it was funny to hear those words from her? Attributing the strange comment to the hefty combination of fatigue and meds, Sid wondered if her interest in it was just a way to sidestep the cumulative effect Mia was having on her.

Sid did not regret that she'd put her hand on Mia's the previous morning. In fact, doing so gave her one of the few truly pleasurable moments she'd had in weeks, and in the virtual tornado of events in the last twenty or so hours, she found solace reliving the tenderness of that touch more than once. Tonight, she'd allowed herself to lean closely into Mia by taking her into a confidence and realized not only how rarely she experienced intimacy but how wonderful it felt.

As she tucked her in just now, Sid was aware of feelings of a decidedly physical nature: she'd had an overwhelming desire to slip under the bedcovers with Mia, to hold and protect and heal her, to let her lean in. It was all Sid could do to walk out the door.

*Now is not the time*, she thought. *It may never be.*

As she walked across the dark house toward her upstairs loft, she questioned whether Mia was even ready for another relationship. *Did she say Riley had passed away two years ago? Does it matter? Don't I have enough on my plate?*

Sid's internal debate stirred up memories of the earlier

subjective vs. objective discourse. Mia had surprised her. She had a quick intellect and strong opinions and was better informed on the subject of art than most people she'd met outside of the industry. For a moment, she felt guilty that their chat had burned energy Mia could have spent on her physical recovery. The debate had obviously exhausted her. Nonetheless, Sid hoped she'd have another opportunity to convince Mia that where the paint landed on a canvas, like provenance, wasn't nearly as important as the artist's intent.

Sid's mind jumped back to the gallery, and she pulled her phone from her pocket. Five a.m. She had a noon call with Ella, and she had to spend at least a couple of hours on the range repairing fences before then. She took the stairs two at a time and didn't bother to undress before falling into bed, instantly asleep.

## CHAPTER TWELVE

Ella Danowski had worked at Northern Lights Gallery for almost as long as Sid Harris. As one of the gallery's associate curators, Ella reported to Sid but never felt like a subordinate. They respected each other and had a shared vision of art.

For a time, Ella wondered if Sid was on the high functioning end of the autism spectrum. She certainly had savant qualities, extraordinary acumen when it came to Canadian art and detectable though slight social awkwardness. But Ella soon learned that the impatience Sid demonstrated was self-directed and extended to others only when they annoyed her. Sid Harris did not suffer fools lightly. She was intellectually adept at moving swiftly to resolve issues, and when confronted with a problem, Ella accepted that Sid preferred to stay in her head until she could present the solution. She reminded Ella of a pointillist, standing in front of a giant canvas and applying each dot of colour with Seurat-like precision yet with a vision for the final work.

Ella realized that people meeting Sid for the first time often mistook her intensity for disinterest. And her unrelenting focus for dismissiveness. But she knew that in spite of these misconceptions, Sid's reputation as the expert in the Group of Seven and contemporaries was unsurpassed, and her clientele quickly learned to love Sid's peculiar, undeniable charm. One artist had become particularly charmed, and as Ella reflected on the almost year-long gallery romance, she found herself wishing that Sid had as discriminating an eye for quality in women as she had in art. Aurora

St. Germaine was a piece of work. Talented, without question, but her behavior was erratic, her lifestyle turbulent, and her commitment to Sid questionable if one believed the ever-churning rumour mill. The artist's abstract canvases evoked the torment of Frida Kahlo and frenetic qualities of Jackson Pollock. She guessed that Aurora's addictions were not terribly different from her influences.

At this moment, though, the bohemian artist was the least of Ella's—and Sid's—problems. It was noon. Ella picked up the phone, took a deep breath, and dialed.

❖

*Sandwiches in fridge. Xoxo, Isabel.*

Mia, awake but still groggy from a restless night, found the note on the kitchen table just after noon. She resolved to put herself on a more regular sleep schedule and to arrange for flowers to be sent to Isabel, whose egg salad was as unexpectedly transcendent as her kindness was appreciated.

Mia curled up on the chair by the kitchen's bay window, enjoying an iced tea and soaking in the sun with Milo beside her when she noticed Sid sitting on a hay bale, her back against the door of the barn across the yard. She was mostly in shadow, but her hair flicked the light as she pushed the disobedient tresses repeatedly back over her ears, moving her phone from hand to hand, ear to ear, as she did.

"Good morning. Or should I say afternoon?" Duncan's jovial voice boomed across the room, and Mia almost jumped out of her slippers.

"It's afternoon." Mia was embarrassed at her poor showing of houseguest manners. "I'm so sorry about disrupting your schedule. It's not like me…I'm usually a morning person."

"Well, you're not your usual self. How are you feeling today?" Duncan propped himself on the window ledge facing Mia and blocking her view of Sid.

Mia took a moment of inventory, lifting her right arm so that it came out from her side and stretching it forward, palm up. She worked to keep from grimacing but was pleased that she didn't have to work too hard.

"I'd have to say I'm much better. Tired but better." Mia smiled with sincere relief.

"And where's *your* other pal?" Duncan said, rubbing Milo's ears; his tail wagged in response with enough energy to almost knock the tea from Mia's hand.

Mia answered. "He decided to stay in the bedroom this morning. I think Milo's energy is too much for him to handle." Mia reflected on the past week or so and noted that Flynn had been spending much more time on his own than usual. "Maybe he misses his own bed. Speaking of which, I wonder if it wouldn't be too much trouble for someone to help me move back to my trailer. I have really loved the company, but there's nothing like a night in one's own bed."

"That's no trouble at all, provided you really feel up to it. You know Isabel will put up a fight, but I'll defend your decision. I think she likes tending to the wounded." Duncan took his arm out of his sling and moved it freely but slowly. Mia's eyes widened as she realized that his range of motion was close to normal.

He winked. "I'm probably going to have to come clean at some point."

❖

Sid had just finished moving Bullwinkle into his official barn stall with the help of Aaron when her phone buzzed and *E.D.* popped up on her screen. She stepped out into fresher air and plunked down on the nearest hay bale.

"Hi, Ella. What's the news?"

"Good morning, Cassidy."

"God, that sounds way too formal. I know this is serious business, but can we please stick with Sid?"

As a way of honouring her mom, whose surname was her given, Sid stuck with Cassidy with most clients but within the team, family and friends, it was Sid.

"Right. Sorry. It *is* serious, Sid."

Sid could hear Ella take a deep breath, and she braced herself.

"Jason set up the deal. It went through."

"Are you sure?" Sid knew she was.

"Yes. And at a record price, so the markets responded accordingly. As soon as the last of Europe's numbers trickled in, I called him into my office. He admitted that he approached the seller. But he denied knowing about our policy regarding first refusal, let alone about the canvas and Mr. Stephens's interest in it."

"I'll just bet," Sid replied, her gut turning.

"He said the buyer's broker was aggressive, and he thought that by cutting out the gallery he was doing a good thing for the seller."

"My ass. Jason knew what he was doing. The boy's not that wet behind the ears, for God's sake. Hard to imagine this wasn't his intent when he applied. And I hired him."

Sid bit down on her sense of shame, trying to keep things in perspective. But she felt overwhelmed by the magnitude of the consequences that were likely to come her way as a result of the situation, and it was difficult in the moment to resist self-flagellation.

"*We* hired him, Sid. And we had no way of knowing. References all checked out. I agree, there's no way this was an innocent mistake. You should've seen his face when I asked him to explain why he violated procedure by cutting the gallery out. I suggest he be terminated immediately. I can start the paperwork." Sid knew Ella long enough to know a recommendation to fire someone, in spite of how justified, was difficult. She was soft-hearted, but with more experience, she would gain confidence. In this case, there was no question this course was the only option. Too bad the damage had already been done.

"I'm sure he has a job to go to, so let's not imagine he's being left high and dry. Dollars to donuts, the purchaser's agent made some promises, and Jason isn't so naïve that he'd think we'd put ourselves at risk again and keep him on staff."

"Fair enough. I'm sorry, Sid. I assume you'll want to let Mr. Stephens know?"

"As soon as the sun is up in Tokyo. Anything else I need to know?" Sid wasn't sure why she was asking.

"Aurora asked when you'd be back." Ella paused, no doubt expecting the reaction Sid was madly stifling. "I told her she'd have to ask you herself. I hope that's okay?"

*The text. That must be why.*

"It's fine. Thanks, Ella."

She ended the call and looked at the screen. There were now two text notifications from Aurora. Sid put the phone in her pocket. Seconds later she pulled it out and carried it into the kitchen.

❖

Duncan and Mia were still laughing when Sid walked in. She acknowledged them only barely before pulling open the fridge.

"There are sandwiches there, Sid," Isabel's voice called from the hallway. "Please eat something."

"I'm okay," came the tired response, "but thank you."

Flynn trudged in behind Isabel. Mia's good spirits changed abruptly when she saw him. He was clearly losing weight. He was oddly listless. Was she so drugged up she hadn't noticed before now? Maybe, like her, he did just miss his own bed...but what if it was something else? Mia felt her throat starting to constrict with worry. She willed herself to relax.

"Isabel, you have been an angel, honestly, but I really have to get back to training before Milo forgets what he's learned. And I admit he hasn't exactly retained his attention to command, as evidenced by yesterday's incident. Was it yesterday? Two days ago?"

"Three," Duncan replied.

"Mia, you're still not well. I promised Beth I'd keep you here until you healed."

Mia put on her brave face and lifted her arm even higher than before. "See, my ribs are fine. And my hand." To demonstrate, she wriggled her fingers and closed her palm. "And no headache today. Honest." *Almost honest.*

"The girl needs her own bed," Duncan said as promised. His arm was back in its sling.

Isabel took a few moments to examine Mia's palm and then

held her face in both hands, looking into her eyes, apparently assessing her pupils.

"Okay, but you are still going to the doctor later today. I will text Beth to pick you up at your trailer. And I will pack you some food to take home with you."

"No point in arguing."

"Dad's right," Sid said, leaning against the kitchen counter, thumbs tap-texting on her phone. "I'll drive you. Aaron is on his way back from town, and I've texted him to swing by and pick me up." She held up her phone as if to prove it. "That way I can leave your truck at your trailer for when you're able to drive."

Isabel jumped in. "No driving yet, little girl. Promise. Not until the doctor says you can."

"Yes, I promise. Thank you. Really." She looked at Sid, who was back to her phone. "Everyone."

Sid's only response was a barely audible grunt and a quick glance in Mia's direction.

*Grey eyes. That's trouble.*

Mia made her way to the guest room. With effort, she managed to dress in the clothes she had worn the day she wrestled with Bullwinkle. Whatever day that was. Isabel had kindly cleaned and folded them, placing them on the dresser. Mia gathered up the clothes she'd been wearing over the past few days and slid them into a borrowed duffel bag, committing to return it and the clothes once laundered. She lingered over the Tragically Hip T-shirt, which had retained its vanilla scent in spite of Mia's recent hygiene challenges. She imagined it must be Sid's. It smelled like her.

She rejoined Isabel and Sid in the kitchen just as Isabel was closing up a large straw picnic hamper.

"Good Lord, Isabel, I'm one woman. How much do you think I can eat?"

Isabel seemed about to defend herself when Duncan's truck door slammed. She turned to the window in time to see him drive by, both hands on the wheel, arm free of the sling, smiling like the proverbial cat with canary.

"Where on earth does that man think he's going?"

"He's off to physio, Isabel." Sid smiled conspiratorially. "The man is on a mission." Then she stepped outside and out of reach before Isabel could react.

"Watch out for these Scots, Mia." Isabel shook her head. "Their stubborn self-reliance will drive you around the bend."

## CHAPTER THIRTEEN

Mia insisted on carrying the small duffel bag to the truck, politely declining Sid's offer to tote it along with the hamper. It felt good to be on her feet and outdoors, the sun on her face and the wind blowing through her hair, making it look like one of those inflatable wacky waving men at the tire dealership, she was sure. She could feel Sid's eyes on her even as the dogs were harnessed in the back.

"I heard you mention bannock the other day, and how your Mom was Métis. If you don't mind my asking, given dominant gene theory, how does it come about that a Métis ends up with blond hair and blue eyes?"

Mia smiled, certain that Sid could have phrased her query a bit more diplomatically. But her curiosity was earnest, and somehow, Sid disarmed her. She also sensed there was something much more important on Sid's mind; maybe she preferred this topic of conversation to whatever might have transpired today with the art deal.

"I don't mind, and you're not the first person to ask. If you'd ever met my parents, you'd really be wondering." Mia attempted to pull herself into the cab but abandoned the effort and accepted Sid's assistance.

Sid gently lifted her onto the seat, and as she was helping situate her, Mia noticed how fit she was. Sid wore a sleeveless John Deere shirt, revealing her defined biceps and deltoids where they rounded the broad shoulders. Sid's muscles molded like clay into a sculpted neck, the source of the vanilla scent on the T-shirt tucked away in the duffel bag. Mia hoped Sid wouldn't notice that she took in as much of the fragrance as her ribs would allow. As Sid leaned over to insert the seat belt, her hair brushed Mia's chest heavily enough to be noticed; her nipples reacted instantly to the touch. While Sid scooted around the front of the truck, Mia pulled her shirt forward so that it bunched rather than hugged her body, hoping to hide the involuntary response.

*Jesus, Mia, get a grip.*

"So neither of your folks were blue-eyed blonds?" Sid asked as she slid behind the wheel.

Mia recalled her grandmother saying that distance didn't separate people, silence did, and it was a lesson she took to heart. It made her happy that Sid was giving her an opportunity to share the story of her heritage. And it was a nice distraction from the occasional rib twinge as Sid slowly started down the driveway.

"No. I am Métis, with a double dose of Scandinavian along the ancestral lines. Many greats ago, like, back in the 1750s or so, a small group of Finnish immigrants arrived near Winnipeg to join in the fur trade. On my mom's side, an ancestor from a Manitoba Ojibwe tribe hooked up with one of those immigrants, a Fin named Keranen."

"Hooked up? Is that what the kids are saying?" Sid smiled as she pulled cautiously onto the road.

"You know what I mean. Are you from a long line of mischievous brats? Or is this a case of nurture versus nature?"

"You've met my dad...you tell me." They both laughed, and Mia barely registered that even the slight rocking of the truck over the road's occasional bumps challenged her core muscles.

"Their descendants ended up, through marriage, on the Six Nations of the Grand River reserve in Southern Ontario. So, that's my mom's branch of the tree." Mia looked at Sid to make sure she was still engaged. "My dad's Canadian tree took root in the 1820s when a Finnish engineer named Jaarvi, escaping the famine, came to work on the Welland Canal. He met and married a Mohawk woman, my great-great-great grandmother, from Grand River. They started the paternal branch. Jaarvi morphed into Jarvis. My last name."

"So, eventually the Jarvis branch meets the Keranen branch… and they *hook up*?"

"My parents become romantically involved," Mia corrected, knowing full well that Sid was just stirring the pot.

"Romance sounds much nicer." Sid cast a look and another charming smile.

"To make a long story short—or at least shorter—my parents are a uniquely Canadian blend of First Nations and Métis; Dad from the Jarvis line and Mom from the Keranen. You can imagine the surprise when the recessive Scandinavian genes claimed the throne, and I was born."

"You wear 'recessive' well," Sid said before making the final turn onto the dirt road. Mia gripped the armrest in anticipation of a rocky ride.

"I promise I'll go slowly." In spite of Sid's best efforts, the road up to the camp proved excruciating. Mia tried to shut out the pain by focusing on her driver and what she'd like to do to Sid. With Sid.

*What Aurora does with Sid.*

Thoughts of Aurora checked her fantasies. She had never, and would never, get involved with anyone in a relationship. In spite of the attraction she might feel. She felt.

"How did you manage to figure it all out?" Sid asked as the truck rolled up to the trailer.

"It took me a bit of time to sort out all the branches, but I am my family's arborist, and to be honest, I had fun doing the research. They didn't have the 'spit and mail-in' DNA testing when I was born, but I did it as an adult. The indigenous community keeps pretty good records now, too, so that helped. Let me know when you're bored…I see you looking at your phone!"

Sid put the phone back on the armrest between them. Her mood had darkened.

"Any news yet?" Mia asked.

"Nothing good. Your family history sounds like it should be made into a movie. Mine pales in comparison. Literally." She laughed and opened up the back doors to let the dogs out before coming around to Mia's side. "How does a whole culture end up with no pigment at all? I swear, we Scots burn just thinking about the sun."

Mia watched as Sid busied herself, suspecting she was trying to avoid what must be eating her up inside. After helping Mia out of the truck, she insisted on carrying the duffel bag, the dogs' supplies, and Isabel's food hamper into the trailer and managed to accomplish all before Mia had walked the distance from the truck. Sid avoided talking about the situation at the gallery, and although curious, Mia didn't want to push. She only hoped Sid would be able to manage the energy to keep it all contained.

*Maybe that late night on the sunporch was a one-time deal.*

"Will you be okay?" Sid asked. "Is there anything you need help with before I go?"

"All good. Can't keep a good woman down, as they say." *Much as I'd like you to try.* "Beth will be by later to take me to the doctor. Jack McMann, Milo's owner, is coming by tomorrow morning." A flash of concern crossed Sid's face. "It's okay. I'm not doing a training session. He's just dropping off some meat."

"Meat?" Sid helped Mia up the two stairs into the trailer but immediately stepped back outside.

Mia didn't like the distance. "I make the dogs' food. From scratch. It's not only more economical, especially if you have an organic cattle producer friend, but it's better for the dogs. And they love it. I even have past clients who still order from me. I ship it frozen."

Aaron's truck was approaching, and Sid began to back away from the trailer.

"Since I'm cooking, how about dinner the night after tomorrow?" Mia said, thinking quickly of a way to see Sid again soon. "I'll be up and around by then."

Sid tucked her hair behind her ear. Mia held her breath, which hurt. "Sure. Unless something blows up. I have a phone call to make to Tokyo later this afternoon, and maybe by then, the news will be better."

Mia wanted to reach out and console her, but she was already turning to leave.

Aaron waved from the cab as he pulled in and leaned out the window. He looked so handsome with the bright sunshine pulling the strawberry out of his blond hair. "How you doing, Mia?"

"All good, thanks, Aaron."

Sid was already in his truck and buckled in, phone in hand. Mia could see she was anxious to get going. Aaron set the truck in gear and turned, careful not to excite the dogs, who were shamelessly campaigning for attention.

"Flynn, Milo, come." The two begrudgingly but obediently made their way into the trailer and snuggled into bed, an exhausted Mia seconds behind.

## CHAPTER FOURTEEN

Jack McCann showed up as promised in the morning with an oversized cooler full of frozen beef and chicken and two large bags of grain. He was kind enough to unload the raw materials into the tent on benches so that tomorrow, Mia would be able to access them without lifting too much. When she asked where in town she could buy butchered steaks, Jack insisted she come by his place tomorrow, and he'd have a special package for her.

"No butcher is going to do better than the Alberta strips I have. Aged longer and grass fed. As close to Wagyu as you'll find around here."

Mia knew better than to resist. Jack was generous and seemed to have become quite fond of her over the weeks. It helped that he wasn't in a time crunch when it came to Milo.

"So, I guess it'll be a while before this fella is going to see a real cow again?" he asked.

"In spite of what happened at the Harrises', Milo's behavior indicates he's ready to work. He's fearless and has amazing instincts, so all we…well, all *I* need to focus his training on at the moment is basic command response. Once he convinces me that he's willing to listen, I'll be more confident he'll be safe with the herd. Give me another week, and he'll be ready to start working with them and you."

Once Jack left, Mia spent the rest of the morning doing stretches the doctor had shown her the afternoon before. Her gauze had been replaced by a wide tensor, and she was instructed to keep it on for the next week but to remove it while stretching and icing. The hand was healing well, the angry red-blistered line now a paler, purply-pink streak. Mia's head was a different story.

"It is likely you were concussed," the doctor had explained. "The scalp wound is abating, but given that you're still having headaches, you'll need to be honest about any symptoms you might experience. Dizziness. Nausea. That kind of thing."

Promising to return if she experienced any of these effects, Mia convinced Beth that she'd be fine on her own and was looking forward to getting back into a routine with the dogs.

Mia was delighted to be back at the trailer, her home on wheels for the past year and a half. The twenty-five-foot Serenity Airstream was comfortable for four people but indulgently spacious for Mia and her dogs. Her pickup easily towed it, and setup was easy. It was self-contained with a mounted gas generator and water tanks. She owned it outright, financing her life on the road with the sale of the Toronto house she and Riley shared, with plenty left in the bank "just in case." So far, her training business had a solid client base, and she hadn't touched her savings. Whenever she reflected on her financial comfort, she remembered something her Granny K once told her about fortune: "A person who finds themselves alone with a bag of money will only be aware of the loneliness." True enough.

Once her stretches were done, Mia took off her shirt and lay in a cushioned lounge chair with a bag of frozen peas propped under her side. She was still unable to put on a bra but was especially thrilled to be topless because the cold felt good against her bare skin. Never one to be shy about her body, camping gave Mia the opportunity to enjoy the kind of privacy she relished. She chose her locations accordingly and felt unencumbered knowing that the dogs would alert her if anyone came within earshot.

She wouldn't let herself nap, as tired as she felt after what seemed like a full workout but was simply taking a shirt off. She had committed to getting her sleep schedule back on track. Instead, she began making lists of what the next few days would involve. After lunch, she'd take the boys for a short hike and maybe find the lake Aaron mentioned. And text Beth to ask for a ride out to Jack's tomorrow and head to the co-op for some grocery items. Tonight, prop open the cooler so the meat will thaw for tomorrow. Tomorrow, train with Milo. And dinner with Sid.

*If she shows. And if she doesn't, that's okay, too.*

The forecast was good for the next few days, so a fireside dinner would be nice. And safe. Mia wasn't sure she trusted herself with Sid in close quarters. It was clear to her that regardless of her self-respect—and her albeit begrudging respect of Aurora—Sid had become an object of her fantasies. She thought about the sensuous but powerful physique and unexpectedly tender touch. She imagined those eyes staring into hers, how soft her lips would be, how sweet. As long as they stayed fantasies, what was the harm? It had been a long time, and she was ready to feel love, sensual, sexual love, again. She would need to stay on guard in order to prevent herself from feeling all of that with a woman she couldn't claim.

Mia tackled the list, first texting Beth, who explained that she was "heading into the co-op tomorrow anyway," though Mia suspected she was making a special accommodation. She would pick Mia up at eleven, promising "a nice lunch in town." Once the semi-thawed peas were back in the freezer, and her side had temporarily numbed, Mia realized how warm the day had become. There was little breeze, and within minutes, the initially loose tank top she'd managed to pull on post-pea-pack was already feeling sticky against her skin and the tensor bandage beneath uncomfortably moist.

"Come on, boys. Let's go find that lake Aaron mentioned."

The walk up the step was just what Mia needed, and she permitted herself to go at a slower pace than her usual march. Her head felt clear, and her legs were marginally weak but seemed as happy to be challenged as Milo was. He took lead, sniffing and marking the trail past the fence opening Duncan had created. Mia kept him close as they came through the pines, and with no cattle within eyeshot, she gave him rein again. Flynn stayed close, keeping up unenthusiastically as they walked along the clear water of the creek. The cut rock on the mountainside was spectacular, forming a half canyon of layered stone and iron-tinged ledges. Small springs flowed into it from the higher elevations, and Mia wondered if they were drinkable. They certainly looked clean, but better to check before risking a dose of waterborne "beaver fever."

As the creek began to bend around a low rise on her left, Milo's ears perked, and his pace slowed. "Milo. Stand."

He lay down, his ears still set on whatever he was hearing. Slowly, Mia made her way up the rise, staying behind a cover of trees in case a predator—a cougar or bear—was the object of Milo's alert. Stepping behind the last tree in the stand, she was relieved to discover not only the lake that Aaron had described but the very opposite of a predator. Sid Harris stood chest deep in the water along the near shore, her back to Mia.

Her hair was pulled into a tight bun that rested just above her long neck. She wore a black, racer-back swimsuit, and as she lifted out of the water, her graceful body arching into a shallow dive, Mia held her breath. Sid's arms drove powerfully into the glassy surface of the water, her strokes economical and her front crawl speed impressive. Barely a splash pushed up from the legs that propelled her across the lake, and before long, she had cleared the halfway point of the thousand-yard lake, headed toward a small red canoe on the far shore with no sign of slowing.

*So, this is her element.*

Mia wondered if Sid's work provided her with this same opportunity for control and if that was how she had managed so prestigious a position at a relatively young age. As she watched, she grew aware of her own responses to Sid's performance. Emotionally, she felt a deep, longing desire to watch as Sid powered through her workout and wondered if Sid chose the solitude or if she was imprisoned by it. The way she attacked the water was competent, but she emitted an energy that reminded Mia of a boxer pummeling a hanging bag.

Mia's physical response was equally curious. Her mouth had become dry, and her breasts swelled against the clinging tank top, nipples pushing against the sweaty cotton. A pulsing sense of warmth began to spread between her legs, and she squeezed her thighs to intensify the pressure. Clearly, something about the intense energy Sid possessed was having an unexpected but very welcome effect.

A soft whine and a nose nudge from Flynn pulled her out of her reverie.

"What's the matter, boy?" Mia bent, and a single spear reminded her that her ribs were not quite ready for such spontaneous movement. "Okay, time to head back." Flynn wasn't the only one who'd reached his limit.

Taking one more look at the lone but capable Sid, Mia turned from the lake and put her right hand in her pocket to stabilize her core as she stepped down the rise and back toward the trail. As she uncurled her fingers, which she'd clenched to protect the palm wound as she slipped it into the jeans, the tips touched a small, smooth, familiar object. She pinched it carefully and pulled it out as she walked. The shiny dime glistened in the sun.

Mia could conceive of no explanation for the find. These jeans hadn't been worn since Isabel had returned them, laundered and folded. As a habit to protect the dogs, she avoided putting coins in her pockets where she kept the reward treats. There was no obvious or logical explanation for this or any of the forty or so dimes she'd found over the years since Riley passed.

When she found the first few, she didn't even know about the odd phenomenon, proof—some believed—that the departed were still with us. It wasn't until she found more than a dozen under equally inexplicable circumstances that she mentioned it to Beth and learned about the superstition. Mia didn't buy in wholeheartedly, but she did admit that the sudden appearance of dimes—not nickels or quarters or pennies, just always and only dimes—was unusual, and that if it was Riley sending her a sign, well, it wasn't unwelcome. She kept every one in the box that held their wedding rings.

Mia smiled wistfully but with gratitude, then palmed the coin and put it back in her pocket, letting Milo lead her and Flynn home.

## CHAPTER FIFTEEN

Mia was curled up on the day bed in her trailer when her phone rang. Leah. "So, how are the ribs? And everything else?"

"Better than when I last texted. Honestly, the first few days after it happened are a fog." Except for certain very distinct images centered primarily on a specific Harris.

"Yeah, I figured that from the insane number of typos in your texts. Mom kept me in the loop on your recovery since."

"Are you home? How's Jim?"

"No, I'm still in Calgary. Discoveries started yesterday. Jim's results aren't in yet. But that's not why I'm calling. You'll never guess who I ran into on Saturday night at the Emily Carr exhibit."

"Spill!"

"None other than Aurora St. Germaine."

*Wonderful.* Mia felt her gut clench.

"Mia?"

"Yes, I'm here." Mia realized her voice was tinged with something akin to envy.

"Guess what?"

"I couldn't possibly." She didn't like this game.

"She was there with another woman. A professor from some Ivy League school. Anyway, not with Sid. Cassidy. Whatever. And by with, I mean *with*. Like, all kissy face. So, unless they have an open relationship, it seems that she and Cassidy Harris are no longer the art world's foremost Sapphic power couple."

Sid and Aurora could very well have an open relationship but she didn't think the choice fit with what she'd observed of Sid. Mia's reaction was mixed. A breakup could explain a few of the dips and crests in the roller coaster of anxiety Sid appeared to be riding. If the two had split, even if the decision was mutual and conciliatory, breakups were difficult. So at the same time as she felt genuine concern for Sid's well-being, the fact that the news sent her pulse racing meant her intense concern wasn't entirely about empathy. Sid's relationship status meant more to her than she was comfortable with. And she wasn't about to admit that to Leah, who had enough distractions at the moment.

*Not quite yet. Stay on the path.*

"Mia, did you hear me?"

"Yes, yes, of course. Well that's too bad for them. How was the exhibit otherwise?"

Leah went on to talk about which of Carr's canvases had been shown and who of the art literati had attended. While they chatted, Flynn managed to pull himself onto the couch and laid his head on Mia's lap. As she stroked him, she noticed that his coat wasn't as satiny as usual.

"So, what date works for you?"

"Sorry?" Mia's voice came from far away, where worries float.

"*Tourtière* date. November twelfth sound good?"

In spite of her crazy workaholic schedule, Leah always made room for the annual baking of the Christmas meat pies. It was a tradition the two had carried since their twenties, the family recipe a treasured one from Mia's mom. Depending on who was around during the holidays, they'd spend a day baking anywhere from five to twenty-five pies, with a few bottles of wine to fuel the fun.

"Are you okay, Mia?"

"Yes. No. It's Flynn. I think I need to take him to the vet. His energy has shifted." Mia's throat constricted, and she felt tears beginning. *Maybe the weepiness has something to do with the concussion.* Or maybe it was because the thought of Flynn being sick was too difficult to imagine.

"Sometimes, I think that Flynn is all that's left of me and Riley." Mia forced the words out, tears now falling onto the phone screen. Leah was the only person to whom Mia would ever have the courage, the trust, to disclose what she just had.

"I get it. You and Riley adopted Flynn together, so of course there's a special connection. Try not to imagine the worst, I believe, is what a good friend told me recently. Admittedly, though, I'm not beyond holding my own pity parties lately."

Mia knew the fear Leah was feeling. Cancer was like a monster under the bed, the mere thought that it might be lurking there as terrifying as if it really was. And as much as Mia felt that the situation with Flynn was a trigger for things deeper, feelings she had been working through as she grieved, she realized she needed to be present for her friend. She thought about the dime in her pocket.

"I have a really strong feeling that things are going to be fine. November twelfth works for me. I'll come to Vancouver if I'm not there already with a new client."

Mia was surprised to hear herself verbalizing the next step in her travels. Yes, she'd started in Toronto, and the jobs she had accepted over the past years were leading her gradually westward. But she realized that how far she would go in her journey was still to be determined. The words of an American philosopher, David Bader, came to mind as she pulled herself off the couch: "Be here now. Be somewhere else later. Is that so complicated?"

## CHAPTER SIXTEEN

Sid loved sitting at the kitchen table at twilight, watching the shadow of the mountains creep across the barnyard toward the Harris house. It was one of the rare times she forgot about all there was to do and allowed herself to feel a thorough sense of accomplishment for what had been done. She and her dad were enjoying a beer while Isabel stacked the dinner dishes beside the sink, a tea towel draped over her shoulder.

"Your father can't retire. He's annoying me already with this shoulder hiatus, and I'm sure I'd have to kill him if he were underfoot all the time." Isabel laughed.

"I don't know how you bear it; you're obviously a saint. I'm just saying that if he is considering selling, he's financially ready. In spite of the recent losses."

"I don't want to sell," Duncan said. "I only brought up the subject of succession because you're here, and well, I was wondering more what *you* might be thinking." He reached across the table and took her hand. "I know you love what you do, Cassidy Lynn, but I also know you love this place."

No question Sid loved the land. But it took her until this recent visit to realize that the memories of her mother's death—visions of the strong woman slowly and visibly destroyed by the cancer, unwilling to leave home for a hospital, knowing that the disease would find her no matter where she was—the awful memories that the young Sid had run to the city to escape, were being slowly replaced by reminders of her mom's life. Beautiful, wonderful reminders. Like the lake they both loved to swim in. The sunny porch where she'd enjoy her morning coffee while Sid talked about 4-H club events or learning to drive a tractor or how dumb the boys—and one particular girl—in her class were. Their weekly horseback ride along the step. Walking along the creek looking for gold. Sid's mom, her mom, the mom before the cancer came, was still right here.

"How about you give some thought to what you'd do with that ten-acre spot up on the step?"

"The lake?" Sid's voice broke, and she stared at her dad in disbelief until her vision blurred with tears.

Sid wiped her eyes as Isabel joined them, sliding a tissue box across the table. "What I would do with it? Why? Are you okay, Dad? You're not sick, are you?"

"Gosh no! It's just that, well, I'm…" Duncan started and then put his hand on Isabel's. "*We're* not leaving here, and you're certainly not going to live with *us*. We enjoy our empty nest, don't we, Isabel? Even Aaron has his own place, though I doubt he's there much. I think that boy is settling down. In fact, he won't say it, but I think he's back with the McCann boy. Glad of that. He's a nice young man."

Sid laughed with relief and then rolled her eyes. "Subtle, Dad." This wasn't the first time her father had given her an opportunity to come out to him by demonstrating how comfortable he was with her cousin's identity. But Sid had made up her mind a long time ago that until there was someone she felt strongly enough about to bring to the homestead, there was no reason to make it a topic of discussion. Sometimes, she felt that there might never be a reason.

"There's plenty of good land up there, and we can leverage a few things to get a house built. Maybe with someone special?"

Sid wasn't sure whom he was imagining. Given the amount of press coverage she had been given through gallery events, there was a chance that he had seen photos of her and Aurora together. Or heard rumours. But with her track record in the relationship department, a partnership wasn't on her radar, and she wondered briefly why it was on his. *Of course, it has to be Mia.* Sid could pretend that she wasn't looking forward to the dinner, but she felt unnerved. And unnerved wasn't ideal; if the cattle losses didn't end, there wouldn't be much left to "leverage," and she owed it to her dad, to her family, to stay focussed. Nonetheless, his offer of the parcel of land stirred a feeling of gratitude mixed with a curious sense of relief and hope. She hadn't experienced even one of those emotions in a while, and she wasn't about to let any of it be stolen out from under her. *Focus, Sid.*

"Isabel, how do you put up with Mr. Romantic here?" Sid laughed.

Isabel shrugged before trying to wrap her arms around Duncan's neck. When he recoiled, she swiped at him playfully with the tea towel.

"Don't pretend your shoulder still hurts, *mi amor*. I know you're better." She hugged him from behind and patted his chest with the palm of her hand, draping the tea towel over his shoulder. "The dishes are waiting for *you*."

Later that evening, Aaron showed up, and they settled in for a game of Texas hold 'em, but before the stakes hit the table, Sid's phone began to vibrate. She checked the number and excused herself from the table.

"Start without me. This may take a while. And Dad? Isabel? Thank you."

## CHAPTER SEVENTEEN

First thing the next morning, Mia called the local veterinarian and was told that Dr. Vandeven was on site until the end of the week, visiting ranches in the area. This wasn't unusual in a rural practice, particularly not toward the end of the summer when cows who birthed in the spring, as many traditionally did, were within the optimal insemination window. For ranchers who didn't have bulls, the vet's service was vital. The vet tech listened to Mia's concerns and booked Flynn an appointment for Saturday morning.

"If his condition worsens, call before bringing him in. Dr. Vandeven stops here in between site appointments to check up on any animals that have overnighted, and I'm sure she'd be able to work Flynn in if the problem escalates."

Mia let Milo out for a run while she had her coffee, and Flynn wolfed down his breakfast. Ten minutes later, as if he knew that a vet appointment was in his future, he nosed the door open and joined Milo in rounding up the morning shadows.

*You're going anyway, old buddy.*

Beth would be coming by soon to pick her up for their trip to the McCanns' and to pick up some supplies in nearby Hinton. While waiting, she spent the time reviewing commands with Milo. The few days he'd had off after the bull incident seemed to make a big difference in his ability to listen. Either that, or his run-in with Bullwinkle fired up his willingness to do whatever it took to be the boss in future meetings. Even Flynn sat watching them attentively, his wagging tail easing Mia's mind about leaving him for part of the day.

Once she and Beth finished picking up a specialized seed order from the supply store, they stopped to enjoy lunch at a little bistro in nearby Hinton. When the server filled their water glasses, Mia was prompted to ask about the springs.

"Is the water drinkable as is?"

"What a coincidence you're asking. Some company called this week asking if they could do an environmental assessment on our bit of acreage on the step. Owen told them thanks but no thanks. He told me the water has been pristine forever, especially now that the mines are down; nothing is likely to change that in the near future."

Mia wondered why a company might be interested in testing water on land that wasn't theirs unless they had plans for it but kept her imaginings to herself. Farmers and ranchers in this part of the province held proudly to their land, not because it was the most productive in terms of yield but because it was a treasured way of life. The farm industry, on the other hand, was comprised of inconceivably vast tracts of land pumped full of whatever it took to turn crops over as quickly as the super-seeds could sprout and ripen. Some of these tracts were still operated by families, but many were owned by seed and fertilizer manufacturing giants who hadn't shown interest in areas like the foothills, nor were they likely to because the conditions and transportation infrastructure weren't conducive to the profit levels they sought. Nonetheless, Mia put a mental bookmark in the subject and finished her lunch.

Beth knew Jack McCann's wife, Nancy, so when they arrived at his ranch to pick up the steaks, she headed to the house for a brief visit while Jack gave Mia a tour of his operation. He knew a great deal about the area and its history, so Mia took the bookmark out.

"How far back do the properties along the step go?" she asked. "Surely not the whole of the mountains?"

"Not the whole, no. Much of it is Crown land, so the National Parks manage it. But the upper acreage does stretch back well beyond the creek. If you need specifics, the land registry will know. Why? Are you thinking of buying a place out here?"

"I'm not saying yes, and I'm not saying no." she joked. *Half joked*. "But I was wondering about the springs up there."

"Heck yeah, the springs are great. Clean. A water company came to see me a few weeks back, asking if I would be willing to let them siphon off some of my own source water. Of course, they were willing to pay. I told them I didn't need the headache. Enough trucks on the road as it is."

Jack loaded a carton of steaks into the trunk of Beth's car, more than the number he'd promised Mia.

"Owen loves a good piece of beef, so make sure he gets a couple of these," Jack said, noting her surprise. He patted the large box with pride.

"Will do. And I'll see you Saturday. Make sure you review the list of commands I gave you. Milo's not the only one I'll be testing!"

As she waited at the car for Beth to finish her good-byes, she pondered what Jack said about the water. His story about being offered money for spring water didn't explain why the Harrises' cattle were taken, but the puzzle pieces were definitely coming together.

## CHAPTER EIGHTEEN

For the rest of the afternoon, Mia set aside her curiosities regarding the water and cattle situation and focused on cooking. She started by brewing some chai tea and then setting some peeled and cored pears in it with a thick slice of ginger, several cardamom pods, and a cinnamon stick.

While they simmered, she set a large iron cauldron on a tripod above the firepit and began to fill it with the meat Jack had given her the day before as well as some fresh milk and eggs—shell and all for added calcium—that she'd purchased at an insane discount from Beth. Given the quantities she'd required, Mia insisted on paying something for it.

The meat contained a good amount of fat, so she didn't need as much salmon oil as she typically used. Once the fire was stoked and the ingredients had started cooking, Mia added several cups of oats, some brown rice, carrots, peas, zucchini, and spinach. She worked extra cautiously moving and lifting in order to keep the spears from hurtling her way. The most difficult part was going to be removing the pot from over the fire, but she hoped Sid would help her when she arrived.

The mere thought of cooking for Sid excited her. It was not an unwelcome emotion but definitely unexpected. She found herself looking forward to spending time getting to know Cassidy Harris—and Sid—much better. She wanted to see beneath the peculiarly distracted yet confident exterior, a strange combination she felt compelled to explore.

*If she'll let me.*

Sid arrived on the ATV just as Mia finished stuffing the mushroom caps. To say she looked radiant would be an insult to light. Her hair was windblown and just barely held as a frame around her face by the aviator glasses she lifted above her forehead. Skinny denim jeans hugged her hips, and her muscled thighs and calves were tucked into a pair of honest-to-goodness Alberta Boot Company square-toed western work boots. Mia owned a pair of ABCs and recognized the brand, but her own boots were more for show than for go.

Sid's jeans were cinched with a leather belt fronted by a silver roper-style buckle with turquoise inlay. Finally, as if Mia wasn't already feeling woefully underdressed in a simple cotton blouse and paisley skirt, Sid sported a sage-colored sleeveless, collared linen shirt, tucked half in, half out. Mia smiled, thinking that this was perfectly in character with the woman whose range of emotion had, in the short time she'd known her, run the gamut. The outfit was a perfectly executed yet curious coupling of elegance and work ethic. Mia's heart fluttered unexpectedly; she couldn't take her eyes away. She hoped, as Sid worked to untie a canvas bag from the storage rack of the bike, that her attentive surveillance was going unnoticed.

Eventually, Mia found words to break the spell. "Welcome! So glad you could make it. I'm curious…have you folks out here never heard of helmets?"

Sid laughed. "Good God, not you, too. I hear that every day from Isabel. No, I'm not the helmet type." Sid sauntered toward her, holding the bag.

"I suppose I'm overly sensitive about heads, given current events." Mia ran her hand through her hair, still aware of the slight pain from touching the residual bump.

"Here," Sid said kindly, handing Mia the bag. "Maybe this will make you feel a bit better."

Mia accepted the mystery gift and placed it on the wide arm of a cottage chair set near the fire, gesturing for Sid to take the accompanying seat.

"May I get you a drink? Pinot Noir?"

"Sounds perfect." As Mia stepped into the trailer, Sid continued to talk. "We really lucked out with the weather tonight. It would have been a shame to be stuck indoors. Is it safe to assume that *this* is not on our menu?"

Mia stepped down from the trailer, drinks in hand, and saw her peering into the cauldron over the fire. "Milo and Flynn aren't much into sharing." She laughed. "But I do need your help with that, if you don't mind. It's cool enough to move into a cooler, but I don't think I should test my ribs yet."

"No worries." Sid had the heavy pot unhooked from the tripod and ready to transport. "You know, this doesn't smell half bad. It's dog food?"

"My specialty. The pot lid is beside the aluminum cooler in the tent. And there's a big bag of ice in the smaller cooler."

Sid lowered the pot into one of the large silver coolers, fitting the metal lid on the stewed meat mix, and poured ice from the other cooler over top. Once the lid was secured, they moved to the chairs where glasses of wine and the canvas bag waited.

"Now, this wasn't necessary," Mia said, untying the drawstring. "I'm the one in *your* debt."

"The pot was not that heavy. I actually felt badly that Bullwinkle scared Milo." She patted him. "You'd better open it before the dogs do."

Mia reached into the bag and pulled out a cobalt blue porcelain bottle. She read the label aloud. "Casa Noble Reposado?"

"I know you're partial to good ol' Jose, but since this camp is decidedly salt and lime free, for some reason I still do not quite understand, I thought you might enjoy some reposado. If you've never tried it, I think you'll like the pronounced blue agave, especially if you let it linger."

Mia fought back a smile. *Did she really just use the word linger?*

"That's lovely, thank you. I promise to stay far from Bullwinkle if I've had too much the night before."

Mia could tell from Sid's smile that she was more excited about something left in the bag than what had already been so sweetly received. She reached back in and pulled out a small wooden box with a flip-style lid. She held it flat and pushed up the lid with her thumbs, revealing a glistening slab of honeycomb and a small wooden spatula.

"There's a beekeeper not far from here," Sid explained. "My mom always kept our honey in a wooden box similar to that, and it's a tradition that's stuck with me over the years."

"It's a lovely gift, and the honey will be perfect with the pears we're having for dessert. I don't think I can wait that long, though."

Mia drizzled a stream of honey off the spatula onto her baby finger and put it on the tip of her tongue, fully aware of the suggestiveness of her gesture. Flirting was not something with which she was well practiced, but she hoped it was having the intended effect on her dinner guest. As much as she was enjoying her own performance, she didn't have the courage to look at Sid. She imagined that if she did, she'd fall into those provocative eyes, and dinner might never end up on the table.

"My God, that's good. Now I can't wait for dessert. Steaks first, though. Would you mind restoking those coals while I go finish the appetizer?"

Five minutes later, Mia emerged with a small platter, which she set on an overturned cut stump that served perfectly as a table. Sid was trying to hide the fact that she had been looking at her phone. Mia appreciated the effort.

"Cashew cheese stuffed cremini mushrooms with arugula walnut pesto."

Mia's description was second only to the compelling arrangement she'd created. On the white background of the rectangular plate, a broad brushstroke of pesto in the shape of an elongated S ran its length, creating a playful counterpoint to the platter's angles. She placed the mushrooms, burgeoned with warm creamy cheese and dripping with a drizzle more of the pesto, were placed along the green swipe like tiny mountains along a river. The rest of the landscape she'd sprinkled with baby arugula leaves, small bits of roasted walnut, and tendrils of delicate yellow sweet clover.

Sid's mouth dropped. "I know that people eat with their eyes first, but you have created a masterpiece."

"Aha! So, does this mean you are reconsidering the importance of the aesthetic?" Mia was delighted to return to the debate from nights ago.

"Perhaps, but I'm not ready to concede just yet. I do need to *experience* the whole story."

With that, Sid picked a mushroom off the plate and popped it in her mouth. *Such a sensuous mouth.* Mia imagined what she was tasting: Creamy with crunch. Earthy with herbaceous notes. Salty and savory. Whatever qualities hit Sid's palate, they were enough to knock her back into her chair, her eyes rolled back, feigning surrender.

"How about now?" Mia asked playfully, delighted with Sid's reaction to her fare. "Does pretty win?"

"What kind of a critic would I be if I failed to complete my research?" Sid asked, smiling and reaching for another.

As the two polished off the remaining mushrooms, Mia decided to broach the subject of the situation at Sid's gallery, hopeful that it wouldn't cast a pall on an evening that had started off so well.

Sid seemed open to her query. "There's still hope. I managed to get a message to the European buyer, which tells me he's willing to talk. To be honest, the most difficult part was telling Martin."

"Martin? Not Martin Stephens! He's your client?" Mia tried not to sound as impressed as she was. Martin Stephens was a celebrity, yes, but she had attended a symposium he spoke at on humor and health when Riley was sick, and his insights helped her with some of her own caretaker issues. Of course, she knew about his art interests, too, as the national arts media covered his activities extensively. Odd that Sid hadn't mentioned he was her client that night on the porch when his name came up.

*A good poker player indeed.*

"Not a client exactly. He's a friend. He has been a tremendous advocate for the gallery, generous to a fault, really. In return, though he doesn't expect it, I help him sort through the complexities of his other deals. I keep him safe. There's plenty of fraud now that prices are high. I wish I could have secured that sketch for him."

"So, *he* has the final canvas? The one inspired by the sketch sold out from under you?"

She tucked her hair behind her ears and finished what was left in her glass. "He does." When her gaze wandered to the foothills, Mia's followed. The pale orange sky now looked like a thick quilt lay along the top of the peaks.

"So tell me about you. How on earth did you end up back in Alberta, training herding dogs?" Sid got up and added a couple of pieces of wood to the fire, petting the dogs as she returned to her chair.

"Where do I start? To be honest, the journey wasn't exactly planned. I did my undergrad at University of Calgary and fell into some postgrad work with Ian Jorden."

"Glad I'm not tonight's only name-dropper…you *are* talking about *the* dog guy, right?"

"The one and only star of public television's *Fetch It Fella*, yes. And yes, he is as quirky in real life as he was on the show. He financed most of his research and that of the psychology department thanks to the show's residuals."

Mia went on to talk briefly about her own research in the psychology of eye and hand gestures and how she'd worked with the Ministry of Defence in Ottawa for a short time, consulting on covert communications. Mia was pleased to see Sid engaged and rewarded her—trusted her—by revealing a bit more about her life with Riley.

"So, she was a military pilot?"

"She was. Loved flying. Pretty good at it too by all accounts." Mia stared into the flames and noticed with some alarm that the fire had burned down to coals again. "Gosh, you must be starving. Would you mind setting the grate just above the coals while I get the steaks?"

"No problem." Sid was quicker out of the chair than Mia, who still moved with extra caution.

Mia flipped open the trailer door, grabbed the sidebar to pull herself inside, and felt a dull thud behind her eyes. She stopped mid-hoist, balancing on the first step, uncertain in that moment if going forward or stepping down would be the best strategy. As the trailer tipped in front of her eyes, she was no longer part of the decision.

"Hey, there! I gotcha." Mia felt Sid against her back, her arms gently sliding under Mia's elbows, steadying her enough that she was able to establish balance on the step. There was something familiar in the closeness, the embrace. The carousel.

*I gotcha.*

Mia turned and found herself swimming in eyes that had transformed into pools of molten jade made even greener by the sage shirt.

"I'm not sure you should be on your feet."

Tumbleweeds were pummeling Mia's very core. "I'm starting to agree," she whispered. Instead of pulling away, she let herself sink closer into Sid's chest. She heard and felt a surprised gasp, then watched Sid's eyes fix on her lips.

"You have a little honey there." Sid nodded at the corner of Mia's lips, then brought a finger to them, tracing the width of her mouth before reaching the sticky residue.

"Waste not, want not," Mia managed breathily, pulling on Sid's shoulder blades, drawing her even closer before lowering her head and brushing Sid's lips with hers. She explored gently at first, but as she felt the reciprocity of Sid's response, a swell of urgency flooded her body. Soon, Sid's hand was in Mia's hair, gently pulling while half lifting her down the step and into her arms.

"Ouch!"

"Oh God, Mia, your ribs! I'm so sorry! Are you okay?" Sid stepped back and held Mia's hands. She clenched in response, taking a handful of short, staccato breaths that reminded her of every Lamaze class she'd ever seen on TV.

As much as Mia wanted nothing to shatter their embrace, the act of nearly falling into Sid gave rise to a rib pain that took her breath even further away than Sid's kiss had already. When the pain subsided and her breathing regulated, Mia pulled herself more upright, loosening her grip on Sid's hands. She smiled weakly. "Well, I can't say I'm glad that's over, but I'm glad that's over."

"I'll get the steaks if you can make it to the chair," Sid offered.

"Deal."

Sid returned to the fireside chairs with the steaks, as well as the bottle of reposado and two wine tumblers. She set the tequila trio on the arm of her chair and gently set the steaks on the grill.

"For the pain," Sid said, holding a tumbler toward Mia. "I thought maybe we could…"

"Drink?" Mia finished her sentence because Sid, for some reason, had frozen in place. The dogs turned, tearing their interest away from the steaks, their ears perked toward the step. Sid set the glass down and took her phone from her back pocket and handed it to Mia, who sat, unclear of what exactly was happening.

"1004. That's my phone's passcode." She was almost whispering.

"I don't understand." Mia mimicked Sid's tone, not understanding the sudden shift. Mia didn't even have a passcode on her phone, so she wasn't sure what was expected. It wasn't until Sid pointed toward a small flickering light not quite a kilometer away near the creek that realization struck. Mia commanded the dogs to stand. They obeyed.

"Call my dad. Please. Tell him to hurry. And if Aaron's there, bring him, too. 1004." Without looking, Sid moved toward the ATV.

"Why, what are you…wait, you're not going up there alone! Sid, don't be—"

The ATV engine fired up, drowning out Mia's plea.

*Reckless.*

As Sid and the machine tore off and sped toward the light, Mia corralled the dogs and closed the trailer door behind them. She found *Dad* in the contacts and phoned. She tried with only minor success to keep the panic from her voice as she explained the situation.

"Stay put," he instructed. "Damn that daughter of mine! Aaron's here. We're on our way."

Mia scanned the hills, picking up the taillight of the quad

here and there, the deep engine roar still audible, echoing off the mountains. The white light, a beam, maybe a headlight or a flashlight, was moving north.

Then the red light fell from sight, and she heard a grinding, whining engine sound followed by sudden and eerie silence. The white light to the north turned and headed toward where the red light was last visible.

It seemed like forever that the night was still. Mia's current inability to drive amplified her frustration and intensified her fear.

*What the hell was she thinking? Why can't I hear the ATV? Is she okay?*

Before she could wonder where Duncan and Aaron were, an ATV followed by a truck roared up behind Mia, who stood transfixed in the direction Sid's taillights had last glowed. Aaron pulled up beside her on his quad, and she pointed toward the white beam, now the only light visible on the ridges. It had turned again and was moving away from where she'd last seen Sid's ATV lights. Duncan tailed Aaron, his luxury pickup not as mountain friendly, but she could tell from the look on his face as he sped by that he was going to put the manufacturer's performance promises to the test.

Mia watched helplessly as the truck's high beams teetered up and down as the vehicle made the climb for what seemed like an eternity. Then its taillights glowed brightly, and the vehicle came to a stop. Well ahead of it, Aaron's quad lights closed distance between the red and white lights until both disappeared behind trees, casting a silhouette against the mountain backdrop. Moments later, the truck's direction pivoted, and its headlights faced toward the camp.

"Godspeed," she whispered into the warm night air.

## CHAPTER NINETEEN

Sid knew the minute she chose that particular ledge that her impulsiveness should have been curtailed and that Mia had been right to try to deter her. But knowing her decision was a bad one, knowing that riding off like a renegade fueled by the hate of whoever was on her mountain in the middle of the night didn't stop the right front wheel of her ATV from dropping. It didn't slow the machine enough to give her a chance to correct. And it didn't stop the inevitable toppling of the machine off the craggy ridge with her on it.

And then under it.

She swung her legs aside as she fell to keep her head from striking the boulders that had tumbled from the mountain generations ago. These same boulders kept the machine from crushing her as it rolled, but the arm she used to cushion the initial fall caught a jagged edge and tore deeply just above the elbow. It felt as if she'd fallen against a branding iron, and the inescapable pain radiated up and down her arm. In the dark, Sid couldn't see the blood, but she felt the warm thick fluid creep down her elbow and forearm beneath her tattered sleeve, and she could smell its telltale ferrous and almost acrid odor.

*Stop the bleeding.*

Once the avalanche of Sid and rock and ATV had stopped, a rush of adrenaline let her feel for the source and stem the blood. She came across something that felt like a piece of wet sponge attached to her arm. She bit back her disgust and replaced the flap of gashed skin over the open wound, then gripped it as tightly as she could. Once the searing heat of the tear dispersed, she began to disentangle herself from the debris, keeping pressure on the gash.

She was on her feet by the time her father arrived.

"Cassidy Lynn!" he began. "What were you thinkin—" He focused on the blood pushing between Sid's fingers and stopped mid-sentence. "Quick. Get in the truck. Do you need help?" Without waiting, he half lifted her into the truck and tore down the mountain toward the trailer. She worried about his shoulder, but it was clearly feeling better than her throbbing arm.

"Dad, I'm fine. Really." She could hear the misdirected anger in her voice.

"If you say 'just a flesh wound,' I'm going to…well, just don't!"

Sid knew the Monty Python reference was a test, and it had the effect she knew her dad was hoping for. Without excessive effort she smiled, and he smiled in response.

As the truck approached the trailer, Mia rushed to her door and pulled it open. They shepherded Sid into the trailer and set her at the kitchen table.

"That's quite the first aid kit." Duncan was staring at the impressive variety of bandages, gauze, ointments and cotton swabs on display.

"I'm a bit accident prone myself, as you know," Mia said.

Sid didn't want to look at Mia, knowing that she couldn't bear her disapproval on top of everything else. And while her dad was a good buffer, Aaron was still out there.

"Dad, please go check on Aaron. I'm fine."

He nodded, his face turning ashen as Mia extricated Sid's hand from around the wound. The blood brightened and dripped onto the table. He excused himself and headed back up the mountain.

*This is gonna hurt.*

❖

"Here, hold this on it." Mia handed Sid a large square of gauze out of the sterile envelope. "Press hard but not too hard."

She went to the sink and soaked a clean white towel with warm water, wrung it out, and tenderly wiped around the held gauze. She nudged Sid's bloody hand away and took a peek. "You'll need stitches," she said, probing at the edges of the flap of skin that held in place over the three-inch gash.

"It's not that bad."

Mia couldn't tell if Sid was saying so because she wanted to keep Mia or herself calm. If it was the former, she didn't have to concern herself. Mia kept it all business, controlling her increasing impatience by acting with clinical, if not chilly, care.

*You're not about to get out of this doghouse.*

She focussed on cleaning the area around the wound, careful not to reopen the jagged laceration. She replaced the now half-soaked gauze with a clean one and wrapped it securely in place.

There was a long silence as Mia repacked the kit and disposed of the soiled towel and compresses. She kept her eyes on her tasks, knowing that she could easily lose her focus; she needed to keep composed until she could figure out how best to sort through the myriad of emotions that Sid's impulsive, stupid, dangerous, yet well-intentioned actions had churned inside her. *What is it they say about good intentions?* Eventually, she could feel Sid's eyes trying to track hers down.

"Are you upset? I'm sorry about ruining dinner."

"Yes, Sid, *that's* what I'm upset about. You *ruining* dinner." Exasperated, Mia sat at the table with another clean warm towel and pulled Sid's still bloodied hand on it, sandwiching it and placing her own hand on top. "This impulsiveness of yours, honestly. You are going to get yourself hurt. Well, you already did. My mistake. So, no, I'm not upset about you ruining dinner." Mia felt her voice tighten. She turned her attention back to Sid's hand and unfolded the towel, using it to wipe the blood that still clung to her fingers until she felt a vibration. Mia cursed under her breath. Sid pulled her hand from the towel and reached for where the phone sat on the table.

"Good thing you didn't injure your phone fingers. I'm sure that call is more important than your health!" The words flew out before Mia could bite them back, and while she felt bad for the cheap shot, maybe it was the only way to get Sid to pay attention and consider the well-being of her cousin and father if not her own. They'd all been put in danger unnecessarily. Who knew what awaited them on the ridge? Desperate people with questionable motives operating in the middle of the night probably had contingency plans. An unarmed woman on an ATV, helmetless at that, not so much.

Mia felt only partly relieved when Sid stopped mid-reach and returned her hand to the towel. *Maybe she does have a lick of sense after all.* An ATV pulling up beside the trailer prevented her from continuing her censure. The dogs weren't barking, so it was someone they recognized. A minute later, a knock on the door and a friendly "Hello" heralded Aaron.

"Come in," Mia shouted, wiping the rest of the blood off Sid's hand with casual efficiency.

"You okay?" Aaron looked at Sid, grimacing at the blood starting to ooze through the dressing. "Guess not. Uncle Dunc's gone home to make some calls. I'll take you back on the ATV. Listen, I saw a few guys and a truck up there. Not one big enough for cattle but still pretty big."

"What were they doing? Did you get a plate number?"

Mia shook her head. Sid was like a dog with a bone; one day, a bigger dog would come along.

"Not sure, but the back of the truck had a bunch of those big blue water cubes on it. I didn't get close enough for a plate, but that truck can't hide for long around here once we get word out."

"Did you check on the herd?"

"They're not here for the cows," Mia said. Sid and Aaron turned to face her. "At least, that's not their ultimate goal." They listened as she explained what she'd come to understand. With this final piece, the environmental assessment at the Millers' and the company approaching the McCanns for water made sense, and Mia was ready to share her theory.

"I think they're here for the water. Spring water. It's the new gold, given global warming. And my guess is you're sitting on a source that somebody wants to tap into. Taking the cows is just a way to reduce bargaining power and get Duncan and others along the source to sell."

Sid was on her feet, pushing past Aaron and heading to the door, already back in fight mode. "Aaron, tomorrow we do our own assessment. I'll make calls tonight and find someone reputable. We'll get Dad to phone around in the morning and see if these assholes left any breadcrumbs."

Mia knew that Sid wasn't about to listen to reason, so instead, she turned to Aaron. "Does her mind ever settle?"

Sid spun, her eyes shifting ominously. "Don't *psychologize* me."

The cold words struck Mia in the chest, stunning her. Without hesitation, she responded equally icily. "Then don't *act* like a cowboy. No offense, Aaron."

Sid turned back to the door, cradled her arm, and stepped out of the trailer. Mia watched her march to the ATV, Aaron falling in behind.

Mia stood in the trailer door, not inclined to wait for a response. "Get her back and make sure Isabel checks her out," she yelled, loud over the engine. "She shouldn't be trusted to look after herself!"

*Watch out for the bigger dog.*

## CHAPTER TWENTY

M ia woke up early the next morning, headache free in spite of the previous night's tumultuous events. Her ribs had finally relented, allowing her lungs to expand without spears. She hadn't had a recurrence of the dizziness, so she took the opportunity to spend time working with Milo. He was showing tremendous skill and restraint, and Mia expected he would be prepared to work safely with cattle by the weekend. Flynn, on the other hand, was still not himself, and Mia planned to contact the vet to see if she could squeeze him in if he didn't show any improvement by the end of the day.

When she returned to the trailer, Flynn and Milo curled up for a snooze. Mia set about cleaning up the vestiges of the previous evening's dinner. The steaks had burned to coal on the grill, far beyond what even the dogs would scavenge, so she dumped them in the ashes. She washed the glasses, setting the uniquely bottled reposado on the table beside the wooden box of honey. Although she had tried since waking not to think about Sid—to keep herself occupied with things that warranted her attention, things that didn't make her crazy with worry and fear—Sid's well-being hadn't left her mind for a minute.

Once the dog food was bagged and in her upright freezer, one of the custom luxuries she had insisted on as an upgrade in her trailer, Mia set about cleaning the pot, a job best done outside with a hose. But when she opened the garbage bin to scrape off what was left of the food, she saw the bloody gauze from the night before. Her heart racked with worry. And her morning plans instantly changed.

Driving was a challenge, but her truck was an automatic, so it only took a bit of maneuvering to shift into gear with her left hand and head down to the Harris farm.

Isabel and Duncan welcomingly intercepted her on the sunporch. "Good morning, Mia. Join us for a cup?" He was on his feet, ready to head to the kitchen, but Mia raised her hand to decline.

"Thanks, but I actually am here to…well…I'm wondering how—"

Isabel smiled. "She's in her bedroom. It's upstairs…toward the front door. Can you manage?"

"Yes, I'm good." Mia wanted to race upstairs but felt she should at least be gracious. "How are you two?"

"I'm great. The physio says I can expect to have my sling off for good today."

Isabel slapped his arm. "You haven't been wearing that sling for days!"

"I know, but Aaron is so much better at mucking stalls than I am." Duncan laughed. "Besides, I have more than a few phone calls to make about our visitors last night."

"You're terrible, *mi amor*." Isabel turned in her chair and looked back up at Mia. "Beth and I are headed out to the casino this afternoon if you'd like to join us."

Mia wavered. "Thanks, but Flynn's not feeling great; I'd like to keep an eye on him. Can I have a rain check?"

"Of course." Isabel nodded toward the archway. "Just head toward the front door. You can't miss the stairs. Her room is on the left at the top. I'm sure she'll be happy to see you."

*I'm not so sure of that.* Mia barely noticed the majesty of the great room as she made her way toward the stairs. Her own impulsiveness of late had at least rivalled Sid's, and in retrospect, her chiding last night was a bit hypocritical.

Mia managed the stairs, holding the banister and moving with deliberate attention to her head and ribs. She was pleased that she made it to the top without experiencing vertigo.

An abrupt but distant "Come in!" was the response to her knock on the door. She stepped into Sid's bedroom and glanced around. She wasn't aware that she had expectations of what Cassidy Harris's room might look like, but what she saw surprised her. Clothes, including the bloody and torn shirt, draped the edges of the bureau, rail footboard, and chair if they hadn't already fallen in a clump on the floor. The bed was empty and unmade, sheets and blankets tangled, a smear of rusty red on one of the pillows. On the night table, a closed spiral notebook, bottle of Tylenol, two glasses, a mug, and a phone competed for space.

The sole oasis in the carnage was in the corner where a desk and office chair stood. The surface of the desk was immaculately ordered, the laptop on and pens aligned beside another spiral notebook. A small row of thick art books, held at each end by western bronze sculptures in the dynamic Remington style, lined up with precision along the wall edge of the desk. An easel stood on the floor between the desk and the French doors leading to a small deck. The canvas displayed a red canoe balanced atop a beaver dam. It was dark and atmospheric, and Mia wondered how well it might fit Sid's mood today.

"I'm in here, Isabel." The voice came from the attached bath.

Mia tiptoed through the disarray and followed the voice. She stopped in the doorway and found Sid standing in front of the mirror in a pair of unzipped jeans and a tight-fitting white tank top, attempting to rewrap her injured arm.

"Not Isabel," Mia said, looking with dismay at the bandage, the same one she'd applied the night before. "And *not* that bandage. Where can I find a clean one?" She avoided Sid's eyes but could feel them.

Sid pointed over her shoulder toward a tall cabinet. "Top shelf."

Mia flipped open the door and took a small step back. The items on each of the six shelves were meticulously organized: towels folded perfectly and arranged by color, then size; bottles placed with the tallest in the back, all facing forward; and small labels on each shelf declared the contents. Like the desk, the cabinet was in dramatic contrast to the post-tornado ambiance of the rest of Sid's space. Mia had to stand on tiptoe to survey the highest first aid shelf but easily located a roll of gauze, a bottle of aloe vera, and a box of gauze squares, all of which she gathered and placed on the vanity.

She worked in silence, cleaning and applying the aloe before redressing Sid's wound. It continued to bleed a bit around the edges and was red and swollen. When she was done, she stood back and looked at Sid's reflection in the mirror beside her own.

"We are a fine pair. The walking wounded, as they say." Mia let the words hang, then advanced again. "Please don't protest, Sid; you have to see a doctor about that today. This morning. It appears infected."

Sid lifted her head and half pushed, half flipped her hair back over her shoulders. Her eyes locked on Mia's. "I will." She sounded sincere and a bit deflated. "I'm sorry about last night."

"No, I'm sorry. I had little right to admonish you about your impulsiveness. I wasn't exactly pushed into that bull pen, you may recall."

"My comments were unnecessary. My actions, too." Sid's eyes cast downward, her fingers picking at the edge of the countertop.

Mia hoped she was referring to how she had bolted, not their brief kiss at the trailer door. Her worry was put to rest when Sid turned, leaned forward, and whispered in her ear, "Some actions."

Mia was shocked at how quickly her words and gesture affected her. She felt her breath catch and her face flush with excitement. Her ear tingled against the warmth of Sid's breath as it floated down her neck, and her bra felt tighter, sending vibrations between legs that now felt pleasantly wobbly. She pressed her cheek against Sid's, the now familiar faint vanilla fragrance filling her senses and commanding response. She gently touched Sid's other cheek, holding her face and kissing her briefly, then more hungrily. Mia's desire was so deep that it flooded her body, her passion all-consuming and her hands eager to explore every part of Sid.

Sid tenderly withdrew her lips, but her thumbs rested beside Mia's mouth.

"What's wrong? Did I misread—"

Sid rested her forehead on Mia's, held her in a close embrace, and let out a frustrated sigh. Mia could hear the phone vibrate on the counter behind her.

"Go," she said, lowering her hand to Sid's chest and pushing her gently back. "It's okay."

Sid withdrew slowly, her eyes lingering as she picked up the phone and stepped around Mia and into the bedroom.

Mia looked in the mirror and composed herself, running her thumb along her swollen lips and taking a slow calming breath before reentering the bedroom. Sid was at the desk, donning a headset and propping her injured arm up beside the computer. She began tapping the keys.

"How firm?" Sid said into the Bluetooth headset. "I'm sorry, can you repeat that?...Yes, he's willing to counter...Under no circumstances use the gallery name in the paperwork, Ella...This is off-book...I know. I'll explain to the director myself when it's done. It won't change anything."

"I'm sorry," she mouthed toward Mia as she stepped over a pair of discarded jeans.

Mia wasn't sure if Sid's apology was intended for the kiss, the interruption, or for the state of her room. She hoped not the former. She smiled and gestured back. "Okay."

Sid turned back to the computer, and as Mia passed the dresser, she noticed a small wooden box, a match to the honey box Sid had given her the night before. It was open. A dozen or so dimes were in it, nothing more.

Dimes. Riley. Flynn.

It couldn't be a coincidence. Was Riley trying to send her a message? Someone else? She didn't perceive anything menacing, but an unease she couldn't shake possessed her, and Flynn was on her mind. Concerns mounting, Mia headed back to the trailer, foot heavy on the pedal. For whatever cryptic reason and as intoxicatingly distracting as Sid was, her focus needed to be on her stalwart companion.

❖

The dogs were happy to see her, Milo bounding outside as she opened the door and Flynn following with slightly less energy but more than Mia had expected. Or imagined. Her concern was disproportional, and she knew why. Flynn was their dog. Hers and Riley's. They had rescued him as a pup, and they'd heaped their love on him as most childless couples did. Predictably, when Riley died, the attachment enhanced, the strengthened bond tying Mia to not only the dog but to the memory of Riley. And as emotional as she felt, she possessed professional objectivity when it came to canine behavior, and Flynn's recent listlessness was not expected of a dog his age; smooth collies usually lived fourteen or so years, and Flynn was barely half that.

In spite of his recent energy spike, Mia knew to trust her instincts. She called the vet's office, negotiated with a calm demeanour, and was told to bring him by the next day around noon when the doctor would be back from rounds.

She checked her fears and spent the rest of the day finishing her chores and working with Milo before turning her mind to her own recovery. She was more in touch with how her body felt and credited her sparked libido. She could still feel Sid's lips on hers, the softness of her caress, and as Mia leaned into a side stretch, arm over her head, she imagined Sid's hands on her sides and relaxed into her breathing, expanding her rib cage with each inhale. She hadn't experienced any further symptoms for almost twelve hours but promised herself to stay aware, and if another episode occurred, she resolved to follow up with another visit to Beth's doctor.

After a frozen pea cool-down, Mia called a shop in Hinton and ordered flowers for Isabel as a thank you for her kindness. She spent the afternoon packaging the cooled dog food and caught up on orders and other emails, then showered and spent the evening by the fire, satisfying what she could of her aroused appetites by polishing off the goodies from Isabel's hamper. She promised herself a renewed and ramped up workout regime as soon as she was able. Maybe swimming? She wondered what Sid was doing but accepted that until Sid had exhausted all options in recovering the sketch, her focus would be elsewhere.

Mia fell asleep fantasizing about how it would feel to be the subject of Cassidy Harris's undivided attention.

## CHAPTER TWENTY-ONE

The next morning, before Mia's coffee beans were even in the grinder, Beth called to invite her for an impromptu breakfast. Never one to turn down her favorite meal of the day, Mia accepted. She gathered that Beth also wanted to make sure she was properly on the mend and admitted that in spite of how she enjoyed her independence, it was nice that someone had eyes on her.

"Beth, if my ribs would allow it, I'd need to run all the way to Calgary to trot off that breakfast. Honestly!"

"I didn't force that last pancake down your throat, little girl." Beth laughed, and both Owen and Mia joined in.

Mia's appetite hadn't relented in spite of the previous night's fireside hamper-fest, and she tore through a stack of pancakes, eggs, hash browns, three sausages, and a pile of maple bacon that Owen had proudly smoked himself. They talked about the springs and the events on the step. Isabel had been in touch with Beth and told her that Duncan planned to meet with the RCMP on Monday morning in Edmonton to discuss what could be done to stop the raids.

"We're going to make a weekend of it. The four of us. Leaving tomorrow morning and returning Monday night. Aaron has offered to stay here and tend to the milking and feed. Sweet boy. Will you be okay while we're gone? Do you need anything in town?"

"I'm good, thanks." Mia drank what was left of her coffee and pushed away from the table. "Sorry, I can't stay. I'm taking Flynn to the vet this afternoon, and I need to work out with Milo first. Not *just* for Milo," she added, sitting back in her chair and patting her belly before standing.

"Don't be ridiculous. You look great, doesn't she, Owen?" Owen nodded and continued clearing the dishes. The strong silent type. Perfect for Beth, a yin to her yang.

*We should all be so lucky once in life, let alone twice.*

"Are you able to drive? Do you want me to take you?"

"I'm fine. I managed to drive down here myself, and the vet isn't that much farther."

"Just keep us posted, okay? I'm glad to see you're feeling better, and I'm sure Flynn will be fine, too. Try not to worry, little girl."

❖

Sid stood in the lake, weighing her odds. She had dropped by the urgent care clinic that morning but only because she was picking up some fence wire at the co-op and found herself driving past. Her decision to have her arm checked certainly had nothing to do with Isabel's insistence or Mia's or the fact that the throbbing gash kept her up half the night.

The doctor was quick to write a prescription for an antibiotic ointment, and he applied a large adhesive bandage, instructing Sid to keep it dry and change it twice a day. She stopped at the pharmacy to fill the script and picked up a box of the large wound dressings. The box label promised "waterproof," which was why she now stood readying herself for her daily swim and questioning whether it was the implausible promise or the prospect of self-inflicted harm that was keeping her from diving in. A large, painful, red and purple bruise had already encircled the injury, wrapping entirely around her upper arm from shoulder to elbow, furthering Sid's doubt about whether she'd have the range of motion necessary to swim.

She looked south across the glassy surface of the lake at the opposite shore. This was her spot now, and she allowed it to fill her with a joy she hadn't experienced since her mother died. She let herself imagine a house on the southwest shore, the morning sun on the wraparound porch, a dog running along the shoreline, sniffing at the banked red canoe and leaping through the high grasses.

How could she make it work?

Sid contemplated what moving back here might feel like. Aside from sorting out a work arrangement with the gallery—provided she was still employed there after the smoke of this most recent fire cleared—would living here alone be good for her? *Alone.* She thought of Mia's strange utterances that night she'd tucked her in. *Funny. Not alone.* The words had sounded strange then, but she'd pushed them aside. She wished she could as easily push aside the feelings she had for Mia. Persistent feelings. After yesterday morning's phone call interrupted their most recent kiss, she did her best to keep her mind on finding a solution for her client, but it was clear that her mind was still on Mia. Repeatedly, she ran her tongue along her lower lip, imagining that the taste of honey remained.

*Why not rent the U-Haul now?*

She laughed aloud at the lesbian first-date reference and walked into the cool water. While thinking about Mia distracted her from the professional challenges she was facing, Sid was careful not to delve too deeply into fantasy. It was fantasy, after all, that had lured her into a destructive relationship with Aurora. She'd heard the rumors about the impetuous artist and wondered if knowing that monogamy wasn't part of the St. Germaine package made the choice to date her all the more alluring. Regardless, if it was Sid's plan to avoid intimacy, it ended up only proving to her how important intimacy was. She was lonelier with Aurora than without her. Would dating Mia be any different? Mia, who only two years ago lost her wife. Mia, who was quite likely grieving and in no position to manage a serious relationship.

*Serious? Did I just use the word* serious*? Whoa back, Harris. You've only had two kisses.*

True. But she wanted more. Her thoughts turned to how critical timing was to relationships and whether love was worth it when it was so easily lost. Her dad crossed her mind, and she acknowledged how he had managed to find happiness again with Isabel. Maybe she could roll the dice, too, and if lucky, stop settling for convenient. Aurora was convenient. And Mia was decidedly not.

❖

Mia had been watching Sid for some time. She seemed deep in contemplation of something perplexing. As she moved closer, Mia wondered at Sid's ability to win at poker; even in profile, her face was far more expressive than most players she'd met. Or perhaps she was now paying much closer attention to its subtleties.

The dogs sniffed along the bank, then moved into the high grasses. Flynn would keep Milo close if the youngster decided to explore too far afield.

She stepped from behind the stand of trees that concealed her. "I was hoping I'd find you here. You may not know it, but I gave you a rain check for the steak dinner." Mia continued appraising Sid's mood as she approached, hoping to lighten it. "If you wait too long, it may expire."

"That's illegal. And I have no intention of *not* cashing it. Sorry, but everything takes a bit longer at the moment." Sid touched her bandage and recoiled.

Mia felt her stomach lurch as if the pain was her own. "Still tender? Mind if I have a look?"

"You don't have to. I did see a doctor."

"I'm impressed." In fact, she was very impressed and not simply because Sid had accepted care. Sid looked striking; even in the afternoon shadows her hair captured the light that bounced off the water's surface. Her black bathing suit clung to her tight frame. Her full breasts packed against the sleek, satiny fabric such that her nipples were easy to detect.

"Still, a second opinion is important, don't you think?" Mia didn't wait for a response. "I won't ask what you're doing in the water. I'm sure the doctor wouldn't have recommended swimming quite so soon."

Her body made all kinds of recommendations where Sid was

concerned. She wanted to make Sid feel better. She wanted to feel Sid. And she could tell from how Sid's eyes were already undressing her that she was welcome to do just that. She unzipped her jeans and lowered them over her hips with her good hand, simultaneously stepping out of her boots.

"How's Flynn?" Sid asked, her eyes fixed on Mia as she dropped her jeans and stepped into the water.

Mia took the oddly timed comment in stride, suspecting, hoping, that Sid needed more cooling off than the lake provided. "He must know he's going to the vet this afternoon because he rallied this morning and insisted on joining us." She pulled her T-shirt up over her bra slowly, still aware of the tenderness around her rib cage. "Dogs are like cars...I'm sure you've experienced that pervasive rattle that becomes mysteriously undetectable the minute you roll into the mechanic's?"

"And then starts rattling again when you're halfway home?"

Mia stood knee deep in nothing but her lacy bikini briefs and matching blue bra, perfectly comfortable in her own skin. "Exactly." She could feel Sid's eyes but continued to speak matter-of-factly. She wasn't sure how far she was willing to go with disrobing. In fact, she'd gone further than she'd imagined in front of a relative stranger, relativity being an exaggeration given the fantasies she'd been having. But Mia loved the feeling of the water, and her libido had been dormant for so long that the sensuality of the moment emboldened her. As she reached to undo her bra, she continued the inane conversation, aware of its absurdity but using it to steel her resolve and keep Sid's welcome attention from straying.

"Have you ever thought of getting a dog?" She dropped her bra on the pile of clothes, thinking how funny it was that it had taken her fifteen minutes highlighted by agonizing contortions to get the bra on and an equal number of pain free seconds to get it off.

"I have, but I don't exactly have a dog lifestyle...back and forth, lots of travel." Sid spoke more softly, and her tongue ran along her bottom lip. Mia could tell she was struggling to direct her gaze elsewhere.

She took a few more steps. "When are you planning on going

back?" Mia wasn't sure she wanted to know, but regardless of what it was, she was here right now. And she wasn't going to waste time.

"Not sure. I have a couple of things keeping me here."

Mia smiled, pleased Sid had dropped the pretense and was now staring at her every curve. Deciding to keep her panties on for no reason other than to tease, she waded until she was waist deep, and stopped only inches from Sid.

"Are you keeping this dry?" Mia touched the area around the arm patch, circling it, then trailing down Sid's arm under the water. She took Sid's hand and lifted it above the surface, placing the wet palm against her lips and kissing it. Sid leaned forward, taking a short step so that her thigh moved between Mia's, the lace pressing against her hip.

❖

"I'm trying." Sid couldn't imagine trying any harder. She was no longer in touch with her ability to reason, and with Mia rendering every rational thought as flimsy as blue lace, she was quite literally in too deep. She tilted Mia's head upward before gently claiming her mouth.

Her body shuddered as their lips met. *Honey.* She could almost taste the wildflowers from which the pollen was gathered. Goose bumps rippled down her arms as her suit pressed against Mia's bare chest. Her other hand moved around Mia's hip, and she pressed it against the wet lace, pulling Mia's pelvis tighter against her thigh.

The water was nowhere near cool enough to temper the heat between them. She released the pressure on Mia's rear, raised her thigh a fraction, then increased the pressure again. Mia moaned, and Sid repeated the motion, angling her thigh so that Mia's weight rested on it. It was clear she was moving further and further from shore.

"Are you sure?" she asked.

"I'm here, aren't I?"

As if to prove it, Mia's tongue slipped between her lips and delicately, expertly, probed the softness inside. Beneath the water, Sid continued to rock, building the pace and pressure as Mia's legs coiled tightly around hers. She wedged a hand between them so her thumb could stroke Mia's hard nipple. It elicited a throaty growl that bolted through Sid like an arrow. She responded by pulling more tightly against her, taking care to avoid pressure on her ribs while trying to remain steady as her own feet shifted into the gravelly lake bottom. Her own mound swelled against Mia's wrapped leg, thick liquid building in the folds of her pussy, her clit growing hard and sensitive.

Mia writhed, and Sid grabbed on to support Mia's lower back, skirting the lace panties. She moved with a swimmer's rhythm, responding to Mia's surges. As they quickened, her movements became equally shorter and more intense. She could feel Mia struggling to maintain their kiss as she moved toward climax. Waves of pleasure rolled through Sid's body and broke, the release even more satisfying because it freed her to focus on Mia, whose head was buried against her neck. Sid stroked harder, her thigh pushing deeper. Mia's gasps became shorter, her moans strained, and her mouth hot against Sid's ear. Faster now. More quick gasps. Then Mia's body tensed.

"Yes."

❖

Mia was outside of her body. She could hear her own voice, now as gravelly as the lake bottom. Water splashed around them, dancing jewels atop the surface, leaping madly in the light of day.

Then she was back in her body, arms wrapped around Sid. She clamped harder with her legs, her butt tightening against Sid's hands. A warm flow, like underwater lava, emanated from between her legs against Sid's thigh. Another shudder shook her, and she relaxed into Sid's arms. Her breath came in heaves as the muscles along her rib cage yielded for the first time since her injuries. It was a relief. All of it was a relief.

The water was still now, both of them waist-deep and slowly catching their breath. After a moment, Mia felt Sid shift and tense as if she'd heard a knock at the door.

"What?" whispered Mia, still in a post-orgasmic haze.

There was a long pause. Mia stayed in Sid's arms, sensing that she needed time to find the right words but afraid of what they might be. "My dad doesn't know."

Mia fought the urge to laugh, sensing that as ludicrous as it might seem for a forty-year-old to worry about what her parent might think, Sid was still her daddy's daughter.

"He doesn't know you...swim?" Mia's pressed a kiss against Sid's neck.

"He doesn't know about me. About...this..."

Realizing that Sid wasn't quite ready for humor, Mia sat back on Sid's thigh and looked into her eyes, noticing how the irises were edged with a darker ring that held tiny specks of gold. "Of course he does." She smiled and tucked Sid's hair behind her ear, delicately tracing the strong and sexy jawline. "You're not as mysterious as you think. In fact, your father probably keeps more secrets than you do."

"Oh, I know about Isabel. I have for years. Terrible poker face, my dad. It's so easy to win his money. Almost criminal." She smiled a little.

"You're fascinating and intricate and more than a bit complicated, but a big secret in terms of *who* you love? Nope. You may be a good poker player, but you have a tell."

"What do you mean?" Sid pulled back, water filling in the space between them.

Before Mia could answer, Milo interrupted with a sharp loud bark. Mia recognized the urgency of his tone and was out of the water and on the bank in a second, Sid close behind. Lying on the moss, with Milo cross-stepping and continuing to bark, was Flynn. His eyes were closed.

Mia fell to her knees beside him "Flynn!" She tried to rouse him, and when that failed, she leaned close to check his breathing, placing her hand on his chest. "Okay, he's breathing," she said, tears almost blinding her. She put her arms beneath him and brought herself awkwardly, painfully, to one knee. Flynn's limp body was slipping from her arms.

"Move, Mia. Please. Let me." Sid's voice was gentle but insistent. She dropped to her knees and transferred Flynn into her arms. Then she stood in one easy motion and hustled with him toward her truck. "Grab your clothes," she yelled back. "I've got your boy."

## CHAPTER TWENTY-TWO

Sid sat next to Mia in the veterinarian's waiting room, stroking her back. She moved over the fabric with utmost caution, recalling what she'd seen, what she couldn't have imagined, when Mia crouched over Flynn an hour ago. The long angry bruises that lashed across her back and around her side were a reminder of the terrifying incident in the arena. They'd eventually heal, but she wouldn't soon forget. Milo sat between their legs, ears perked toward the doors Flynn had been taken through when they arrived.

Mia sighed deeply. "What is taking so long?"

As if on command, the office door opened, and Dr. Vandeven stepped through and sat down beside Mia. Milo circled her anxiously. "Flynn is fine at the moment. We're giving him fluids and running a bit of blood work. He seemed dehydrated, and whether that's the culprit or not, we'll soon know. I'm glad you brought him in when you did. I'll be back when we know something further." She put her hand on Mia's knee, rubbed Milo's head, then disappeared back through the door.

Mia sighed again and wiped a tear away. "I'm sorry. I'm sure this seems silly to you. But Flynn was our dog."

Sid sat quietly, trying to think of the most consoling thing to say, wanting to take away the fear but reminding herself she was in no position to fill the hole Riley left in Mia's life. Maybe no one could. And wasn't that best anyway? No strings. Casual. Maybe it was all she was capable of. In fact, Sid thought, if she hadn't been distracted by the shambles that her tryst with Aurora had become, maybe she would've kept her eye on the ball. Maybe—

"Thanks for mentioning my clothes back there. If you hadn't thought to remind me, I might've ended up here half naked. I feel a bit odd going commando, but my underwear was wet." Mia smiled and set her hand on Sid's knee.

Sid was happy Mia didn't wait for the words she hadn't yet found. And in spite of herself, she was delighted by Mia's touch. *Keep it light. Don't make it a thing. You'll never be Riley.* "I confess, I fought my instinct to remind you. I enjoyed your naked half. And the not so naked other. I guess I should be grateful I left my jeans and tee in the flatbed. I can't imagine sitting here in my wet bathing suit." She winked. "May I say, you are exceptionally good at dressing in the confines of a pickup cab. Is it safe to assume you've had prior experience?"

Mia squeezed her knee, making her jump. "You know, Cassidy Harris, you really should let people see this delightfully mischievous side of you more often."

"Yeah, I know. I've been in a bit of a funk lately."

"Technically, you've been a bit of a bitch lately. I like this bratty side, though. Looks good on you."

"You bring it out in me, to be fair. Not sure why, except that you're somewhat ravishingly sexy." Sid held up a single finger. "A great cook." A second finger, then a third. "But mostly aggravating…"

Mia grabbed Sid's counting hand and squeezed it hard. "Aggravating? *I'm* aggravating? Have you ever tried to have a conversation with someone whose phone takes priority?" Mia's tone seemed light, but Sid accepted that the comment wasn't too far off base. She was on her phone a lot.

"I'm sorry. I've heard that before." The digital distraction had been the subject of numerous nasty disputes with Aurora, who in fairness had plenty more egregious preoccupations. Nonetheless, Sid often found herself wondering if she'd been unable to commit fully to Aurora because she was constantly on the phone or if she had been constantly on the phone because she'd been unable to fully commit. If there'd been any intimacy between them, it had the qualities of a thick oil paint recklessly slathered in splotches and streaks on the canvas of their relationship. It took a year for Sid to accept that there was too little white space for her to appreciate the work and too much white space for Aurora. Eventually, they agreed that nothing significant, certainly no masterpiece, would come of their affair, and soon after, Sid spoke the necessary good-bye. At least she hadn't done that over the phone.

"The phone is a bad habit," she said, returning Mia's gaze. Oddly enough, she didn't even know where her phone was at that moment. Likely still back at the lake. It felt good, almost decadent, to be out of range of the device and wholly within range of Mia.

"No, I'm sorry. I know what you've been dealing with, and that comment really wasn't fair." Mia rubbed Sid's knee. "I'm glad you're here. And I'd understand if you have to leave to tend to business."

Sid didn't budge. They sat quietly after that, Sid periodically distracting Mia with quizzes from the stacks of *Oprah* magazines that littered the waiting room. Mia checked Sid's bandages and rounded up some clean dressings from the receptionist, changing the wet and mud-spattered gauze for a more sanitary wrap. The wound beneath had reopened, and Sid guessed it was when she'd scooped up Flynn. *Thank God for adrenaline.*

A couple of hours passed before the doors opened again, and Milo was first to his feet.

"Okay." The vet took a deep breath. "Flynn seems to be fine now. Once the electrolytes we gave him kicked in, he perked up. Has he been eating properly?"

"He seems to be," Mia replied.

"The tests showed a bit of a blood sugar issue, and I'll give you a script before you leave for an oral insulin. Is this fella new in the house?" The vet squatted and rubbed Milo's face.

"I've had him for three weeks or so. Why?"

"Try feeding the two separately so that this one doesn't eat all of Flynn's food. You wouldn't likely notice unless you stand and watch them eat, but a younger dog can easily become an alpha at the food dish. You wouldn't notice his weight gain because it's expected."

"So that's all it is?" Mia leaned against Sid's shoulder.

"Likely. I'll need to see him in a couple of weeks to do more blood work. The sugars may resolve themselves if he's eating his usual amount of food. I saw in the admission form that you make your own dog food, which is great. High protein, low carb for Flynn right now to keep his sugars level. Maybe a bit of extra calcium given his age. Egg shells are perfect. And it won't hurt Milo to have the same but with some added carbs, at least until he's finished growing. That might be enough to keep him from stealing from Flynn's bowl. We'll have your boy ready for home in fifteen minutes."

❖

It was dark by the time Mia made it back to the trailer. She wanted Sid to stay but she sensed that after a half day without a phone, Sid felt a compulsion to find it. She compromised. "I've already taken up so much of your day, but I'm happy to throw those steaks on the grill if you're hungry. That said, I know your phone is out there wondering where you've gone, so your rain check is still good if you'd rather do it another time." Her invitation had enough polite outs that Sid couldn't possibly feel badly if she needed to decline.

Sid's eyes widened, and she smiled. "I would rather do it another time. And another time after that, Mia."

Mia also smiled, realizing that Sid was not talking about dinner.

"But yes," Sid added, "I do need to find my phone. Just in case—"

"I understand. Another time, then." Mia leaned across the cab and kissed Sid good night. She felt disappointed but was grateful she was there when Flynn collapsed.

The thought of losing Flynn had unearthed fear. *He was our dog.* Mia had always managed the various challenges that cropped up from time to time when alone, but having Sid in that moment resurrected the notion that it was time to consider a change. She found herself thinking about a life with Sid, wary that she might be setting herself up for heartbreak. No doubt there was chemistry between them, but sadly, there would soon be distance. Sid would be heading back to Toronto, and she'd be looking for her next Milo.

Mia swallowed hard and winced, aware of a lurking headache. The almonds she'd eaten in the waiting room hours ago were all she'd had since breakfast, so as soon as she fed the dogs, she would look for sustenance. She took a deep cleansing breath, and stroked Flynn's head. Wherever the path took her, she was ready.

Mia supervised the dogs' feeding closely. Sure enough, Milo gobbled his down and would have trundled down the length of the trailer to help Flynn finish his had Mia not intercepted and showed him the door. Just then, her phone rang. It was Leah.

"Two calls and a visit all in the same week? Is Jim okay?" Mia could feel the panic welling in her, but didn't let her voice show it.

"He's fine. I just got off the phone with him. Results should be in tomorrow morning."

"Saturday morning results? That's great news." Over the six months Riley had been sick, Mia had learned more about medical protocols than she'd ever wanted. At the beginning, dealing with cancer was like a cruel puzzle. It took time to realize there were pieces missing, like things unsaid by well-intentioned medical staff trying not to speak the awful truth. But she quickly learned to listen not only to what was said but what wasn't. "It usually suggests they've been relegated to administrative staff who aren't allowed to deliver bad news."

"Well, that is certainly a positive spin. What on earth has gotten in to you?"

Mia tried to dial it back. After all, she had no idea if Sid and she were, well, she didn't know what they were exactly. It was just too early to tell. "Not sure what you mean. Flynn is okay, by the way. We just got back from the vet. Milo was stealing his food, and it threw his blood sugar off."

"We?"

*Does nothing get past her?* "We. Yes. Sid drove us. Long story." Mia hoped for a reprieve so she wouldn't have to delve too deeply into things. The headlights from a vehicle flashed against her kitchen wall, and she jumped at the opportunity. "Look, Leah, if you're okay, I have to go. Someone's here. It might be Milo's owner. Are you okay?"

"Yes, I'm fine. But we'll talk again tomorrow, okay? I know there's something you're not telling me."

Apparently, Mia was not the only one who knew when pieces were missing. "Absolutely. Love you, Leah."

"Love you back."

❖

As Sid rolled the truck up to the lake, she tried to recall a time when she'd been this long without her phone. Or even thought about it. It felt good to have Mia lean on her the way she had in the waiting room. Yes, people needed her at work, but with Mia, there were other needs being met. Needs she didn't realize she had. And Sid wasn't just thinking about what had happened earlier in the day.

She hated turning down Mia's dinner offer but until she found her phone, relaxing with Mia—as much as she craved it—would be out of the question. She also sensed that Mia might appreciate a bit of time to settle Flynn.

*He was our dog*. The words echoed in her head. Mia and Riley's dog.

With the help of her headlights, she was able to find her phone on the shore where she'd left it. As expected, there was a series of texts from Ella advising that nothing was firm, but the purchasing dealer agreed to broker for a percentage higher than customary.

Sid sneered and shook her head. "Mercenary."

Now all she needed was an agreement by the new current owner to sell at a fair price plus fees and what Ella referred to in one text as "other considerations." Sid made a note to ask Ella about that in the morning.

There was also a text from Aurora. Sid left it unopened.

Next, she called Aaron.

"I think we scared them the other night, cuz," he said. "No losses today. Tomorrow, Greg McCann is showing me how to use his drone."

Sid could hear his smile through the phone. "Yes, I'll just bet he is."

"Very funny. But drones will help us get eyes on whoever these guys are."

Thanking Aaron for taking the initiative, she threw the truck in drive before noticing a small clump between the passenger seat and the stick shift. She wedged her hand in and extricated a damp pair of lacy blue underwear. Instantly, her mind went to Mia. And instantly, she felt hungry.

"Aaron, I gotta go. Call you tomorrow."

## CHAPTER TWENTY-THREE

Mia stepped out of the trailer, the incoming vehicle so close that the high headlights blinded her, and she turned her head. The heavy truck door slammed shut, and the driver, silhouetted and still unidentifiable, approached.

"Do these belong to anyone here?" Sid's voice was husky and full, a quality in perfect harmony with her overt beauty. Mia found the whole Sid Harris package irresistibly attractive.

From Sid's extended hand dangled a piece of crumpled, lacy blue fabric.

"Guilty," Mia said. "With apologies to the court. What are you doing here? Don't you have some business to deal with?"

"A girl has to eat, right? And I have both my phone and a rain check."

Mia accepted her underwear and kissed Sid on the cheek, taking her hand and leading her to the firepit. "You get it started, and I'll grab the steaks." Mia said a silent thank you to Jack for the extras and turned toward the trailer.

"Hang on a minute, beautiful." Sid pulled Mia toward her and took her face in both hands, thumbs brushing lightly across her lips. Registering the desire in Sid's eyes, Mia tamped down her surprise and stepped closer. Sid's warm body trembled, and Mia wanted her to know that she invited her touch, her lips, and her body. She waited, feeling each second of delicious anticipation, for Sid to kiss her. When she finally did, Mia felt no hesitation. No resistance. The hunger rose in her core, the heat building between her legs and sending shivers down her arms. She heard a soft growl and realized it was her own. Her lips parted, inviting Sid's tongue to slip past them and explore the soft fullness of her mouth. When the kiss ended, Mia stood with her eyes closed as Sid placed soft kisses around her face, ending with one on her chin.

"Mia, I am starving. And tonight, I promise, I am not leaving without dessert."

Mia went inside and returned a few minutes later with a tray piled with foil-wrapped potatoes, two steaks, a small bowl of butter, the wooden honey box, two glasses, and the bottle of Casa Noble. Flynn and Milo joined them by the fire. As Sid banked the coals, Mia set the potatoes against the surrounding rocks.

"I think we have time for a drink, no?" Mia said, handing Sid the bottle.

Sid caught Mia up on what she'd learned from Ella and Aaron as she twisted open the silver ball atop the blue bottle and poured a healthy shot into the wine tumblers. Mia accepted the glass, letting her fingers touch Sid's as she did, and held it under her nose.

"This is a very different tequila than what I'm used to."

Sid waited until Mia sat down and then joined the dogs at her feet, leaning against the chair between Mia's legs and resting her head against a thigh. She held the glass so that the flames danced behind it as she swirled the yellow liquid. "Would you like me to tell you about it while it rests?"

Mia raked her fingers through Sid's soft hair, delighting as Sid almost purred at the touch. "Of course." Mia was curious about a tequila that needed to rest.

Sid seemed pleased to elaborate, telling Mia about its flavour notes, how a reposado is stopped in the aging process just short of becoming an añejo so that its woodiness and agave spirit prevailed. "It can be a great shooting tequila, but in small quantities and without window dressing," Sid explained.

Mia was engaged as she listened to the differences in process between it and Jose Cuervo.

"Go ahead," Sid said at last, tipping her head back to look at Mia's face. "Try it."

Mia sipped, the liquor warming her mouth enticingly. She detected the barrel oak Sid had described, and although she'd been a tequila drinker since university, Mia felt as though this was her first. "I think Jose is planning to retire," she declared, bending down and kissing Sid's ear.

Instantly she felt a sharp pain on the back of her head and a burst of vertigo. She gripped the arm of her chair and pulled herself upright. It passed as quickly as it struck, so quickly that Sid hadn't seemed to notice. It'd been over a week since she'd banged her head. It was likely a flashback to her overindulgent night with Leah. *Maybe keep the tequila to a minimum tonight.*

"So do you really think I'm a cowboy?"

*Well, that was out of the blue.* Mia thought back to her angry words the night that Sid tore off. She'd felt relieved that Sid wasn't more seriously injured, but what plagued her were fears of what might have happened if Sid had encountered the trespassers. She wasn't without her own impulsiveness, but even the six-year age difference between them had provided Mia with a perspective that came with time and experience, much as she hated to admit it. And a little bit of self-reflection. Sid was justified in her anger, too, and although they'd both accepted apologies, it seemed Sid had held on to Mia's words, taking her fear-fueled comment very much to heart.

"First, let me say that I am very fond of cowboys, including those of our preferred gender. The hats, the boots, the works." She felt Sid's shoulders relax, leaned down, and kissed her forehead, continuing to stroke her hair. *No dizziness. Good.* "I have worked with herding dogs for years. It's amazing to watch as they work cattle toward a path of least resistance. The dog and its team work as one, and I don't think the cows ever feel denied; they rely on the team to keep them safe. It's a trust relationship." She paused and rubbed Sid's shoulders, losing herself in their soft curves before continuing. "Some dogs can't work in a team. They have too much lone wolf in their blood. I've run into a few over the years. They're plenty sweet, but I've had to suggest that the owners make use of them for jobs other than herding because they not only put the herd in danger, they put themselves in danger."

"So, I'm not an impulsive cowboy; I'm a lone wolf?" Sid asked, her intonation a mix of disappointment and disbelief.

Mia nudged Sid aside and stepped toward the fire, stirring the coals and rolling the potatoes closer, taking the time to measure her response. She took a seat on the ground, leaning against the chair beside Sid and placing her hand on Sid's knee. The dogs shuffled and, with no space to curl up in between them, ended up flanking them.

"I don't think you're any *one* of those things. I think you're much more complex than that. More, well, human. Do you think I've been without impulsiveness? Even to the point of recklessness? Do you think anyone has?" Forgetting her pledge, she sipped her tequila and let the questions sit with Sid. "These aren't solely negative qualities, nor are they necessarily positive qualities. Many of our great leaders, boundary-pushers, have held them. We're not so black and white, we humans." Mia jostled her knee until Sid looked at her. "And to be honest, I was afraid of what could have happened to you that night."

"You must've worried about Riley all the time, yes?"

"But her training taught her to see not only the horizon but the path. She was wired to know exactly when to yield and exactly when to advance. It was her nature."

"Situational awareness," Sid stated, rising and setting the cast-iron grill on the fire. "I don't think I could have done anything differently where the sketch is concerned. How could I know what Jason intended? But you may be right about that night on the step. I could have exercised more patience and waited for Aaron or my dad."

Mia refilled their glasses and handed Sid the steaks to place on the grill. "My Granny K, my mom's mom, used to tell me the creation tale of Andek the crow, when I was a child," Mia said, putting her arm around Sid's shoulders. "Since you like stories so much, I'd like to share it with you."

"Please." Sid settled back into her place in front of Mia.

"Andek didn't feel like the other flyers that the Great Spirit created, the eagle, the hawk, and the loon." She kept her voice soft and low. "As soon as he was old enough, he ventured into the forest and came upon a squirrel. The squirrel was sad and feeling drained about his life, so Andek took him to Mkwa the Bear for some medicine and Miskwaadesi the Turtle to rediscover his spirit and wisdom. It wasn't long before the squirrel felt balanced and returned to his purpose revitalized and with a refreshed spirit."

Mia took a breath, staring at the coals. Sid sat so still that she could almost hear her heartbeat.

"Andek then came across a rabbit who was living in such fear of the fox that she wanted to die. Andek explained to the rabbit that her purpose was in her long ears and strong legs; the first would allow her to hear the fox coming in enough time that her speed would carry her to safety with ease. The rabbit's confidence was restored, and she no longer lived in fear. Through his travels," Mia said, "the crow discovered that his purpose was in helping others either find or renew their purpose."

"Are you telling me this because I am the squirrel? Or the rabbit? Drained? Or fearful? Stuck?"

"Do you feel that way?" Mia asked. She could sense Sid struggling and gave her time to think.

Sid paused before stroking Milo's head. "Do you think *I* need training?"

Mia laughed. "Not at all. I just think you need to recognize that more often than you think, there is an easier path. Maybe your purpose is to simply choose it once in a while. If we all did this, we'd spend a lot less time feeling like a scared rabbit."

Sid handed Mia her glass and rose to flip the steaks. "'Walk a good path, and you will be guaranteed to find your life's purpose.' You become your purpose by doing what feels good with good intention. So say the elders."

"I like the sound of that." Sid leaned in for a kiss. "I like you, Mia."

"I'm glad you came back tonight, Sid Harris."

❖

The steaks were barely salvageable by the time they disentangled themselves, but the potatoes were fluffy and encased in almost nutty skins, charred perfectly by the coals and slathered in butter. Sid gathered the dishes and watched with interest as Mia served the poached pears.

"I hope you like chai tea because the pears have been steeping in this syrup for two extra days," Mia said as she dropped a dollop of mascarpone on each, then twirled streams of Sid's honey on top.

Sid was amazed by how well each component was elevated by the other and tied closer by the fragrant undercurrent of cardamom. She tore through it with the speed of Milo and spent the next several minutes watching Mia finish hers while contemplating the story of Andek.

When the feast was done, she grabbed a blanket from her truck, spread it by the restoked fire, and invited Mia beside her. They lay on their backs, watching the sparks fly and float like lightning bugs against the black sky.

"I think you may be right about me being stuck."

"Your words, not mine, cowboy."

"True. I love my work at the gallery, but I love it here, too. I don't want to give up either, but I can't figure out how to do both and not feel resentful." Sid took a breath. "And to be honest, I feel a bit panicked."

Mia propped herself up on an elbow. "You love to swim, right?"

Sid wondered where Mia was going with this but answered in the affirmative.

"And when you swim, do you focus on the shore you're headed to or each stroke you take?"

"I feel each stroke. I guess because I trust they'll get me where I aim to go."

"As you think about the decisions you're facing, maybe it would help to consider that same approach. When you swim, you're aware that the water resists, but your will, your experience and strength, guides you without you being aware of it. When you're in your element, you stay on the path. You feel it under your feet, even in water."

"You're talking about being in, staying in, the moment. If I had a dime for every time I've heard—"

Mia let out a gasp and dropped softly onto her side. "Did you say dimes?"

Sid listened as Mia admitted noticing the box of dimes on her dresser, told her about finding the most recent dime in her pocket, and asked if she knew about the superstition.

"I didn't know for quite some time," Sid said, "but after the first six or so I found following my mom's death, I mentioned them to Isabel. She's a tad superstitious." Sid smiled, holding her index finger and thumb together, then separating the two until they were at their widest span. "She filled me in on the various interpretations. The number ten symbolizes the circle, so some say the dimes suggest a fulfillment of the cycle of life. Others take it as a warning to stay aware. Most folks, Isabel included, see it as proof that there is life beyond and that dimes are left by our loved ones as sign that they are still here. Watching over us."

As Sid spoke, a wave of shivers crossed her shoulders and traveled down her arms. She reached for the edge of the blanket and curled more closely into Mia, feeling unusually vulnerable.

Mia reached around her and drew her into warm arms. "I used to think that. Leah and I both found dimes for several years after our parents died. Now I think Riley has taken over, but rather than leaving them to remind me that *she* is still here, I think she leaves them to remind me that *I* am still here. And that my path continues, even though hers has ended."

"It's easy to lose sight of that. Of still being here. I hadn't considered that interpretation, but I like it almost as much as I like the thought of those who go before us keeping an eye on us." Sid lay back, thinking about her mom. She'd felt her mother's loss so deeply that she lost her way and wasn't sure she wanted to find her way back. It was as if a grey fog had crept over the mountains and deluged her, surrounding her with darkness. With each dime she'd found, the fog thinned, then lifted. She treasured each one.

Milo licked her arm before nosing beneath it and curling up against her. Sid turned and watched Mia reach for the honey. Using the spatula, she scooped out a piece of the honey-laden wax and let it fall slowly into her mouth.

The sensuality of the act mesmerized Sid and made her aware of a rhythmic pulse between her thighs. She stared wordlessly as Mia rose and straddled her. The pulse intensified. Mia pushed the piece of comb between her lips, her teeth clenching the wax, and the honey oozed out, falling in a syrupy trickle toward Sid's mouth. She clenched her butt, and the pulse became a powerfully pleasurable throb. She lifted her head, sticking her tongue out to take in the honey before claiming Mia's mouth. She bit into the comb, splitting it in two. It released another gush of honey and a sigh of pleasure from Mia, whose body shook before collapsing into her arms. A single breath later, she came with a deliciously slow easiness.

The lightning bugs continued to dance above them like drunken comets. Sid moved onto her side so that she could run her fingers through Mia's hair. She chewed the wax, thinking of nothing more than the woman beside her.

"Two desserts in one evening?" Sid managed, tossing the spent wax into the coals.

"Three if we're lucky."

## CHAPTER TWENTY-FOUR

It had already been a crazy, messy, wonderful day. Breakfast at the Millers', the lake rendezvous with Sid, then Flynn's collapse and diagnosis. Now, here she was, having just made love with Sid but still feeling inexplicably energized. Not only was she fatigue-free, but she was on a high similar to those she'd experienced when she'd hit and then overcome the ominous runner's wall. Triumphant. Tonight, any wariness about moving forward was washed away by the adrenaline coursing through her. Touching Sid, her body revved with sexual drive. She wanted nothing now the way she wanted to feel Sid's hands on her body again. She needed to feel the same flesh she'd leaned into at the lake.

"Sid," she whispered, "I need to feel you." She hoped she didn't sound as desperate as she felt, but she was willing to risk it.

Sid was bare beneath her T-shirt and jeans, so Mia grabbed the scruff of her collar and pulled it over her head so that her breasts were exposed to the starry sky. Sid complied wordlessly, her eyes ablaze with passion. Her nipples hardened and goose bumps formed down her arms and up her neck, and Mia could feel her own juices pooling between her legs.

Mia wriggled, freeing herself from her shirt and bra with Sid's help. As soon as it was off, she pressed into Sid, kissing her deeply and hungrily. As Sid's hands moved around her back, Mia could feel her hesitate.

*The ribs. Of course.* "Sid, I want you. All ways. Every way. On me. Over me. Under me. In me. You won't hurt me. And I promise I won't hurt you. Can I please have you tonight?"

Mia punctuated her request by grabbing Sid's hair and pulling it back, exposing her neck and nipping hungrily down to the clavicle. She ran her tongue along the ridge before tracing a route between Sid's breasts. Her back tensed, and Mia could feel her anticipation. She stopped, amazed at her restraint, and waited for Sid's answer.

"Can I please have you tonight?" she repeated, her finger circling the soft flesh.

"Yes. Mia. Please."

"Good. Because I've been wanting to touch you here." Mia kissed lightly around Sid's breast. She laid her tongue flat against Sid's nipple and areola and held it motionless while her finger and thumb found the other breast, tracing circles before lightly flicking the nipple.

"And here."

Sid's body arched, and as it fell, Mia began to swirl the rosy nipple, delighting as it grew harder and fuller before capturing it between her teeth and flicking it with the tip of her tongue.

Sid writhed. "Oh, yes!"

Mia pulled her leg up and over Sid's hips so she was straddling her as she played with her breasts. She could feel Sid's heat and wetness through their jeans, and this further bolstered her confidence. She moved her hips lower down Sid's thighs and unzipped her to reach around and squeeze between fabric and flesh. She kneaded Sid's softly sculpted ass, pulling tighter against her before pushing the denim down over her hips to her knees.

Mia placed one knee between Sid's legs, then the other, spreading them so that Sid's followed suit. Slowly, hungrily, she eased down the blanket until her head was poised above Sid's pelvis. She took in the trimmed mound of fine hair before descending, smelling the musky vanilla as she leaned her shoulders against Sid's inner thighs.

"And of course, I've wanted to touch you right here."

She lifted Sid slightly while gently spreading her open. She slid her tongue into the folds, exploring the delicious valleys around Sid's swollen clit. Sid moaned, and Mia pushed more deeply into her, engulfing warm wet flesh, her tongue rippling to create long, broad, upward and downward licks. As Sid tensed, she stopped to dip back into the valleys before broadening again to continue the onslaught.

Mia pulled a hand out from under Sid and slid her fingers into the wetness along with her tongue. When Sid's pelvis tilted, Mia entered her, first with one finger, then another. Sid moved up and down in rhythm with her tongue, so Mia slowly circled and pressed higher. She hooked her fingers until Sid's throaty gasp told her that they'd found her G-spot. As she continued to tease Sid's clit, Mia pushed her knuckles farther with each slow thrust.

Mia noticed the moment Sid was no longer in the room. Physically she was there. But her body had almost stilled, and the electricity flowing between them moved in only one direction. She placed her palm on Sid's lower belly, pressing down lightly to feel waves rolling beneath it. *Present, but not present.* She didn't know exactly what had caused Sid to check out, but she would wait patiently until she returned. She kept her tongue on Sid's pussy and let her fingers relax in place.

Within a matter of seconds, Sid stirred. "What? What's wrong?"

"Nothing is wrong," Mia replied. "I'm still here. Where are you?"

Sid grabbed Mia's hand and squeezed. The electricity was flowing again. "Please, Mia, please, fuck me. You feel so good. You make me feel good. Please don't stop. Tell me what you want me to do."

"I want you to breathe. Stay right here, with me. I want you *with* me."

"Yes, yes. I…please, Mia, don't stop."

"I won't." Mia kissed Sid's mound and felt her impassioned response. "Instead of paying attention to what I'm doing, try to focus on what you're feeling. All of what you're feeling. Be with it. And stay with me."

Mia fell back into rhythm, using her thumb to slowly circle the swollen clitoris as she moved in and out. Sid's breathing became slower, deeper, and she relaxed into the blanket.

Mia let her fingers, thumb, and tongue dance with Sid as she trembled and pulsed, moaning with ecstasy, her wet pink folds opening up like a late spring tulip, inviting deeper and stronger strokes. Mia responded accordingly, driving deeper, stroking more rapidly. Sid's moans became louder.

"Mia. Yes."

She maintained a consistent pressure and speed until Sid's buttocks began to clench, and her legs quivered. Then she plunged as far and hard as she could until Sid fell silent, and her body seized, curling into Mia and then arching away, contracting and expanding with wave upon wave as she came.

"I'm here!" she cried, her voice broken and throaty.

"Yes, Sid, yes."

Mia slowly extricated herself between Sid's convulsions and moved beside her, grabbing the blanket and rolling into her. They curled together in the blanket by the fire under the stars. She'd need to talk with Sid about where she might have gone for those brief moments during their lovemaking, but now was not the time. A fierce headache that had been circling her since she'd tried to lift Flynn settled behind her eyes. Sid's vanishing act was a runner's wall she would have to tackle another day.

❖

As soon as Mia fell asleep, Sid's mind began to churn. She hadn't wanted to leave, certainly not while every inch of her body was attuned to Mia's touch, her desires prowling, hunting for immediate release. She wanted to feel it all, harder and faster and completely. But at some point, she'd gone somewhere in her mind. It had happened before. Sometimes, she didn't know when it happened, but this time she did. It happened the moment Mia's fingers found their way to the place that took away all distance between them. Her mind turned to all those wasted moments when she resisted surrender, believing it was weakness. Poised at a precipice with Mia, she was in the past, taking in for the first time the places she'd been. It overwhelmed her. Making love with Mia was so far away from the ambivalent mercenary transaction that she'd experienced with Aurora. This was new ground, and for a split second, she was afraid of where she might be heading.

But Mia had noticed. And not only did she notice, Sid realized with amazement, she stayed. She smiled and pulled Mia closer. *New ground.*

## CHAPTER TWENTY-FIVE

Once the morning breeze followed the sun up the rise, Mia couldn't get close enough to Sid to stay warm, as much as she tried. The fire had long ago died out, so she roused a spent Sid and led her into the trailer. Sid collapsed in the bed, pulling Mia under the covers, spooning her gently with her injured arm across Mia's uninjured side before falling back into a dead sleep.

Mia smiled. It was clear from Sid's physical responses the night before that she had not forgotten how to please a woman. The moment Sid had vanished was surprising, and when the time was right, she'd ask about it. For now, the fact that she'd returned and fully connected reassured Mia about how wonderfully things were unfolding. Even the fears she'd held about sex with someone after Riley, fears that she might think about her, call out her name, or worse, compare her new lover, had been put to rest as deeply as Sid now slept. Riley was gone. And Sid was Sid. She felt, smelled, and tasted different. She was different, and she made Mia feel different.

Mia's mind was racing, so when she was unable to fall back asleep an hour later, rather than disturb Sid, she decided to feed the dogs and take Milo out for his final command session before Jack came by that afternoon. Flynn made his own decision about how he wanted to spend his morning; as soon as he'd finished his breakfast, he jumped into bed with Sid and gave Mia a "yep, this could've been you!" look.

❖

Somewhere in the tangle of linens, something was vibrating. Half asleep, Sid thought it might be her, the effects of last night still resonating in her body. She rolled deeper into a fuzzy comforter, reaching out but realizing after completing a snow angel that she was alone in the bed. Except for something furry, which licked the foot that had gently kicked it. And the vibration of the? What?

*Phone!*

Sid jumped up and began ferreting through the sheets. She found it and flipped it screen side up. She read the text message before realizing it wasn't intended for her. It wasn't her phone.

*Pick up, Mia! Please. Results in. Need to talk.* It was from Leah, and seconds later, the phone vibrated again, this time indicating an incoming call. Normally, Sid would never touch someone else's phone, let alone read a message or consider answering it, but it was impossible to ignore the sense of urgency.

Sid pressed answer. "Hello, Mia's phone."

"And who might this be?" Leah asked, drawing out the query.

"Hello, Leah. This is Sid."

"Sid Harris. In the morning hours." Leah's tone was that of someone expecting it might be Sid, though Sid was perplexed to understand why. "What have you done with my friend?"

"She's not here at the moment." Sid looked around the trailer, spotting a piece of paper with her name scribbled on it propped up on the window frame at the head of the bed. She unfolded it. *Out with Milo. Didn't have the heart to wake you. Back at ten. Xo Mia.*

"She'll be back at ten. She's out with Milo. Would you like to speak with Flynn?"

Leah laughed. "I know now why Mia was in such a strange mood last time we spoke."

"Strange?"

"As in happy. Happy strange. I'm guessing she got past hating you? And maybe you decided against pressing trespassing charges?"

"Possibly." Sid wasn't entirely sure how Mia felt but wagered that as close as the two childhood friends were, Leah knew more than she did at this point.

"You will treat her nicely, right, Ms. Harris? Because I know where you live."

"I think that's a good bet." Sid paused, weighing her next words. "I hope you don't think I've taken advantage, or that it's too soon since Riley—"

"*No*. No one thinks that. No one who knows and loves Mia. She's worked hard to find her way again, and it seems like you're a decent enough person. I'm sure you two will figure out a plan for when you head back to the big city, if that's what you both want."

Sid had been trying to figure out a plan to keep Mia close since their first kiss. "I'm sure we will," she replied, hoping a solution would appear now that she'd admitted how much Mia meant to her. It didn't. *Think, Sid. Find a way. Abandon convenience.*

"Good. I'll hold you to that. Now, would you please ask Mia to call me the minute she's back?"

"I will do that. Oh, and Leah, I'm sure your mom has already asked you to come to my dad's birthday bash, but it would be really great if you could make it. It's next Saturday. It would be a nice surprise for Mia, and it's going to be one hell of a party. And bring your man!"

## CHAPTER TWENTY-SIX

Sid hung up and rolled back under the covers. Flynn settled in beside her, resting his head on his crossed paw, and staring at her with his big blue eyes.

"Yes, I know. You're right." Dogs always were. She'd eventually have to go back to Toronto and her job at the gallery, but thinking about it tied her up inside. For most of her life, she'd connected the ranch so closely to her mother's death that sadness was all she could see. It was only on this trip that she'd been able to experience the memories without the pain. The Harris homestead felt again like home, so the thought of leaving brought about a different sense of loss.

*And then there's Mia.*

Sid burrowed deeper in the bed. She wasn't sure why Mia affected her so. She worried it was a rebound. After all, it had only been a couple of months since Sid salvaged what was left of her self-esteem and ended things with Aurora. It had been a torrid affair, and one that shouldn't have gone beyond the carnal. Now, she wanted something real. Deeper.

Mia was real. And beautiful. And passionate. Perhaps she was the other pea in Sid's pod. It'd be easy to lie in bed all day reflecting on the amazing night, but another vibration from a phone on the kitchen counter pulled Sid out from the sheets and back into her current reality.

It was Ella, calling to let her know that Martin needed to talk that afternoon. He was on set in Hawaii, but she could call him late-day. Sid found her clothes and threw them on. She'd need to put a few more pieces in place before she spoke to Martin and needed to be back at her desk to do so. She thought about calling Mia, then realized that Mia's phone was still in the trailer, so she flipped the "out with Milo" note over and wrote her own.

"Keep the bed warm, buddy." Sid ruffled Flynn's ears and left the note on the kitchen table propped against the tequila bottle before heading out.

❖

"I can't believe that is the same dog, Mia, really. You've done wonders." Jack McCann stood beside her, shielding his eyes from the bright noon sun, his mouth open as he watched Milo work the herd. Milo's focus was sharp, his energy high, and he was attentive to the twenty or so head but most importantly, to command.

"Bring them around, Jack." Mia was now training the partnership, proud to hand the responsibilities of the lead to Jack. Milo moved the cattle from right to left, using one of the fences in the Miller's two-acre stockade, a space that was perfect for this point in his education.

"Come-bye, Milo."

Jack commanded him to go to the left of the stock, clockwise around them, which would redirect them away from the fence and take them to the right. This step tested the bond of dog and owner because the herd was no longer up against a fence. Milo moved with speed and agility, darting from side to side across the head of the herd and making use of the intimidation stance he'd first tried on Sid's ATV, this time with great effect. Halfway through the turn, one steer began to splinter from the whole.

"Milo, walk up." Jack directed him to approach the herd more closely to maintain cohesion. He did as asked and routed the stray back in, managing his position so that the fence was again supporting his efforts.

"Good job," Mia said. "We'll try one more. Even dogs with

Milo's energy get tapped out when they first start working, and it's important not to diminish his dominance. Right now, the cows respect his authority, and for safety, it's best to keep it that way. Ask him to bring them back and use the hand signal so that we start to build visual responses, too. It comes in handy on a windy day or when the herd is large."

"Away to me, Milo." Jack accompanied direction with his index and middle finger, thumb tucked in.

Milo conducted the redirection, keeping himself positioned so that no cow had the opportunity to splinter. *That dog is catching on quickly.*

"That'll do." Jack showed index and pinkie, rotating his wrist back and forth.

Mia smiled proudly. Milo trotted toward his owner with swagger. Working dogs weren't driven by reward but by the heredity of their breed, assets born thousands of years ago when dogs ensured their species' survival by capitalizing on the symbiotic relationship with humans. Mia enjoyed that the relationship was truly give and take. Domesticated dogs were sheltered, fed, and protected in return for their service, be it retrieving, hunting, or herding.

"Milo, you have every right to be proud of yourself. Good boy! You too, Jack. You obviously put serious time into studying the signals."

"Sure did, and I'm just so impressed at how he seemed to respond."

"You'll see it again when we try it next time without the vocals."

"Not that I'm in any hurry to see you go, but I'm wondering when we'll be wrapping things up? Greg, my son, has been experimenting with drones to secure and herd cattle and, well, not that I'm opposed to modernization, but I'm excited to show him how capable Milo is."

Mia felt as though her mind hadn't registered his words. Or their meaning. This was the second time her mental acuity had faltered today; earlier, before Jack arrived, she'd struggled to recall a command sequence. *Coincidence.* She asked him to repeat his question.

"When do you think Milo will be ready to graduate?" He didn't seem to have noticed the momentary lapse.

"Another week, I expect, based on his progress. We have some of the more complicated functions to work on like finding cattle in the bush, casting, and separating animals. But now that I know he's safe around the herd, that'll come quickly with practice."

*I'm fine. It's just fatigue.*

"And then what are your plans?" Jack leaned into the cab of his truck, reaching for his sunglasses on the dashboard.

*Good question.* Mia's mind flashed to the night before. And then to the note she'd found that morning when she'd returned to the trailer:

*Hated to leave. Work to be done. My turn to make dinner. Come around seven and bring the boys. Call Leah.*

So, Mia knew what she was doing that night, but beyond that, she wasn't sure. *Is it too early to wonder how Sid might fit in with my future?* "No plans yet."

"Well, I wonder if you'd consider something a little different. I hope you don't mind, but I mentioned your home-cooked dog food to my oldest daughter. She's got a great mind for business and the credentials to boot. Her ears perked up as high as Milo's when I told her how much he prefers your recipe over the stuff I was feeding him. Our family has connections to suppliers. But Jesse is all about manufacturing, marketing, and distribution. She's visiting us next week from Saskatoon. Would you be interested in stopping by and meeting her?"

Mia had never contemplated going to market with her dog food, but she knew that trying to find a natural food that Flynn would eat was hard, if not impossible, to find in stores outside of a few major urban centers. Even online offerings were meager. "Why not? Sounds interesting."

"I'll warn you, she's like her brother Greg. She doesn't always hoe a straight row. All about organic this and non-GMO that. Imagine, a vegan in a house full of beef producers!"

Mia could easily do that. The vegan and vegetarian bandwagon was now a brigade, rolling into rural areas and finding serious consideration and receptivity where there used to be none. She'd even started to experiment with natural plant proteins, working them into Flynn's mix more and more over the years.

"See you Monday, then," Jack said. "Come for lunch. I'll make sure there's something other than tofu on the table."

Mia waved as he drove off and then started hiking up the road to her trailer. After only a few minutes, the hill seemed unusually steep. To avoid thinking about it, she turned her mind to the decisions she'd soon need to make. It was high season for ranchers, so most wouldn't have the time to spend on their dogs until the fall. That left her with almost two months to sort out her next move. Until just hours ago, when Leah shared Jim's results, she thought she might go to Vancouver to spend time in support of Leah and her husband. But Jim's clean bill of health was the best possible reason to have to change that plan. *To what, though?*

After another few minutes, she found it simpler to curse the hill again. It wasn't that she couldn't think of what she would do next—or where she would do it—that bothered her most; it was the looming realization that her ability to make decisions quickly and rationally felt compromised. The doctor had mentioned that concussions could cause temporary impairment, but she hadn't had any other symptoms so had dismissed the possibility.

By the time they arrived at the trailer, Milo was ready for a nap. And so was she. Her sleep cycle had been commandeered by her injuries and meds. Could that also account for the odd disconnect between Jack's words and her cognitive processing? Maybe these strange challenges weren't symptoms but side effects. Two more days of the antibiotics, and she'd hopefully be back to herself. As she stepped into the trailer, she was aware of a profound lack of energy and thought back to last night when she wasn't just tireless; she was boundless. Perhaps it took the right carrot, because right now, she was dragging. Flynn, on the other hand, had been in bed all morning, and as much as Mia wanted to shower and catch up on her sleep before dinner, she was responsible for his needs. She took him outside and played with him until his fatigue matched hers.

"Glad you're feeling better, my boy. But I think Milo has the right idea. Time for a nap."

Mia set her alarm, giving herself plenty of time to get ready for the evening. Her mind floated back to the night before: the taste of tequila and honey, the feeling of Sid beneath her hands and tongue, the sound of her breath and the gold specks in her eyes flashing like fireworks as she came. Even now, hours later, Mia found herself aroused. She could smell Sid in the sheets, and she immersed herself in them, comforted by the presence of the woman she already missed. Knowing she wouldn't find peace until her urges were sated, she let her fingers roll and ramble through the wetness between her thighs. Fantasies of Sid beneath her tongue quickly escorted her into a quivering release, and she soon after surrendered to sleep.

## CHAPTER TWENTY-SEVEN

Sid would've preferred to stay in Mia's bed all day, but as adorable as he was, Flynn was no substitute for the woman who'd captured her heart. Besides, she had work to do, and the sooner she put her plan into place, the better. By the time she'd cleaned up after tending to the ranch chores, the sun was already over the yardarm. She sat at her desk and reviewed the plan. She read and reread Ella's latest missives, then reached out to a few foreign contacts to make sure all the pieces needed to resolve the problem were in place.

*Hopefully, Martin will still trust me.*

Martin Stephens was the only person in her professional realm aside from Ella whom she'd invited to use her abridged moniker. Not even Aurora had called her Sid. Martin had always been genuine with her, and as they'd developed a friendship, she felt comfortable reciprocating. It was late afternoon when she placed the call to him.

"Sid, I can't tell you how much I appreciate what you're doing," he said after she'd laid the new developments out for him.

"I'm just glad there were breadcrumbs to follow. You do know that no one at the gallery knew what this idiot was doing, right? Nonetheless, he put us in a terrible spot, and I hope to get us out."

"Do you think my offer is fair?"

"I think it's better than fair. I spoke to the buyer this afternoon. Fortunately for us, he has ultimate respect for provenance, so the proviso that gives him back right of first refusal if you ever decide to sell the two pieces will be well received. I feel confident of that. Just know that this proviso includes private and public markets. The fox in the henhouse here is the broker. He wants extra fees, likely because we've interrupted other moves he may be involved in. I won't lie, Martin, things are still volatile."

"Which is why you've asked me to keep an eye on the market at my end. I owe my friends at least that much."

Martin had a lot of friends, people whom he had convinced to invest in Canadian works, primarily the Group of Seven but also Emily Carr and other contemporaries. They trusted him just as he trusted her, which was why she felt it imperative to make it right.

"Thank you, Martin. I appreciate you entrusting me with this. I can't say sorry enough for dropping the ball."

"Don't be ridiculous. You didn't drop the ball in the least. In fact, you didn't even hold it. You work for the gallery, and the purchase wasn't under your purview. The piece was privately owned, and if the broker in all of this mess had even a speck of the integrity you have, my dear, he would never have leveraged the deal. You know that. I know that. And soon, everyone will know that."

"Duncan Harris didn't raise me to work without integrity. I promise I'll call when I have a response. The buyer is in New York this weekend. So, likely Tuesday or Wednesday?"

"Perfect. Talk to you then. And Sid? I want you to think about what I said earlier this week. Whether you make this deal or not, I can tell you're ready to leave the gallery. I can set you up with clients. You know I can. And I'd be honored to. Just say the word."

How Martin knew that she was restless, Sid could only guess. She was learning that people knew more about her than she thought. Nonetheless, she was touched by the faith Martin had always shown in her and relieved that she was making progress. Now she could only wait as the shadow of the trees outside her window fell slowly across her desk. And then it struck her. The shadows were over the house.

*Dinner with Mia!*

## CHAPTER TWENTY-EIGHT

Sid was hurriedly tucking her shirt into her pants as she flew down the stairs, then slid in her sock feet partway across the great room's hardwood toward the kitchen. She'd had a choice to make: dinner on time or clean and fresh. She chose the latter.

"Slow down there, cowboy! Where you going in such a hurry?"

Sid's heart skipped at least a beat and not solely because Mia—who stood next to a freshly built fire—had taken her by surprise. She was a vision in a cobalt blue midi dress with a skinny-strapped, satiny bodice that displayed her cleavage exquisitely.

"You look..." Sid couldn't find the words.

The dress flowed at the waist into a two-layer skirt, the crochet lace overlay cascading to just below Mia's knees and the sheer hem showing off her legs from just above her knees down. Mia always looked lovely, even when she was wrapped in an old tee and a bathrobe. But standing barefoot in the living room, she was drop-dead, breathtakingly gorgeous. Sid couldn't look away, nor could she complete her sentence.

"Hungry?"

*Yes. Hungry.* "I was going to say exactly that, yes." Sid felt conspicuous, one hand still half-tucked with her plaid shirt inside her distressed relax-fit jeans. She pushed her hair back over her ear and moved, entranced, toward Mia.

"Are you *really* a good poker player?" Mia looped her fingers in the belt loops on each side of Sid's waist, pulling her into a kiss.

Sid could think of little else than how Mia—in that dress—was making her feel. "Why do you ask?"

"I haven't known you long, but are you aware of your tell? Just before you shift gears, at times when you're having trouble staying on task—"

"When I'm distracted like I'm distracted right now?" Sid licked her lips, her mouth suddenly as dry as a bone.

"Yes." Mia smiled. "Like now. Did you know that you have a habit of tucking your hair behind your ear?"

Sid smiled and crooked her head. "I'm not sure I'm comfortable with you noticing that. I don't like to think of myself as predictable." She said it only half jokingly. A lifetime of relationship difficulties had given her insight into a destructive habit: she didn't like being truly seen. And being seen as acutely, as intimately, as Mia apparently saw her scared Sid. She shuffled a step back, but Mia pulled her close again and kissed her. At first, the kiss felt reassuring. Then inviting. Then it rolled with passion. Sid's body crested, and she let the wave carry her until she could find bottom. Mia released her, and she steadied.

"I get paid to pay attention to signals," Mia said. "I'm skilled at it. Your tell is subtle, and it's not likely others have noticed. The proof is in how much you leave the table with, right?" She smiled, yanking on Sid's jeans. "Besides, I enjoy predictability; sometimes it's like a warm quilt on a cold night. Speaking of which, I could still smell you in my bed this afternoon. We took a short nap together."

*It's hard to stay annoyed with this one.* "Fair enough. I'm blaming tonight's hair tuck on how amazing you look." She ran her index finger behind one of the shoulder straps, then along the border of the bodice. "Maybe I should stop playing poker. I would lose my shirt if you were at the table."

"That wouldn't be such a bad thing, would it?" Mia's hands moved around her waist and up and down her sides beneath the untucked hem of her shirt.

"It won't be, I promise. But I promised you dinner, too, and I haven't eaten today, so I'm starving. Again." Being around Mia always stirred an appetite of one sort or another.

She led Mia into the kitchen and poured a glass of wine, explaining what had gone on that day with the art deal while pulling various things out of the fridge and scattering them onto the counter.

Mia laughed. "Do you have a plan, here, or are you free-styling?"

Sid confessed that the day had gotten away from her, but Isabel's leftovers were infinitely better than anything she could create. She began to prepare vegetables for a crudité.

"Something tells me you're underselling your abilities in the kitchen. Those aren't the knife skills of a culinary amateur," Mia said, then picked up a mushroom and tossed it toward her. She deftly speared it on the end of the knifepoint. Mia shook her head in disbelief. "Seriously? Are you slow-playing me, Harris?"

"Honestly, chopping is easy. If you have the right technique, anyone can do it with eyes closed. I'll prove it." She placed a cutting board on the counter, put a celery rib on it, and handed Mia a chef's knife. "First, make sure the target is stable." Sid turned the celery so that the curved side was up and the cupped side faced down. "Now, hold your fingers near the end you want to cut, on top, like so." Sid demonstrated on her board. "Tuck the tips of your fingers in, and rest the side of the knife against your knuckles. See, you couldn't cut your fingertips if you wanted to. Now work the blade cyclically, like so." Sid pushed the knife down and forward through the rib, then came up and back, forward and down. "And slide your fingers down the rib slowly, letting the blade but not the edge find your knuckles. If you keep the tip of the knife on the board as you work, you're not in danger." She was pleased with how quickly Mia mastered the technique.

"Shall I close my eyes?" Mia asked.

"I'm not sure I can trust you...yet. You look like a peeker." Sid grabbed a clean tea towel out of a drawer and spun it diagonally. She pressed her hips into Mia's backside and placed the towel over her eyes, tying it at the back but keeping Mia held between her and the counter. She felt a stirring where their bodies touched.

Mia wielded her knife in the air like a blind pirate. "And you say there's no one else here? I ask in case one of us gets hurt."

"Duncan and Isabel are in Edmonton with the Millers, gathering supplies for next weekend's party. They're staying over at the casino. And Aaron…well, he's getting a lesson from a friend about drones, so he says. I'm not sure I believe that, but I do know he won't be coming here tonight. He's looking after the Millers' dairy cows so he's staying at their place. No one is getting hurt." Sid wondered briefly how she could keep that promise. "Now stop stalling and start cutting." She leaned further into Mia, caressing her shoulders, lips brushing against her skin.

❖

"I'm not willing to lose a finger over this," Mia said. "You're making it hard to focus."

"I'd hate for you to lose a finger, too, beautiful, given how adept they are with other tasks."

Mia couldn't help but smile. Sid's playfulness was charming. Her fingers traced the seam of fabric just above Mia's breasts, then retraced the route, but this time, they caressed her skin. The touch was erotic, and Mia did her best to focus on chopping. The temporary blindness heightened her other senses. Her skin tingled behind the trail of Sid's touch. The sound of the celery crisply yielding beneath her blade was almost deafening. The smell and softness of Sid's hair against her neck and cheek was distracting, and she could feel her knees weaken. She dug her bare feet into the kitchen mat to hold her ground.

Sid pushed more firmly against her butt, one hand moving down her waist and squeezing between her upper thigh and the counter edge; the other moved around her bodice and up toward her breasts. Mia pushed back against her to allow the hand more space and tipped her head back, leaning to the side, exposing her neck and inviting Sid's kiss.

Mia's knife stopped mid-cut as Sid bent lower, her mouth claiming the skin below Mia's ear. Her hand cupped her over the fabric between her thighs. The heat and dampness increased as Sid's finger's pressed more deeply.

"Oh, Sid. Your touch. God, I love it."

Mia's breast was captured beneath her bodice, and as Sid moved over the nipple, she convulsed. The knife fell to the board, the celery scattering. She put both hands on the counter to brace herself, conscious of nothing more than Sid's hands moving across her body and under her dress. Mia reached over her head and entwined her fingers behind Sid's neck.

"Kiss me," she pleaded, but she slurred the words. In spite of her libido having found a second gear, she was exhausted, even after her nap. But her arousal was deep, and she wasn't about to choose the corporeal over the carnal.

Sid's mouth felt hot against hers. Sid's fingers had slipped beneath her lace underwear and into her wetness. She gasped, breathless as Sid found her clit and began to stroke it expertly, agonizingly slowly. It was so, so easy to melt. As Sid changed pressure or speed or moved a fraction of an inch, Mia's body relented, telling Sid, without words where to touch her. Where to find her. Once she did, Mia fell back into Sid's arms, shuddering, her hot flow releasing in Sid's hand. When her rippling orgasm calmed, Sid lowered them to the kitchen floor, cradling Mia tightly. Mia's head felt as if it was floating, her body drifting nearby but also far away.

❖

"Well, Sid Harris, that was some appetizer," Mia mumbled, pulling herself into Sid more tightly. She had awakened, unsure if awakened was the right word. *Had she slept?*

"I am a terrible host, aren't I? Let's see what we can find for a main course." She hauled Mia to her feet and kissed her before turning her attention to the pursuit of edibles.

"If you don't mind, while you work your kitchen magic, I'm going to let the boys out." Mia's legs were wobbly, and she leaned against the porch door, watching as Milo goaded and prodded Flynn, who refused to give ground. The dogs and Sid shared the same headstrong determination, and it made her reflect on her own decisions. Yes, her choice to pack up and immerse herself in canine training a couple of years ago was a good one. The love and companionship of dogs was easy, uncomplicated, and it gave her what she needed at the time, a chance to find the ground beneath her feet again, to exercise control, and to live at a pace she could manage. Her ultimate goal wasn't to forget her loss, not to forget Riley, but rather to put the hospitals, trials, specialists, and finally the terribly dashed hopes of a future she'd imagined, into a healthy perspective. She had to challenge herself to really live again. As she watched the dogs, she knew that emotionally, if not quite physically, she was ready for more conflict, more tension, than even an unfettered puppy like Milo could provide.

When Mia came back inside, she felt revitalized. The dogs returned to their warmed spots on the sun porch. Sid had scavenged the various containers from the fridge and put together a mosaic of food on a large platter: roasted peppers, olives, a chunk of parmesan cheese, salami, celery and carrot sticks, and a bowl of leftover spaghetti, which she'd set in the middle of the odd assortment, spearing it with two forks.

Mia grabbed the bottle of wine she'd brought, uncorked it, and carried it and two glasses into the great room. She dimmed the overheads, then set the wine on the side table while she flicked on the stained glass lamps. Waiting on Sid, who was putting final touches on the dinner tray, Mia admired the great room. It was aptly named, the impact of the size elevated by the vaulted ceiling, which was crisscrossed with thick wood beams joined by dark metal braces that looked hand-hammered. The walls were a green she recognized as mountain forest, a hue made famous by Frank Lloyd Wright's Fallingwater palette, the perfect complement to the robust, oak, craftsman-style chairs padded with warm green and rustic red leather cushions. Opposite the fireplace, a wall of large windows ran the length of the side of the house, facing the mountains and a second wall at the front.

The room's two sitting areas, one near the fireplace and the other near the windowed wall, were separated by one of the largest harvest tables she had ever seen, the wood worn from use. A beautiful dried flower arrangement, bold bulrushes towering over a base of nettles and puffy hydrangeas, was large enough to act as a divider for the large room, creating intimacy in spite of the tremendous space. In a corner on the fireplace wall, several chairs clustered around what looked to be a well-used game table.

The tone of the room was strong and masculine but also soft and functional. As she took a spot on the couch, she noticed the large canvas above the timber mantel. The foreground was a collection of earthy mounds topped with a stand of tamaracks that took up at least half of the space. The observer would have to look past or through these trees to see the lake, which was represented by a thin band, maybe one brush-width thick, of light blue paint that crossed the landscape roughly a quarter the way up. On top of that was a darker blue, almost purple mash of paint that evoked a solid wall of indistinguishable trees on the far side of the lake. This took the eye to about halfway up the image where the cloud-spattered sky—still shrouded by trees and painted with the same blue as the lake—completed the depth of the work. Like the room, strong impressionist influences were made soft by the artist's choice of light and color.

Sid joined her on the couch, placing the large platter between them and sitting sideways, legs crossed, facing her. "*Tamaracks*, 1915. Thomson."

"Did you pick it out?" Mia asked, picking up an olive and baiting Sid with it.

"I did. It was a gift for my dad. Not an original, of course, but a good reproduction." She snagged the olive and smiled as she chewed.

"Why? I mean, why did you pick this one?" Mia broke off a piece of parmesan and wrapped it in salami, handing it to Sid before making one for herself.

"This was the piece I fell in love to…with the Group. And Thomson. When I saw this particular work, I noticed for the first time his choices. Where he put paint and where he didn't. The ochre undertones. The representation of Canadian light. I saw between the brushstrokes. I guess you could say that I heard the artist's voice. I was wholly and helplessly smitten." She sat still fondling an olive as she stared up at the canvas.

Mia saw more than infatuation. She saw love and a bit of sadness. *Where is she now?* "They seemed like artists who knew how to forge ahead and make new paths." She leaned forward and put a hand on Sid's knee. "Are you struggling with something?"

"What?" Sid looked into her eyes, and Mia could see the striking warmth there.

"With your path, maybe? Are you still struggling?"

"Yes, I guess so. With change. I think things will have to change for me." Sid stopped short of a hair tuck and reached for a forkful of spun spaghetti instead.

Mia marveled at her ability to self-correct so quickly. Perhaps self-correct wasn't the right term; after all, there was nothing incorrect about a hair tuck. *Except that now, maybe Sid is aware that I'm seeing her.*

"Remember the story of Andek?" Mia said, taking Sid's hand "According to legend, we can't find our purpose if we sit on the path. The crow is meant to remind us that work and dedication, step by step, will show the way to the purpose we seek."

"I'm not sure I'm on a path, let alone which path it might be."

"Look at that picture. That lake was probably hundreds of miles from where the artist lived. He and his friends, they made a new path with their art. Could it be that now is the time for you to surrender?"

Sid took a moment, her eyes on the Tamaracks. "They did find their purpose."

"Exactly. For some, like this one artist, the path was too short. Thomson drowned when he was still a young man."

"The path was too short for your Riley, too." Sid spoke with a genuineness that melted Mia's heart.

"So it goes for everyone who loses a love, but I can't be the rabbit anymore."

"Neither can I. Hopefully, I can make the changes I need to."

She wanted to ask what Sid meant but decided to let her share when she was ready and popped an olive in her mouth. It was salty and oily, but Sid had tossed it with finely grated lemon rind and fresh chopped rosemary. She had a gift for elevating what was naturally delicious.

*She has a lot of gifts.* "You're great in the kitchen," Mia said, tugging one of Sid's socks off.

Sid pulled her bare foot back. "What are you up to?"

Mia grabbed the remaining foot before Sid could retreat. "I'm curious about whether your talents extend to the living room." The second sock was tugged free and tossed beside its mate on the floor by the fireplace.

Before she knew what was happening, Mia found herself beneath Sid on the couch, watching the discard pile grow. First, a pair of cream-colored underwear. Her own. Then a pair of jeans. Sid's. A flannel shirt. Also Sid's. By the time Sid's cotton boxer briefs landed, Mia was wholly occupied by much more interesting things to watch. And do.

## CHAPTER TWENTY-NINE

One of Mia's hands was beneath the pillow under her head. With the other, she twisted the hot white bedsheet. That was where Sid's naked body had been for most of the night. Now the early morning light crashing through the drapes was keeping the spot warm while Sid ignited another spot. Mia's.

"Whoa, cowboy. That's enough. Are you trying to kill me?"

"But I'm still hungry."

Mia unwrapped her legs from around Sid's shoulders as another tremor passed through her body. Sid rested her head on the inside of Mia's splayed thighs, running her fingers through the small tuft of hair.

"Do you think there's any more spaghetti?" Mia asked, realizing that they'd not managed to get much beyond a forkful and a few olives before feasting on each other. No wonder her thoughts were muddled; blood sugar could do that.

"For breakfast? I can think of better things to nibble on."

Mia cuffed Sid's head, then pulled Sid up toward her, propping up pillows against the headboard so they could semi-recline. Sid kissed her on the way by, and Mia could taste herself on Sid's luscious lips. Her juices begin to surge.

*God, not again.*

Twenty minutes later, Sid pulled her from under the covers and up in the bed. Mia must've fallen asleep after that because Sid seemed to materialize in the doorway with a tray loaded with two bowls of spaghetti, a stack of buttered toast, and two cups of coffee. She was naked except for the ragged Etheridge tee, and Mia wondered how it was possible she could look so effortlessly gorgeous.

"I wasn't sure what would whet your appetite, so I brought options." She set the tray down on the bed.

*Whet. Wet.* "That is the biggest lie you've ever told! You've been whetting my appetite for the past…" Mia looked at the clock on the night table. "Oh my God…twelve hours. The dogs!"

"I fed them, don't worry. There was still some of their food in the fridge from when you were here recuperating. And I let them out."

"Mmm. I like that. My own personal lackey."

"Hardly." Sid handed her a cup of coffee and held out a piece of toast until she bit into it. "Flynn seems much better. Milo tried to get at his bowl, but your boy stood his ground. Tough bugger."

"That's for sure. Thank you. Did you check your messages?"

Sid was back in bed, her phone beside her "I did. I'm thinking I may need to take a trip." Sid tucked her hair, then, catching Mia watching her, untucked it.

"To see the person who bought the sketch?"

"Yes. I want to make sure that I've done everything, and I mean everything, in my power to make sure this deal goes through."

"And the personal touch can make a difference. Is that what you're thinking?" Mia twirled a fork of spaghetti, already missing her.

"Exactly. I only need a couple of days. If I can find a flight, I can leave today and return mid-week."

Mia handed her the fork of pasta and slipped out of bed, went to the desk, picked up Sid's computer, and brought it to her.

"Find that flight, Cassidy Harris."

Sid smiled, flipped open the laptop, and started searching. Mia slipped back under the covers and surveyed the room as she nibbled another piece of toast. Her energy was good. Maybe the erratic swings had finally levelled out. Her gaze was drawn to the red canoe in the painting; a sunbeam now streamed across the canvas.

The canoe sat atop a tangled mass of grey, brown, and greenish branches stretching diagonally from foreground to back.

Small indistinguishable red splotches of paint caught by the debris suggested maple leaves traceable to the small tree on the far shore beyond the dark, almost black, pool above the dam.

Several large boulders garrisoned by a solid wall of pines took up the entire upper half of the space, each tree standing like slightly swaying sentries, shoulder to shoulder, unyielding even in motion to what might lurk beyond.

Below the dam, in the bottom right corner, was a black pool reflecting the twisted and trapped flotsam below the dam. The diagonal lines of the barricade and the unapproachable background seemed intended to draw the viewer's eye to the canoe. It struck her as odd, this single object in a landscape otherwise devoid of human presence. Because it was empty, it elicited an immediate question: *Where is the canoeist?*

"Mia? You okay?"

"Yes, great. Really great." *Sort of.* "Tell me about that painting?" she said, taking Sid's hand. "If you've finished booking?"

"I'm leaving later this afternoon, so there's plenty of time to set Aaron up with a list of to-dos. I'll call him from the truck." Sid fell back into the pillows and nodded toward the canvas. "What do you see? How does it make you feel?"

"Moody. A little dark. And curious. I know you didn't choose it for the aesthetic."

"That is true. But maybe the story will shift your perspective a bit. *The Beaver Dam* was painted by J.E.H. MacDonald—a friend and contemporary of both Lawren Harris and Tom Thomson— shortly after Thomson drowned in Canoe Lake."

"I can understand why he might have been inspired to memorialize his friend. But why is Harris important to the story? You're not going to tell me you're related, are you?"

Sid laughed. "I wish. No such luck. You know he was obscenely wealthy, right? His family manufactured farm equipment. In fact, my dad has an old Massey-Harris tractor rusting out in the back forty."

"Okay, so what's his significance to this painting?"

"Well, with all his money came privilege, and with privilege came exposure to a popular Eastern theosophy centered on the three highest levels of being. Consider him the John Lennon of the early 1900s. He shared those somewhat transcendental concepts with his friend MacDonald."

"And those ideas influenced *The Beaver Dam*?"

"Do you see how MacDonald created three levels in this work: the pool below, the dam itself, and the upper pool? That structural aspect mimics the highest spiritual aspects. That's why I don't see the work as moody and dark. I see it as ascendant, celebratory. I see the intent. The story."

Mia was captivated by the way Sid's mind worked and how deliberately she explained her perspective. "I think you just won me over. Is the canoe meant to be Thomson's?"

"Actually, Thomson's canoe was grey. We can't always interpret art precisely or literally. If we did, this piece could be seen quite differently, in that we neither ascend or descend; we just stay…well…damned."

"But that's not how you see it?" Mia asked.

"Not at all. I think the solemnity of the tribute was intentional, but see the red leaves on the surface of the higher pool? How they appear to be moving? I've always interpreted this as MacDonald's attempt to draw attention to the importance of 'place.' The canoe is a quintessential Canadian symbol, a part of the history of its people. So it's front and center. And red. The red maple leaves are another symbol. There are many stories in this work, but it reminds me of where we are and how important it is to move in life. Like the water moves. Like canoes move. Like a country moves. Spatially. Spiritually. Through time."

"God, Sid, I love that notion. It's beautiful. I've always felt that when people are comfortable in their own space, they become more grounded, more resilient. And being aware and comfortable with the here and now helps people withstand even terrible circumstances." She ran her fingers through Sid's hair, pushing the tresses behind her shoulders and settling it behind her ears.

"Sometimes, I think it reminds me that being stuck is a human affliction. I think that's why I like it so much. The painting, not being stuck." She laughed. "I have the same canvas in my living room in Toronto. It reminds me of here. Of the lake. And the lake reminds me of my mom. I feel her love there like nowhere else. I think that's why I stayed far away because here reminded me of how much I missed her. Now I hate the thought of leaving."

*I hate the thought of you leaving, too.*

"When will Milo be ready for Jack?" Sid's voice was unsteady.

Mia knew what she was asking. *So much for the here and now.* "I'll be here when you get back, cowboy. In case you haven't noticed, I like being in your space."

Sid kissed her palm and stroked the faded red line that would be there for a while longer, if not always. "I have a few thoughts about that, if you're serious. Can we talk about it when I'm back?"

"Of course. Now go pack before I chain you to this bed."

Sid smiled mischievously, one side of her mouth turned up, an eyebrow raised.

"Go," Mia said in her most commanding tone. She watched Sid pack with surprising precision given the helter-skelter motif of most of her bedroom. She wondered what Sid's unspoken thoughts were, but she had her own. She was thinking about tomorrow's meeting with Jesse McCann and had considered mentioning it but realized it might be better to wait until she knew exactly what the deal might entail. If there was to be a deal. She realized with a heavy heart that she had her own expectations.

*Or are they hopes?*

Regardless, she filled in the conversation with talk of Leah and Jim and their good news. She told Sid about Milo's progress and how Jack was learning, too. "Proving yet again that you can teach an old dog new tricks."

"I can think of a few more," Sid teased, throwing her computer bag over her uninjured shoulder and grabbing a small carry-on bag. "Tricks, that is."

On their way to the door, Mia spotted Sid's phone and grabbed it. As they turned at the bottom of the stairs, Mia stopped dead and surveyed the great room and the kitchen beyond. It could easily have been mistaken for a crime scene. Evidence of the night before might tell a strange story: celery scattered on the kitchen floor, one knife tipped with a speared mushroom, a pile of socks and underwear near a cold fire, unfinished food abandoned on the couch, a white bra dangling from a bulrush on the harvest table, matching white underwear beneath the same table, an empty wine bottle on the third stair leading to the bedroom, a blue satin ribbon on the fourth, and at the end of the trail, a blue dress haphazardly strewn on the landing. As she looked at the individual pieces, Mia had trouble reconciling them. Connections were jumbled. She blinked hard, hoping to create sense of the chaos, hoping to remember exactly what had gone on. Sid had hastened ahead.

Not wanting to alert her to her to what was too difficult to put into words, Mia turned to the practical. "Don't worry about the mess. I'll make it look nice before Isabel and Duncan get back." Mia followed her, shaking her head as she tried to recall the evening's activities. "I have until tomorrow, right?"

"Yes. And the party is Saturday, don't forget."

The irony didn't escape Mia, but there was no point tipping her hand until she knew exactly the cards she was holding. Maybe her symptoms were side effects. Maybe they were perfectly normal and would fade in time. Sid had plenty of other things to concern herself with. Mia made a mental note to make a doctor's appointment and hoped she'd find it once Sid was on the road.

Sid threw the suitcase in the passenger seat and turned. The dogs had followed them and worriedly circled Sid's feet.

"Joni Mitchell looks good on you," Sid said, her eyes directed at the tee but mostly on Mia's cleavage. "I'll teach you those new tricks when I get back."

After giving each dog a head rub, Sid reached for Mia, who felt an odd vibration as she leaned in for a kiss. Only then did she remember she was carrying Sid's phone. She looked at the display as Sid settled into the driver's seat.

A cluster of texts and phones, all from the same contact. Aurora St. G.

"Is this what you mean by tricks?" The words flew from Mia's mouth on the wings of contempt. She could hear them slap Sid's face. At the same time, it felt as if her heart was being torn from her chest. She turned the display toward Sid.

Unable to shake the odd perceptions, self-doubt flooded Mia's mind. How could she have imagined being the only one in Cassidy Harris's bed? Or heart? The astonished look on Sid's face told her all she needed to know. Sid wasn't available.

Impulsively, she filled the silence. "I know I'm not Aurora. I can't give you the kind of life you have with her."

"Aurora doesn't give me anything, but sometimes I think maybe all I deserve is Aurora." Sid's voice sounded defeated and anguished. "I'm not really sure where I'm going or even who I am. But I'll never be Riley."

Mia felt as though she'd been gut punched. The long silence that followed gave her a moment to think that she'd set up an impossible expectation. *No, that's not it.* She didn't feel that way deep inside. She'd never compared Sid with Riley. She took a breath and tried to look at the situation from Sid's perspective, seeking to understand how things had become so terribly convoluted. Her anger, she knew, was disproportionate to the situation. Wildly.

Then the phone display lit up and another buzz shot up her arm. It felt like an electric shock. She threw the phone across Sid's lap onto the passenger seat and took a measured step back. *Stop reacting. Be calm.*

Instead, she exploded. "I can't believe I'm saying this, but I was wrong about you. I thought you were struggling with picking a path. Now I wonder if you're even interested in being on any path." She held up a hand before Sid could speak. "Don't say anything. Go catch your plane. And while you're gone, why don't you take time to figure out what you want? Think about where you are." Mia thought about the red canoe, and angry tears began to build. "Then maybe you'll be able to see where we can be. If we can be. Where *we* are."

She turned, walked to her truck, and loaded the dogs without looking back until Sid's truck had rumbled down the driveway out of earshot. She would keep her meeting with Jesse but wouldn't make any commitments. If Sid was going back to her life in Toronto, then staying in Alberta wasn't going to be in her plans either.

❖

Sid was behind the wheel, but the truck seemed to have a mind of its own. It ran a stop sign. It crossed the painted lines twice. And it found the soft shoulder on several occasions. By the time she was five miles from the ranch, it occurred to her that if she wanted to make it to the airport at all, let alone in time for her flight, she needed to pay attention. Even so, it was difficult not to replay Mia's words over and over, and it was impossible not to imagine what she could have said if she'd not been so shell-shocked.

*If we can be.* "If?"

*I know I'm not Aurora.* "Thank God."

*I don't know if you're interested.* "I'm very interested. I'm only interested. In you."

She'd only seen Mia angry twice before: the day they met and the evening she'd rolled the ATV. And now again, Sid hated that she was the reason. She wished she could blame everything on Aurora, but she knew she'd reacted badly. *I'll never be Riley.* "But I want to be with you."

She raced to the gate just in time for her flight, with no time and no words that would begin to resolve things with Mia. She worried she might not be given a chance. *Is this it, then? Is it over?* The flight was smooth, but with nothing to focus on except her rising panic, she spent the first few hours choking back nausea. Any ending was preventable and sat squarely on Sid's shoulders. She'd put so much in place so she could build a life with Mia, but she'd failed to share those dreams. How could she be surprised if Mia felt alone? Maybe it was time to surrender because the thought of losing Mia was more than she could bear. Something had to change. She was already having doubts about making this deal and was fearful of failing the people closest to her. Her dad. Martin. And now Mia.

She closed her eyes, and a black crow appeared in her mind,

flying over the lake. She thought about swimming and remembered what Mia had said, "When you're in your element, you stay on the path."

She realized that her doubts would do nothing but disable her resolve. So in an effort to keep the rabbit from running wild, she opened her eyes and grabbed a magazine from the seat back. She flipped it open to an article promising the secrets to Calgary's best steakhouses. As she spread the pages apart, something shiny wheeled down the crease of the spine, and landed on her thigh. Sid's jaw dropped.

It was a dime.

She wasn't alone. It was time she started acting like it.

❖

Mia was loading her truck with samples of dog food when Sid's call came. She felt sick about their earlier exchange. It was hard to think about the incredible twenty-four hours that preceded it, but she'd needed to stand her ground. Even though she had nothing more to say, seeing Sid's name on her phone tugged at her in ways she couldn't ignore her. She pressed answer.

"I don't want you to say anything, Mia. It's your turn to listen. Please. Aurora started texting me a few days ago. Before that, we hadn't been in touch for over a month, and even that was gallery business. Clearly, she wants something because that's the kind of person she is. But I wouldn't know for sure because I have no interest in reading her texts, let alone replying." Sid paused as if to let that sink in. Mia let it. "You were right when you said that you're not Aurora. There are a million ways you're different. You possess unfathomable kindness. You're wickedly smart and deceptively strong in spirit. You have patience enough to see me, to truly see me in a way that makes me want to be seen. At *least* a million ways, Mia. But the one that matters the most is that I don't love Aurora. I never did, and I never will. I love you."

There was a split-second pause, a break so small Mia couldn't fit in a word before Sid filled her in on Martin's offer. She clearly didn't expect reciprocity, and it was obvious there'd been more going on in her brilliant mind than Mia had ever imagined.

"I have pieces that still need to come together, but I have a lot of support, and I really think my plan can work. For both of us. I'm sorry I didn't tell you about this before now. I know I should have. I really want you—"

"Sid, where are you?"

"I'm on the path, I promise. I will make this work for us. No, *we* can make this work—"

"No, I mean where are you physically? Your meeting. You have to be there in twenty minutes, don't you?"

"Crap. Yes. Hopefully New York traffic will be flowing. Okay, I have to go. I love you, Mia Jarvis."

Again, not a split second before the phone went silent. Mia sat staring at it, thinking about what Sid had said and realizing that she had a path to follow as well.

## CHAPTER THIRTY

"Come on, Harris, haul your cute little ass out of that water!" Mia held Sid's towel at the edge of the lake. She was already wrapped and dried from the evening swim. The time had flown. It was Tuesday night, and Sid had returned from her trip just hours before. As soon as she arrived at the trailer, Mia and the dogs were summoned into the truck.

"We're going to the lake!" Sid had yelled from the cab. Unable to resist the joyous demand, Mia had grabbed towels and the comforter from her bed, along with a small picnic basket, before jumping in with Sid, Flynn, and Milo.

Now, Sid marched slowly from the water, reminding Mia of every kid who'd been called to shore before they were ready. "It's warmer in the lake!" She was shivering as Mia wrapped her in the towel.

"Yes, but I missed you, and I have alternative ways of warming you up." Mia winked and sat up on the tailgate, patting the spot beside her.

"I'm sure that's true. But tell me what you've been up to while I've been in the Big Apple."

"With the exception of your flights, we texted or Skyped almost nonstop the whole time you were there."

"True. And yet you missed me. So, tell me more about this mysterious meeting you had with Jack's daughter."

Mia had carefully avoided texting about why she and Jesse McCann were meeting in the first place but only to keep expectations to a minimum. Since the meeting had gone so well, she had one less excuse to keep her plans a secret, but she still felt unsure of how Sid would take the news. Planting roots here might make things more difficult if Sid's plans didn't work out and she ended up back in Toronto.

*Better to just blurt it out.* "It looks like I'll be staying here awhile."

Mia went on to tell Sid excitedly about the ideas Jesse had for the craft dog food business and how her involvement would be consultative, based on her experience and connections with the kennel club and various breeders. She detailed how there would be a funding aspect, tying profit percentages back to humane societies and sustainability initiatives, and wrapped up by sharing Jesse's provocative ideas for developing and marketing organic and plant-based products.

Sid's eyes widened at the mention of alternative proteins.

"Relax, love. Jesse reminded me that we're deep in cattle country, so maybe we keep that little tidbit under our hats until we develop a financial model that works for the whole community, including ranchers like your dad and hers."

"Mum's the word. And that is fantastic." Sid put an arm around her and slid closer.

"I know! Imagine me being part of a cutting-edge craft dog food empire."

"Easy to do. I've smelled your work. I would have eaten it. But that's not what I meant when I said fantastic. What I meant was…" Sid lifted Mia's chin and turned it to face her. "What I meant was, it's fantastic that you're staying."

Mia felt herself blush, pleased at the progress they had both made. "I'm so glad things went well with the seller. Have you told Martin yet?"

Sid had texted from New York after the meeting with the seller, who opted to meet with her without his insistent "but expendable" broker at the always-elegant Gramercy Tavern. They'd come to an agreement on the terms over farmstead cheese and a unique bottle of Barolo Pira, chased with a decadent wedge of mile high peanut butter pie and blood orange jam. Now all they needed was the signed contract, paperwork he assured her would be signed and faxed in the morning.

"Tomorrow afternoon. I'll have the paperwork, and Martin will be awake. He was on his way back from Tokyo, so I figured, given the time zones, I'd wait to tell him then." She slipped off the end of the truck and picked up a floating dog toy, tossing it into the lake. Milo and Flynn launched after it.

"You know, my mom was a marathon swimmer when she was my age," Sid said. "I used to sit right about here when I was a kid and watch her swim the lake, back and forth, for hours. Not that I don't love the city…and maybe it's because you're here…but if I can find a way to stay, that's what I want to do more than anything."

"Sid, home is where my trailer parks. I'm afraid, too," Mia said, wondering if the goose bumps creeping up her arm were because of the cool night air, the risky conversation, or the anticipation of Sid's touch. "The horizon is a promise, but the path is beneath us right now. Sometimes, it's hard for me to feel it because you sweep me off my feet."

Sid smiled and squeezed Mia's hand. "Speaking of strange perceptions, how is your head today? Any more symptoms to report?"

"Very minor swings. Aside from the meeting with Jesse, I rested while you were gone, just as the doctor ordered, and it helped. The MRI results were clear, so now it's just a matter of time and careful symptom management." Mia returned Sid's squeeze. "I'm very sorry about my reaction to Aurora's texts. I wasn't in my right mind. The doctor explained that post-concussion syndrome sufferers sometimes notice their symptoms as instances, but the cumulative effect isn't as obvious to them. Stubborn self-reliance apparently doesn't help."

Sid rolled her eyes.

"You see, sometimes I have trouble surrendering my ego, too," Mia said. They both laughed. "And I have to admit that the fear of losing you triggered the panic I felt when Riley's doctor broke the news to us about her prognosis."

"That's all very normal—"

"I know, but my reaction was not. Thank you again for understanding."

Sid leaned in and kissed her neck, nibbling on her earlobe before pulling slightly back and locking eyes. "I love you, Mia Jarvis."

Mia knew at that moment she'd never be good at poker. Her eyes stung, and her pulse pounded against her throat, the goose bumps spreading rapidly now to her shoulders and down to her chest. *Let the cards fall where they may.* "Cowboy, I love you, too."

They sat on the tailgate, holding hands, legs dangling as if they were toddlers on a park bench. It wasn't until they both shuddered against the mid-August night that Mia convinced Sid to abandon their towels and wrap themselves in the large warm comforter, moving up in the bed of the truck and leaning against the back of the cab.

"Did I tell you Aaron is planning to install a few cell-based cameras in behind that ridge?" Sid pointed over the tree line toward a ridge that overlooked an elevated paddock right where the mystery truck had been spotted the previous week. "And he's going to try the drone tomorrow. They're all app-based, so he can monitor with his cell phone."

"I guess we'll have to make sure we keep our clothes on, then, won't we?" Mia said, pulling the comforter higher around her neck.

"Tomorrow." Sid smiled and pressed her naked body the length of Mia's. "I'm pretty sure he said tomorrow."

## CHAPTER THIRTY-ONE

The morning sunlight sliced between the barn boards, creating a geometric pattern that ran the length of the stable's interior and cross-hatched the grills of the stalls. The only other light came through the alley doors and the loft windows, both of which were latched open. For that, Mia was especially grateful. It was another hot and sunny Alberta day.

"I guess it's all hands on deck, Mia." Aaron's voice boomed from across the barn. "Is it all you dreamed of?"

"Well, when I agreed to help get ready for the party, I thought I'd be setting up tables or helping in the kitchen. I sure didn't guess I'd be knee-deep in cow dung. Or is it horse?"

Aaron poked his head around the wall separating the stall he was mucking. "It all looks like crap to me. Without Sid the last few days and with all the extra time I'm spending with the cameras and drone, it did pile up a bit. Literally. Now I'm so busy getting the barn cleaned up, I haven't even had time to check the video feeds from last night."

"I'm starting to think Duncan is playing us."

"I think both Harrises are. Where is Sid?"

As if on cue, Sid appeared in the main doorway, phone pressed against her ear. She signaled that she was at the end of her call and raised her voice. "Please have the shippers there by end of day, and make sure it's crated and all the customs paperwork is done right as usual. But don't bill the gallery…Right…Have them send me the invoice…There's a ticket for you at the Western Airline desk. And a car at the rental desk…It's the least I can do, Ella…See you on Saturday…So glad you can make it. Bye."

Sid tucked the phone in her pocket and took a deep breath. Mia stood at the door of the stall, leaning on her shovel, watching as Sid's expression turned to relief, her shoulders lowering and her head tipping back to take in the morning sun.

"Are you going to make me ask?" Mia called.

Sid walked down the main aisle, stepped in front of Mia, and wrapped her arms around her, almost lifting her clean out of her muck-mired rubber boots.

"Careful, cowboy, the ribs are not quite one hundred percent." Sid lowered her but kept her arms around her waist. "Can I assume the news is good?"

"It's the best. The best. And in a few hours, I can call Martin and tell him."

Aaron stepped out of his stall and handed Sid a shovel.

"Congratulations! You've won this beautiful previously used shovel and the chance to use it." He wiped his hands on his jeans, pushed his hat back, and smiled. He had all the charm and humor of a Harris. "I am off to find out where our cattle are disappearing to. Hopefully."

When he was gone, Sid stepped into his stall, and they continued to clear each of the forty stalls and pens. Mia listened with delight as Sid talked nonstop, sharing her plans to leave the gallery.

"Clearly, the business needs brokers who possess integrity, so that's the niche I'm targeting. I need to build clientele, of course, but I have an iron in the fire that might spark something. Regardless, I want to work from home. From here."

Mia stopped dead in her manure-coated boots, rested her hands on the top end of the shovel, and put her chin on her hands. Watching Sid so happy and hopeful, Mia felt warmth spread through her body and she realized it was not a result of the hot Alberta sun. This was one of the rare times since Mia had known her that she seemed in place.

Two hours later, the stalls clean, and they sat on a couple of hay bales, Sid telling Mia about her dream lake house. "It would face northeast so the porch would catch the morning sun, but the mountains would still be in view."

"You've put some thought into this, haven't you?" Mia said, smiling in the knowledge that Sid probably had every detail already planned from the cellar floor to the roof shingles.

Sid, though, still had the ability to surprise. "There's just one thing missing. And I'm not ready to break ground until I know for sure that I can arrange it." She pulled a piece of straw from the bale, twizzled it in her fingers, and handed it to Mia. "You."

"I come with a dog," Mia said, accepting the straw.

"I'll take you any way I can get you. And just so you know, I already asked Flynn, and he said yes."

Mia accepted the straw with a kiss, knowing that more than the heartfelt proposal, it was listening to Sid's dreams that reassured Mia about the future. *Our future.* "How could I possibly refuse?"

"Funny, that's what Flynn said!"

They spent the next few hours in the barn laughing and talking excitedly about their plans. "You don't think it's weird, do you? Planning to live together when we've only known each other the better part of a month?" Mia was surprised at how sure she was about a future with this incredible woman but couldn't help but wonder how certain Sid was. After all, she had more pieces to set in place in order to clear her path.

Sid was transferring the grain from the buckets into the feed trays when Mia noticed her stop. She dropped her bucket, removed her gloves, and lowered her head closer to the feed. She pushed her hands into the oats and began digging and sifting, the grains falling through her fingers and bouncing off the floor. Mia couldn't figure out what she was doing but gathered she hadn't heard the question.

"Did you hear me?" she repeated, taking a few steps closer as Sid continued to ferret through the feed. "Do you think it's weird?"

Sid didn't answer. She pulled a clenched hand from the grain and walked toward Mia, turning the clenched palm up and revealing the object she'd pulled from the trough. "Do I think it's weird?" she replied, shaking her head. "Not even a bit."

Mia plucked the silver dime from Sid's palm and looked up

through the loft window. *Yes, Riley, I'm still here. I'm very much still right here.*

She pulled Sid toward her and tucked the dime into her front pocket before planting a long, loving kiss on lips that never failed to stir her.

"Me neither."

## CHAPTER THIRTY-TWO

The Harris kitchen was hopping. Mia was practicing her newly acquired knife skills, chopping onions and garlic for Isabel's marinade. Beth joined them, rattling the seeds out of dried chili peppers. The party was only two days away, and she could feel that everyone's spirits were high. Like hers.

"So, we'll have *pollo barbacoa*, *carne asada*, and *pozole rojo*. *Arroz al poblano con espinacas*, a grilled corn and avocado salad, and *chiles rellenos*, of course, for the vegetarians." Isabel listed the menu, and Mia gathered she was doing so as a mental checklist for things yet to prepare. "Cinnamon cake with *dulce de leche* ice cream for dessert. Do you think we'll have enough?"

"Enough for the entirety of the Princess Patricia's Light Infantry," Beth said. "Did you know, Mia, that we were having the Canadian military drop by?"

"Very funny, *mi amiga*! We're expecting eighty, so I'm cooking for a hundred."

"Plenty, Isabel, plenty. You have to enjoy the party, too!"

"I will. Duncan hired serving staff; that's his contribution." She laughed. "They'll be here at six the night of, so we can all enjoy the evening."

"What about tamales?" asked Aaron from the hallway. "My favorite."

"I know, and you'll get them on *your* birthday." Isabel smiled and kissed him on the cheek.

Duncan followed, emerging from the office where they'd been since Aaron had arrived from the barn. "We have some news," he declared. "Where's Sid?"

"Present." She came in from the porch, canine companions at her feet, a smile across her face, and her eyes sparkling. Mia could tell that her most recent conversation with Martin had gone as well as expected.

Once the meal preparations stopped, Duncan took the floor. "Let me start by saying that I may have doubted Mr. Technology here." He patted Aaron on the shoulder. "But the drone and cameras really paid off. We have enough video evidence to support Mia's water theory; turns out, there is a very extensive, very lucrative system of springs through our back property. It wasn't the cattle these folks were after. They were trying to make their inevitable bid for the land more enticing. We talked to the RCMP again and emailed the videos. They weren't surprised, but they sure were grateful. Apparently, we're not the only victims, but we are the only ones with footage showing licence plates, vehicles, and faces clear enough to identify. Sid and Aaron both worked like dogs to fix those fences, and Sid even gave blood in pursuit of the truth." Duncan glanced at the bandage on Sid's arm. "I want to thank you. Sid, I hope you're considering my offer. Aaron, you know that parcel of land on the east side is yours if you want it. It'd be a good step for you to manage your own if you were planning on staying in the area for a while. You might even consider the water business."

❖

Sid was on top of the world, and she loved the feel of it beneath her feet. But if she'd learned anything from the woman she loved, it was to let people see who she really was. She'd kept so many secrets over the years. The worst was when her mom passed, and she'd hid her grief so deeply that it almost swept her away. Now she wanted to take a new path, and she needed her family to see her for who she was and wanted to be. Once the cacophony of chopping and laughter died down and the palpable relief at Duncan's news abated, she took a seat at the table beside and beckoned everyone to join her.

"Go ahead, *bella*, I'm just finishing up the dishes," Isabel called from the sink.

Sid put her hand on her dad's. She wasn't nervous; uncertain was more like it. She knew it wasn't her job to protect everyone and was sure that whatever the reaction, she was prepared to accept it.

*Start with one small step.* "Dad, I'm very grateful for your offer, and I'm even more delighted that I'm able to take you up on it. I'm leaving the gallery. I'm going to start my own brokerage. There'll be many trips to and from the airport, but I'm going to run it from here."

Duncan winked. "So our empty nest is no longer empty? Isabel, did you hear that?"

Sid wasn't looking for approval, but it pleased her that in his funny way, he'd given his support. She was less sure of how he would receive the next bit of news.

*Take one more step, Sid. You're not alone.* "Actually, Dad, Mia and I…" She put her hand on Mia's. "We'll be staying in her trailer while the lake house is built. So your nest will be empty again."

"You two are going to live together? In sin?" Duncan turned to Mia, his melodrama clearly intended to rankle. "For God's sake, Mia, when do you plan to make an honest woman out of my daughter?"

Sid could feel her shoulders lower, relief lifting the burden she'd carried since she'd kissed her first girlfriend. She was flustered, though, by her dad's question. When? She felt certain that in every way she and Mia were partners, but aside from asking somewhat sideways for them to live together, they'd never talked about marriage. In the rush of the past week and with all the talk of the house and the new businesses, it hadn't been a topic of conversation. *Maybe it should be. Or maybe it's a given.* Sid looked at Mia, confused and apologetic. But Mia was beaming, and the levity of the comment settled Sid's scattered thoughts.

Mia squared herself at Duncan, reminding Sid of Milo. "When are you going to make an honest woman out of Isabel?"

Duncan let out a rolling laugh and pointed to Isabel. She pulled her hand out of the dishwater and toweled it off, displaying an enormous ring on her engagement finger. "Guess who won big at the casino on the weekend?"

## CHAPTER THIRTY-THREE

Preparations continued at an easy pace on the morning of the party. The weather was splendid, and the coals had continued burning beneath the cauldron through the night. Mia held tightly to the wooden paddle, circling the contents inside of the large iron pot as Isabel incorporated a thick, shiny paste that swirled like the aerial view of a tropical storm. The paste was dark like chocolate but deeply red from the peppery notes.

The color reminded Mia of Sid, its spicy properties reminding her of how Sid had managed to find numerous hot and intoxicating ways to keep her in bed that morning. If it wasn't for the final push to help with the party, they'd no doubt still be at the trailer. Instead, they dutifully appeared in the kitchen by ten. Each was assigned a list, mostly final touches, and they went their separate ways.

While Sid and Aaron placed hay bale benches around the courtyard, Mia worked with Isabel on the large cauldron of *pozole rojo*, a Mexican stew with aromatic hominy, slow-cooked pork, and wild mushrooms.

"See, little girl, this is how we make it *rojo*...red...with *anchos*," Isabel proclaimed proudly as she emptied the last of the pepper slurry into the pot. Before long, the shredded meat and chunks of mushroom bobbed contentedly in a heady red ocean thick with corn grain and peppers.

Mia kept an eye on the slow-cooking *pozole* through the kitchen window while she stuffed poblano peppers with a cheese mixture, but her attention was on Sid, who'd moved from the bales to the barbecue. She stood more casually than Mia had ever seen or thought possible: one hand in the side pocket of her overalls, the other playfully twirling the set of tongs as she attended the chicken on the grill. Her hair was tucked through the ball cap Mia had first seen her in the day they met. The Sid Harris that day had a power about her, the kind that had churned with derision and arrogance. So much had changed since then. The woman Mia had come to love had a new, easy power, a relaxed strength and confidence that she wore comfortably, like the white cotton tank top beneath her denims. This Sid Harris had her feet on the path, and Mia had fallen hopefully and helplessly in step with her.

Mia turned to survey the buffet in the great room. With the exception of the *pozole*, which was doled straight from the cauldron, the feast was set out on the harvest table in chafing dishes, platters, and bowls beautifully decorated with corn husks and wide green and gold ribbons.

By mid-afternoon, everything that could be done in advance was set and ready. Sid had gone upstairs to shower and change, but Mia elected to spend the next couple of hours at the trailer. She fed and walked the dogs, showered, and scavenged her closet for something nice. She settled on a simple, cap-sleeve, swoop neck T-shirt dress that clung comfortably to her body and stopped mid-thigh beneath a Navajo print sweater of the same length.

Never one for bling, Mia had made one exception, a sterling silver feather necklace she'd bought while on a mountain biking trip with Riley in Arizona. Created by a consortium of Navajo artists, the medium link chain held twenty or so silver feathers of varying sizes and shapes, some with turquoise inlay, others in a silver overlay design. She took it out on special occasions, and this was the first time she'd worn it since Riley was diagnosed. She slid her bare feet into a pair of sling-back sandals, loaded up the dogs, and headed back to the Harrises'.

Mia parked behind the barn, and she and the dogs stepped into the circle of bales just in time to see Sid emerge from the main house. The sun hadn't crossed behind the mountains yet, so it lit Sid up and stopped Mia in her tracks. Sid was radiant in a white linen two-piece, her bare midriff crossed by two thin straps that connected the halter top with an ankle-length dress slit down one side from the hip. Her height and broad shoulders gave her the perfect body for the outfit, showing off her fitness and femininity. She was barefoot, a silver ankle bracelet on the slit side echoing the large silver hoop earrings that emphasized her long sensual neck and wavy auburn tresses. She was holding a white pashmina with thread of emerald woven throughout that would set off her beautiful eyes.

"Good God, Sid. You are…well, you sure are."

"I'll take that as a compliment." Sid smiled, kissing Mia as if no one was watching. "And you sure are, too. Very. Would you do me a favor?"

"There's nothing I wouldn't do for you right now, gorgeous."

Sid pulled a bandage out of her halter and handed it over. "I couldn't put it on without getting it all wrinkled. Would you mind? Isabel was so busy that I hated to bother her."

Sid's wound was healing nicely, and fresh aloe coated the red jagged edges. Mia carefully opened and applied the fresh bandage, the color of which matched Sid's fair skin. She kissed it as she completed the seal, then planted an equally soft kiss on Sid's bare shoulder.

"Is the outfit too much? I can put on this wrap…"

"If you so much as *try* to cover yourself up, I will undress you completely, no matter who's watching." Mia smiled, drinking in the thought before continuing. "You look ravishing, cowboy. Beautiful, truly." Mia leaned in for a kiss but was interrupted by a loud, throat-clearing cough.

"Ahem. Is this a private party?"

Mia recognized the voice and ran to Leah's open arms, hugging her before wrapping her arms around Jim. "I am so glad you're here," she managed, feeling tears welling. "But how? I mean, when, why?"

"Well, I was going to fly home, but when we got the good news, I figured a detour was in order. Handsome and I are going straight to the Miraval from here for a bit of pampering."

Mia knew the Arizona spa well, having retreated there for a

whole month before buying her trailer and hitting the highway. It was a much-needed luxury, and it gave her the headspace to figure out her path. It was astonishing that she'd not even begun to imagine then that this was where that path would lead.

"Jim, I'd like to introduce Cassidy Harris. Sid."

"Yes, please, call me Sid. Nice to meet you, Jim. And, Leah, glad you took me up on the invitation."

Mia shot Sid a puzzled look, but Leah took her hand and pulled her toward a table set with bottles, kegs, and ice. "Come on. I bet there's a bottle of tequila on that bar!"

❖

The night was magically lit by stars and thousands of fairy lights that Aaron and Greg had strung in the trees and along the buildings' edges. Music from a local folk band filled the air, echoing off the distant mountains. Sid was cajoled into drinking a shot of tequila with the besties teaching the bartender how to make a baja fog, a mind-numbing combination of tequila, Corona, and lime. According to Mia-Leah, this was the only exception to Riley's rule. Sid bowed out to mingle and help Isabel with last-minute details. She'd attended more than her fair share of galas, but this was an evening full of surprises.

She figured the whole neighborhood had shown up to rejoice in what had originally been planned as a birthday party but was now her dad and Isabel's elopement celebration. At one point, there was hardly room on the makeshift dance floor in the arena. As much as Isabel had been teased about the menu, she was right to have cooked for a brigade; there wasn't an owner in the region who didn't come by at one point or other throughout the evening to wish Duncan and Isabel happiness together.

Sid was excited to welcome Ella, who had accepted the invitation at her insistence but seemed thrilled to be far from Toronto. Sid could imagine what the smoldering fires at the gallery in Toronto must have been like in the aftermath of Jason's treachery. At least she and Ella had doused the inferno.

"There's no way I could turn you down," Ella said. "And while I appreciate it, you didn't have to pick up the tab for my flight and hotel. It makes me wonder if you've got some business you'd like to discuss?" She smiled conspiratorially.

"I'd only like you to spend time in this beautiful place thinking about where you'd like your future in the art world to be spent." Sid was sure Ella was reading between the lines. "Because you never know where a new path might take you."

Later, she was surprised to see that Ella's path, in the short term, had run straight into Jesse McCann's. The attractive entrepreneur managed to monopolize most of Ella's time at the party, including more than a few tequila-fueled, extra-close turns on the dance floor.

Just when Sid thought nothing more could surprise her, her dad came around the corner of the house with Martin Stephens, each carrying a hefty crystal lowball of what was most likely a single malt from the Harris family collection.

"Look who I found," Duncan said.

For a moment, she thought she was hallucinating. "Oh my gosh, Martin, how on earth did you…I mean, you're of course very welcome. But how…I thought you were in Hawaii."

"It wasn't hard to find a Duncan Harris in Green Creek, Alberta. And they make these machines called airplanes." He laughed, wrapping his arm around Duncan as if the two were fraternity brothers. "I got on one last night after you and I spoke, and now I'm here. You are a sight for sore old eyes, Sid. I've never seen you looking more lovely."

Duncan laughed along. "Marty's here for my birthday."

"Dad, I'm sure Martin doesn't—"

"Relax, Sid…your father and I know each other. We go back at least an hour ago, wouldn't you say? It was at least a single 'single' ago." He straightened and held his scotch toward Sid, who lifted her glass in response. "To Thomson," he said solemnly.

Once Duncan excused himself to tend to hosting duties, Sid and Martin stood slightly out of sight of the crowd to ensure—at least for another few moments—some privacy for the celebrity and a chance for the two to catch up.

"I don't know what to say," Sid said. "It's so nice to see you, and I'm sure your being here made this a party my dad will never forget."

"He's a good man. I genuinely like him. And he clearly loves you. As you may have guessed, I didn't solely come to celebrate his birthday…correction, marriage. I'm actually following the example of a business associate whom I greatly respect, a woman who took a trip to New York recently to make a deal, knowing that sometimes a personal touch is needed. Consider this *my* personal touch. It's important to me that you know I stand firmly behind my offer." Martin's tone was serious, and his eyes were fixed on Sid's until he glanced over her shoulder. She turned to see Mia approaching from the dance floor.

"Now, who is this lovely vision?" Martin asked.

Sid took Mia's extended hand. "Martin Stephens, this is Mia Jarvis, my fiancée." She shot Mia an expectant look, and when she smiled, continued. "Mia, this is Martin Stephens."

"Please call me Marty. Can I assume, lovely Ms. Mia, that I should be asking for *your* help in persuading Sid to leave the gallery and help some of my good friends patronize the arts?"

Mia smiled. Sid hadn't filled Martin in on the complete business plan she was developing, but if her vision was financially viable, it would involve Martin as more than simply a conduit to purchasers. She had no desire to use her friend that way. Sid trusted Mia to keep those details under wraps until all the pieces were in place. *She trusted Mia, period.*

"Yes, you should." Mia winked at Sid and took Martin's arm "But I must warn you, the stunning Sid Harris has a mind of her own."

"Well, I am ever the optimist. So when we are successful," he said as she turned to lead him toward the dance floor, "how shall I repay you?"

Sid almost laughed out loud when Mia, who did not miss a single beat, replied, "Have you or your friends ever given thought to investing in dog food?"

❖

The embers beneath where the cauldron had been glowed like falling dominos as the warm night wind blew across the courtyard. It was so quiet that Mia could hear the almost ripe wheat spikes in the distant fields dance against each other as if the band was still playing.

"Stand right there. Don't move. I'm turning off the lights."

Mia stood in the middle of the courtyard. The last group of guests had pulled out of the driveway a half hour ago, and Duncan and Isabel had retired shortly after, vowing to be up early for cleanup. The twinkle lights went dark but had been replaced by a sky full of stars.

"We don't need music, do we?" Sid's voice fell softly, wrapping around Mia like a blanket. She reached around Mia's lower back, pulling her into her arms, and they began to sway. "Is this how it feels?"

"How what feels, my love?"

"The ease? The way in which we fit."

"If you let it."

It seemed clear that Sid was expecting a more elaborate response. "Is it hard for you to be in love again? To let yourself?"

Mia knew what she was asking. "I don't want you to love me like Riley loved me because I don't love you the way I loved her. I love *you* the way I love *you*. And I want *you* to love me the way *you* love me." She looked at Sid's downcast eyes and lifted her chin. "A thousand painters can look at the same landscape, and what ends up on the canvas is unique. I think you told me that once."

Sid nodded and smiled.

"And any one unique rendering is perceived equally uniquely."

She could see the wheels turning as Sid considered her answer. "True."

"I think that's true with love. You are seeing me, loving me, as only you can."

"So just let myself?"

"Yes, my love."

"And you'll do the same?"

Mia felt a profound sense of wonder at how much love had come her way simply by keeping her heart open, and there wasn't a single doubt in her mind that she would find a lifetime of ways to love Sid.

"Always."

## EPILOGUE

The winds were strong but warm. Unseasonably warm for northern Alberta in early April. The lakeside house had been framed and the exteriors completed before snowfall the previous year. Between the two-by-fours of what would be the front entrance, Sid and Mia sat enjoying the rising sun.

"You'd think we were back at Martin's," Mia said. They'd just returned from a month in the British Virgin Islands, a vacation arranged by Sid's new business partner. It was a much-needed respite.

During the first seven months since the party, Sid had been working hard with Ella to lay the groundwork for the new brokerage, Harris and Friends. She had also started fundraising to create a Fine Arts Management program at the university with Martin as a lead course designer and sponsor.

Sid was glad Mia was equally occupied. Since the day Milo graduated, she'd been buried in research, testing recipes, and consulting with the province's veterinary college to develop a series of specialized feeds while Jesse McCann put the marketing and distribution pieces into place.

"If only the Chinooks blew all winter long." Sid tipped her head back, imagining her long hair blowing back as if she were in a Mariah Carey video. As a young girl, she'd taken full advantage of the strange and unpredictable phenomenon akin to California's Santa Ana winds by stripping off her winter gear and skating on the still-frozen lake in her shorts and T-shirt. The thought of reliving those treasured times was interrupted when Flynn, who'd been sniffing through the shell of the house, let out a warning bark.

Sid caught the sound of a truck pulling in behind the house. "Who's that?" She wasn't alarmed. The rustling issue had been put to rest, the culprits apprehended shortly after the drone videos were handed to the RCMP. But she was curious about who knew they were here.

"Aaron," Mia said. "I have one other thing I'd like to add to the house."

"Incorrigible! I thought I had trained you better."

Mia flashed her a look and smiled. Sid reflected on the many custom design touches they'd made since construction started, and how Aaron and Greg—new partners in the construction business and in life—had been the most patient and flexible contractors imaginable.

*Nonetheless…*

"The boys are going to kill us. *You*, actually," Sid continued. "They're going to kill *you*. I love you so much but don't think I can protect you. I promised there would be no more changes, and I have to keep my word. Don't force me to use my veto power."

Mia appeared to be ignoring Sid's good-natured caution, stepping down from her perch on the unfinished threshold.

"I'm pretty sure you're going to approve," she said over her shoulder as she and Flynn rounded the corner of the house out of sight.

Sid was enjoying the sun too much to budge, listening instead to the truck door slam, a brief exchange of familiar voices made indecipherable by the warm mountain wind, then another door slam followed by the truck driving away.

Mia reappeared, Flynn weaving around her feet, his eyes glued to her chest. She held a blanket, and as she got closer, Sid could make out tiny furry ears amidst with the fabric. "Sid, I'd like you to meet Poco. The pick of Milo's litter."

Sid jumped from the ledge, her heart melting more quickly than the sun-warmed mountain peaks at the sight of the small blue-eyed puppy. "Oh my gosh, he's adorable!" Sid peeled back the blanket; the puppy struggled out of its cocoon and into Sid's open arms.

"She, actually. Poco is short for Pocahontas, which translates from Algonquin, meaning 'mischievous one.' I thought it was apropos, but she's yours to name."

"Poco is perfect, thank you. I love her, and I'm sure Flynn will learn to love having another puppy around. I think he misses Milo, though he'd never admit it. Would you, boy?" Sid rubbed Flynn's ears, and he wagged in response.

They perched on the foundation, Sid holding Poco and trying to fight back tears of intense happiness. Mia wiped away those that ran down.

"Did you know that the Chinook winds were once rumored to cause psychosis?" Mia asked.

"Is that why I'm so crazy about you?"

"Quite likely, cowboy. But I'll take you any way I can get you."

"Well, you're stuck with me now." Sid twisted the platinum band on her ring finger.

Mia brushed her lips with tear-salted fingers and leaned into Sid. "Right where we are."

Sid looked across the lake and scanned the horizon. There was something about being with Mia that made the mountains look even more majestic and the fields as endless as the possibilities. This was her path.

"Always."

# About the Author

This is Annie McDonald's first novel. A proud Canadian, she plans to celebrate her country's incredible diversity by writing novels set in each of the ten provinces and three territories.

She is encouraged by the nation's ongoing commitment to respect and inclusion of all people and by the many recent heartfelt acts undertaken to reconcile with Canada's inspiring First Nations, Metis, and Inuit peoples. She holds strongly to the late Maya Angelou's words of great wisdom: "Do the best you can until you know better. Then when you know better, do better."

She currently lives in the Niagara Region surrounded by grapevines and their promise.

# Books Available From Bold Strokes Books

**Face Off** by PJ Trebelhorn. Hockey player Savannah Wells rarely spends more than a night with any one woman, but when photographer Madison Scott buys the house next door, she's forced to rethink what she expects out of life. (978-1-63555-480-9)

**Hot Ice** by Aurora Rey, Elle Spencer, and Erin Zak. Can falling in love melt the hearts of the iciest ice queens? Join Aurora Rey, Elle Spencer, and Erin Zak to find out! A contemporary romance novella collection. (978-1-63555-513-4)

**Line of Duty** by VK Powell. Dr. Dylan Carlyle's professional and personal life is turned upside down when a tragic event at Fairview Station pits her against ambitious, handsome police officer Finley Masters. ((978-1-63555-486-1)

**London Undone** by Nan Higgins. London Craft reinvents her life after reading a childhood letter to her future self and, in doing so, finds the love she truly wants. (978-1-63555-562-2)

**Lunar Eclipse** by Gun Brooke. Moon De Cruz lives alone on an uninhabited planet after being shipwrecked in space. Her life changes forever when Captain Beaux Lestarion's arrival threatens the planet and Moon's freedom. (978-1-63555-460-1)

**One Small Step** by MA Binfield. In this contemporary romance, Iris and Cam discover the meaning of taking chances and following your heart, even if it means getting hurt. (978-1-63555-596-7)

**Shadows of a Dream** by Nicole Disney. Rainn has the talent to take her rock band all the way, but falling in love is a powerful distraction, and her new girlfriend's meth addiction might just take them both down. 978-1-63555-598-1)

**Someone to Love** by Jenny Frame. When Davina Trent is given an unexpected family, can she let nanny Wendy Darling teach her to open her heart to the children and to Wendy? (978-1-63555-468-7)

**Uncharted** by Robyn Nyx. As Rayne Marcellus and Chase Stinsen track the legendary Golden Trinity, they must learn to put their differences aside and depend on one another to survive. (978-1-63555-325-3)

**Where We Are** by Annie McDonald. A sensual account of two women who discover a way to walk on the same path together with the help of an Indigenous tale, a Canadian art movement, and the mysterious appearance of dimes. (978-1-63555-581-3)

**A Moment in Time** by Lisa Moreau. A longstanding family feud separates two women who unexpectedly fall in love at an antique clock shop in a small Louisiana town. (978-1-63555-419-9)

**Aspen in Moonlight** by Kelly Wacker. When art historian Melissa Warren meets Sula Johansen, director of a local bear conservancy, she discovers that love can come in unexpected and unusual forms. (978-1-63555-470-0)

**Back to September** by Melissa Brayden. Small bookshop owner Hannah Shepard and famous romance novelist Parker Bristow maneuver the landscape of their two very different worlds to find out if love can win out in the end. (978-1-63555-576-9)

**Changing Course** by Brey Willows. When the woman of her dreams falls from the sky, intergalactic space captain Jessa Arbelle had better be ready to catch her. (978-1-63555-335-2)

**Cost of Honor** by Radclyffe. First Daughter Blair Powell and Homeland Security Director Cameron Roberts face adversity when their enemies stop at nothing to prevent President Andrew Powell's reelection. Book 11 in the Honor series. (978-1-63555-582-0)

**Fearless** by Tina Michele. Determined to overcome her debilitating fear through exposure therapy, Laura Carter all but fails before she's even begun until dolphin trainer Jillian Marshall dedicates herself to helping Laura defeat the nightmares of her past. (978-1-63555-495-3)

**Not Dead Enough** by J.M. Redmann. In the tenth book of the Micky Knight mystery series, a woman who may or may not be dead drags Micky into a messy con game. (978-1-63555-543-1)